SAMANTHA HARVEY

The Western Wind

VINTAGE

1 3 5 7 9 10 8 6 4 2

Vintage
20 Vauxhall Bridge Road,
London SW1V 2SA

Vintage is part of the Penguin Random House group of companies
whose addresses can be found at global.penguinrandomhouse.com.

Penguin
Random House
UK

First published in the UK by Jonathan Cape in 2018
First published by Vintage in 2019

penguin.co.uk/vintage

A CIP catalogue record for this book is available from the
British Library

ISBN 9781784708030

Printed and bound in Great Britain by Clays Ltd, Elcograf S.p.A.

Penguin Random House is committed to a sustainable future for our
business, our readers and our planet. This book is made from Forest
Stewardship Council® certified paper.

SAMANTHA HARVEY

Samantha Harvey is the author of three previous novels: *The Wilderness*, *All is Song* and *Dear Thief*. She appeared on the longlists for the Baileys Women's Prize for Fiction and the Man Booker Prize, and the shortlists of the James Tait Black Award, the Orange Prize, and the Guardian First Book Award. *The Wilderness* won the Betty Trask Award in 2009. She is a tutor on the MA course in Creative Writing at Bath Spa University.

ALSO BY SAMANTHA HARVEY

The Wilderness
All is Song
Dear Thief

Contents

Day 4
Shrove (also Pancake) Tuesday, 17th February, 1491

Bulrushes

Dust and ashes though I am, I sleep the sleep of angels. Most nights nothing wakes me, not til I'm ready. But my sleep was ragged that night and pierced in the morning by someone calling to me in fear. A voice hissing, urgent, through the grille, 'Father, are you in there?'

'Carter?' Even in a grog, I knew this voice well. 'What's the matter?'

'A drowned man in the river. Down at West Fields. I – I was down at the river to see about clearing a tree that's fallen across it. A man there in the water, pushed up against the tree like a rag, Father.'

'Is he dead?'

'Dead as anything I've ever seen.'

I'd slept that night on the low stool of the confession booth with my cheek against the oak. A troubled night's sleep, very far from the angels. Now I stood and pushed my skirts as flat as they'd go. Outside looked dark; it could have been any time of night or early morning, and my hands and feet were rigid with cold. I shifted the oak screen enough to let myself out of the booth – which isn't even a booth as such, but an improvised thing made of props and drapes – and there was the flushed, worried, candlelit face of Herry Carter.

'Went to find you in your bed but you weren't there,' Carter said, words tripping. 'I wondered if you might be here.'

I wanted to tell him that I didn't usually sleep upright in this booth, I didn't know what had happened exactly that made me do it that night. But Carter had the look of somebody who couldn't care less, he only wanted to get back to the river.

'Maybe there's a chance for Last Rites,' he said, with lips set sullen and thin.

'You said he was dead.'

'But if we could get a bit of holy wine down his dead throat – '

A dead throat isn't amenable to wine, I thought, but thought without saying.

'If we could do at least that,' Carter said, 'maybe he could have died a half-decent death. Otherwise – '

Otherwise his fate would be ugly, and his time spent hanging like a lifeless rag off a fallen tree would seem like a happy memory. Herry Carter was right to wish for better. So we two left the church and ran.

The first thing I noticed was the wind, which was strong, bitter and easterly. It was coming up to dawn and the sky had the slightest of light. We ran down the track towards West Fields, which is nearly a mile away and much of it diagonally across the ham. The river itself takes over two miles to cover the same distance. Myself, alb flapping heavily in the wind like a sail, bottle of holy wine sloshing in my right hand, holy oil in left, quick-moving, if breathless and with thighs full of fire. Like a deer, my father used to say, with a wink, because he liked to shoot deer. Carter, young, short, strong on his legs, blond hair blown sideways, trouser knees hardened with another day's mud, all plain, buttery boyhood. He sprinted ahead with his arms pumping.

The ham was flooded, but not as much as it had been; the wind seemed to have pushed the water back into the river. Above

4

us a huge, fast sky that'd be blue when the sun rose, and every-thing but the wind was wet – the track, the grass, the earth, our feet and ankles, the tree trunks, the nests and the fledglings within. My toes were frogs in a swamp. When we reached the boundary of the lush grazing land at West Fields the world got wetter – sodden sheep with shivering lambs, cows paddling upland in herds trying to find drier ground so that they could eat without having to drink, Townshend's horses standing four-square in bog with their muzzles resting on each other's drenched flanks. Only the wind itself was dry, dry and so cold, and blowing away long days of rain.

'There,' said Carter, and he pointed off towards the river seventy or eighty paces ahead. 'I left my axe to mark it.'

Not much of a marker; with its blade rammed into the river bank, it barely stood a foot above the ground. You'd have needed a marker to find it. But Herry Carter had young eyes and his mind was focused on nothing else, just that axe, and that bit of river that had delivered up a poor old rag of a dead man. Carter upped his pace with the wind at his back and was there near the axe, striding this-way-that-way along the bank, ankle-deep in water by the time I caught up.

'It's gone,' he said. Desperate-sounding man, a rasp working at his voice. 'The body. It was there.' *There* being the fallen tree, in the crook of a branch. The river was high and fierce and roiled around that branch; nothing could have stayed in place there, nothing. Not a man's body, not even a cow's body. How could Carter have thought it would? But then, what could he have done? He couldn't have rescued the man on his own.

'Where's it gone?' Carter was saying, over and again. Rushing up and down like a sheepdog. Then he stopped, looked plain at the water and his tone fell flat. 'Where's the body gone? It was right there.'

My once-white alb was soaked and muddy almost knee-high and I felt something like defeat, because I'd have to ask Carter

5

now, and I didn't want to have to ask. I'd wanted to see for myself. The words came to my throat and stuck and wouldn't be dislodged with any amount of swallowing. I'd have looked anywhere to avoid the sight of his pitiful, aimless running. Anywhere: downwards, upwards. Upwards, to the stars that were fading with the dawn.

When I looked back at Carter finally, he was to my left, twenty yards downstream, standing knee-deep and thunder-struck by a thick cluster of bulrushes leaning in the wind. Only then, coming closer, did I see he was holding something of brightish green, a piece of cloth or clothing, which he lifted feebly. A shirt.

'Found this there,' he said, a curt flick of his hand towards the bulrushes. 'Just hanging there.'

So then I didn't even have to ask the question I hadn't wanted to ask, because the shirt made it clear who the drowned man was. We both knew who owned it; even in the poor light, that shirt belonged to one man only. Everybody else had beige shirts or brown or grey, of a wool that had never managed to look unsheeply. Nobody else had one of good linen that had once been as green as the swaying meadow of flax that gave rise to it. Faded now, yes, but all the same it was a fine Dutch shirt. Even before Carter found the shirt, from the moment he saw the drowned man, he must have known it was Newman. How many other poor, bloated dead men could there be floating down this river? How many other men disappeared into it three days before?

But it's our nature to deny what frightens us, and it's not wicked or dull. Isn't there always a bright, willing part of us that keeps hoping that what we know isn't true? Carter tried to fold the shirt into a neat and reverent square – Newman had led an ordered life, even if his death was disorderly. The shirt was too wet to hold shape and went loose and roomy in his hands. With some mumbling he bid his fumbling fingers to fold

6

it again, and again it fell slack. Then he shoved it in the waist-band of his trousers and ran downstream along the edge of the bank, howling Newman's name, splashing through water that was pink with the first glint of sun.

Oh, to throw the holy wine and oil into the river! Bad enough that the dead man didn't get to confess, but what hope was there for him if he couldn't have a drop of wine in him? Carter was right, it might even have been enough to have it in his mouth, on his lips. A cross of oil on his forehead. And now there was Carter, possessed by demons, up and down the bank and the wind was unkind and constant and our legs were soaked, and the day had a despairing mood.

Soon Carter came back, panting and angry, and he sank to a crouch.

'It's gone,' he said, not for the first time. 'He's gone.'

'He'll be halfway to the sea by now,' I replied – which we knew wasn't possible, but the point was the same. After the five bends and two oxbows past the village the river straightens and quickens, and with days of rain it was as rapid as a cart downhill, with no regard for things in its way. Carter nodded, and crumpled into himself.

A boy, really, and a good one at that. One who'd had the spirit knocked out of him that morning. Newman was his friend and a father figure, and in the three days since he'd drowned, Carter had dabbled with the notion that though his friend had died, he might still be alive. After all, the body hadn't been found. If a dead body disappeared, then so did death itself, so Carter seemed to think, and I'd been touched by this optimism, even if it was made of crooked timbers.

That river was cunning and of too many moods – throwing itself thickly over a dead man so that we couldn't say our dignified goodbyes. This was the second time I'd run to its banks to find Newman's body, and the second time I'd failed. By my estimations, if nature thwarts you more than once in

7

the same endeavour, you may have to start wondering if it's something other than bad luck – but I didn't drive this point home to my friend. 'Be strong now, Herry,' I told him, and affection drew my hand to his head. We stayed like that with our backs braced against the wind, and my alb, despite the mud and wet, flowed keenly outwards and forward. The bulrushes bent and hummed. Even in my despair, I liked it that the wind made them do that.

We went back across the fields. In that direction my skirts flowed out behind me like a bridal gown while the cassock underneath slapped at my shins – and I beg pardon for talking so much about what was happening at my lower leg, but so would anyone whose skirts weighed the same as two buckets of water and behaved like something living. I was ashamed to be feeble and wheezy from a fever the month before, and string-legged. I knew the sight of my hair in this wind – a mass of dark, wild curls around the tonsure. I was the one who looked possessed now, not that Carter was paying any attention. He, like me, had set his whole cause against the wind, which was hurling itself at our chests.

Carter's face was stone and refused conversation. He refused even to look at me. In the improved light, and moving slower, I could see better the cut in front of his right ear that he got a few days before; he slipped while fixing the roof of the church porch and caught it on a piece of slate. It was a sharp slash the length of half a finger and I didn't like the redness and depth of it, the slight greenish weeping and conkerish swell.

We reached the track again, where it forked left to the bridge and right to the village. We turned right. There was a pair of hands pushing me forward, away from that half-built bridge where Newman, we supposed, drowned, and when I glanced that way the clouds were thick old brutes, whereas ahead they were high and sparse and turning fair.

Then the sun: a bronzy song rising unseen behind Oak Hill, the long woody ridge we also call the Lazy Dog (sometimes just The Dog, if we're lazy). The ridge runs along the north-east edge of Oakham, which means the new sun can never be seen from the village, but its light spreads a wide glow over the trees on the ridge, as it did in that instance; a glow that starts small and hot, and turns cool, rosy and vast, in a way that always made me think the sea was just the other side. Off the open ham the wind had less fury and we walked together in silence, Carter reaching behind him from time to time to make sure the shirt was still in his waistband. I wanted to comfort him, but how, without prayers and parables? They were all I had. It was clear Carter didn't want any of that. Grief had made him angry and impatient.

'That cut,' I said, 'by your ear. Doesn't look to be healing.'

'It's healing,' he said.

'To me it looks worse.'

'It's better than yesterday.'

'I don't think it is.' He forged on ahead, short of temper, long of stride. I said, 'I don't like the look of it much.'

'Then I say don't look.'

And he stopped, there at the corner by the birches that were festooned with rags once bright, and knelt on the stones of the track. In front of him, in the longer grass, was a dead dog. He turned to me, turned back. 'Was that here when we came?'

'I didn't see it,' I said, 'but it must have been. We were running, we wouldn't have noticed.'

It was sunrise and I had first morning prayers to give, then confession to take, and I couldn't linger over a dog. But Carter put a hand to the dog's ribs. 'Cold as clay,' he muttered. Yet it had a healthy black sheen that made it look like it would get up and run, and we'd have been convinced

9

it would, if not for the lolling tongue and lack of breath. Mostly, when you see a dead dog – or a dead anything – you can assume it starved or was beaten, or was hit by a galloping horse, or dropped dead through age or demoralisation. This one looked thin but not starved, not beaten, not injured, not old, in fairly good humour. It just lay as though dropped from above.

'Wouldn't we have noticed it?' Carter said, his hand flat on the animal's side.

'It was still dark.'

'And we were running.'

'We were frantic.'

For a few moments we stood, and my grip was tight around those small bottles of oil and wine; we'd both been so jittered by this thing with Newman, and now we patrolled like sheriffs over the corpse of a dog as if it was a strange or sinister thing.

'It might – ' Carter tried, 'I might – ' He put his hand to that shirt and was tugging at it. 'Maybe I was mistaken about what I saw in the river earlier.'

'No,' I said. 'No.'

'I might not have seen a body caught in that tree, maybe it was just a shadow – people are going to say that maybe it was just a shadow.'

'And the shirt?' I asked. 'Was that just a shadow?'

'But you said it yourself, you said it – it was still dark. If we didn't see a dead dog that *was* there, maybe I *did* see a dead man that wasn't?'

I didn't want to upset Carter, but there was something to be said for facts. 'On Saturday dawn a man was seen tumbling down that river, Herry,' I said, as kindly and clearly as I could. 'It was Robert Tunley who glimpsed him and he said it might well have been Newman. Newman hasn't been seen since and he's the only man missing from the village. We know it's unlikely

10

to have been an outsider who drowned. God knows we don't get many passers-by.'

Because there were no outsiders, because the river cuts us off. But this wasn't the time for lamenting our fallen bridge, much as the urge rose in me.

I put my hand on his shoulder. 'And now a body washes up downstream – '

'Not far *enough* downstream,' Carter appealed. His foot prodded at the dog's belly. He shrugged my hand away. 'You can see how lively the water is – in three days a body would've got much further.'

'And you can see the journey it would have to take, round the oxbow at Odd Mill, the other at Burn Wood, a body could get lodged anywhere along there, hooked on fallen branches, run against banks – '

Carter turned his shoulder from me. 'People aren't going to believe me when I say I've seen Tom Newman's body, it'll be me who's the laughing stock.'

'You found his shirt,' I said. 'You have it there. What are people going to say about that?'

We stood without words, and it was cold. His shoulders were dropped so low my hands almost went to lift them and my arms to go around him in comfort. Forget what others think, I wanted to say. You saw what you saw – others don't matter. I clutched the bottles to me; the wind whipped and rattled through the birch copse. Such sadness then swept me, and I didn't know how trees kept enthusiasm for growing, when the wind, rain and snow harassed them all winter like that.

It was by some wordless consent that Carter and I began moving, prompted perhaps by the smell of cooking fat that came faint and fleeting. It might have been imagined because it came only once, for a moment, but all I knew suddenly was eggs, was bread scooped into the warm fat of the previous day's bacon, and with one smell I gained a horse's hunger. Carter might have felt hungry too because he sped up and walked at a pace I couldn't match in those heavy, wet vestments. By the time we were at the village, I was some thirty paces behind.

Carter raced towards his home, a quick pelt from the church. Probably wanted to show his wife the shirt and get her to wash it, so he could hang on to it, some sorry keepsake and trinket of a giant love that'd gone from him, swept up like a twig in a crow's beak.

'Carter!' I wanted to offer to anoint the shirt at least, though it was a blunt idea, anointing a piece of old linen. 'Herry! Herry Carter!' But Carter didn't respond. He was holding the shirt above his head and waving it about as if there were people to see him.

Go ahead and suffer then, I thought – not cruelly. Men and women clasp to their right to suffer, and sometimes it's better to let them for a while. I would mention Newman again in Mass and arrange to have that tree cleared from the river. Not that day, though; that day the hours were going to pass before we knew it; I needed half an hour's sleep. Try not to dream of that body getting dragged downstream, try not to be heart-broke over how savage death is. Think only of the pink light on the bulrushes where the shirt was found, and think only of how good it was that the shirt was found there, *there*, in the gentle holiness of the bulrushes; it was the best of all possible signs, and if a man had to die such a violent and unresolved death before disappearing as if swallowed into the whale, at least something of his appeared draped – caught, held, salvaged, saved – in that crowd of rushes, like a man who had fallen back into the arms of his people.

Was the light on the rushes even pink? Maybe not, but in my heart it was now and would always be. There in my thoughts,

12

on the way home, was my sister's voice wise and soft: *The tongues and pens of men must fall silent in wonder.* Why I should have heard this I can't say, except that I was tired and sad and glad and angry and comforted all at once, and when I opened the door to the church I let myself cry over Thomas Newman, and was surprised by how long it took for the tears to stop coming.

Superstition

'A priest is also a judge and a sheriff, whether or not he wants to be.'

'So he is,' I said, without surprise, because I'd got used to the dean appearing before me in the church, waiting, with nothing better to do. This time he was leaning against the pillar near the opening to the vestry, winding around his child-sized fist the spare rosary that he must have lifted from the nail in the porch.

'I hear Newman's body has reappeared? Or – *had* reappeared,' he said. 'Before it vanished again.'

'Word reaches you quickly.'

I'd left Carter only shortly before – come into the church, gone to the vestry to find dry things to wear. Hidden my tears in the stole that hung from a peg til the white silk was grey in patches. When I came out the dean was already there; he had what they called a nose for the nasty. I stood in front of him with the new alb folded on top of the new cassock, a great heavy pile of cold cloth to take home and change into. Nothing to be done about my shoes.

'I saw you and Carter running back from somewhere,' he said, 'and I was, well, curious. So I asked Carter where you'd been.'

'Clearly *you're* the better judge and sheriff.'

He looked at me. He, small and neat like a field mouse brushed by panicked dash through wheat and grass. Its little heart always pounding in a tiny, courageless chest. I, tall and precarious, my eyes made raw by tears. Robes mud-smeared and stained, shamefully, with goose-fat.

'This is the last day,' he said, and then he took from his burse a small roll of paper, which he unravelled. It was the pardon that had been pinned on the church door since Saturday. 'You know, don't you, that a man like Newman can't die without explanation?'

I went to speak; he didn't allow it. 'And you're going to say that there is an explanation – the river is high, the rain's been hard, men aren't fish. They fall in, they drown.'

'They do.'

'But Newman isn't the kind of man who falls in a river.'

I went to the altar to rest the vestments there; they were heavy. I was wet and cold. I asked wearily, 'Is there a *kind of man* who falls in a river?'

'This is the last day,' he repeated, and I looked up at our east window, which allowed a morning light that was wide, thin and silver. He flourished the piece of paper as if I'd never seen it before, and as if it hadn't been pinned for three days to my church door. 'This pardon is our best hope of luring the murderer to confession – '

'There isn't a murderer.'

'So we think, until one is lured. As I said, this pardon is our best hope of luring the murderer to confession, and it isn't going to be offered after today. Tomorrow, too late. A good pardon, Reve – the most you or I could offer, the most anyone in this sorry parish is ever going to get. I can tell you there are plenty of people here who need it, murder or not. You aren't a village that's going to crowd heaven. Do you know purgatory has a waiting room? They call it Oakham, there are so many of you there.'

When I was a boy I'd thought that anger lived in large men; my father was a large man. It was still strange to me when men like the dean, pale and trivial men with narrow faces, could house so much anger. It sat beneath cool skin, in blue-veined hands that shook so slightly most wouldn't notice. But I noticed; the pardon between his fingers tremored like a catkin.

'If you hate Oakham I suppose you could leave,' I said. 'Not everybody likes it that you've taken up in Newman's house anyway.'

Eyebrow raised, a wristy wafting of the pardon and he said, in a voice trying to aim a tone lower than was natural to it, 'I have a death to investigate.'

'Oh yes.'

'If I went away now, on the last day of confession before Lent, on the last day a generous pardon is offered, after all this hard work – ' He paused, and I was left to wonder what hard work he imagined he'd done. 'Well, I don't want to beat the bushes so that others can get the birds, if you understand me.'

You don't want to leave before somebody is tied to a stake, I thought. You don't want to leave on this of all days, this day of celebration, in case the village runs in wild riot, like the animals we are.

'Oh, I understand you,' I said. I bent to pick up a finger-length of dogwood that must have fallen from the chancel pillar sconce, where they faded slowly with the witch hazel and winter-sweet – my sister's wedding flowers, now dying. Then I didn't know what to do with this bit of claret twig, so I held it uselessly. I wanted him to feel that it was more worthy of my attention than him, though I don't think he noticed.

Towards the west of the church, on the north wall opposite the entrance, we have a wall painting of St Christopher carrying the child Jesus across the water – a huge figure, a giant or as good as, with the child scooped in one arm, feet crossed in the saint's palm, the size of a week-old lamb. It covers the whole

16

of that wall, from rafters to lintel. Pinks, reds and yellows. It's been said that if you saw it within a day of your death, it was as good as Last Rites. If your death was sudden or solitary, and you had no Last Rites, no holy oil, no sacrament, sight of St Christopher could still let you off hell. If Newman had seen it on Friday, before he drowned, his soul would be in safe transit to the afterlife by now. Had he seen it? Nobody but Newman could know; I'd flayed my memory trying to find the answer, but no answer would come. Nothing. I took up the bundle of vestments again, and went to the painting and knelt.

The dean watched, and turned away in frustration, and watched, and sighed, and handled the chalice that he'd taken absently from the altar, rolling its stem between his fingers, with the rosary still around his knuckles. I should say *our* rosary, Oakham's. A gift from Robert Tunley. He put the chalice down with a sudden impatience, walked to the chancel pillar, scratched his nail at the stone, swirled on his heels, peered down the length of the small church towards the confession box. I didn't desist from my prayer, but I knew everything he did because I knew how to see without looking, while he only knew how to look without seeing. I knew he was about to lose patience and would come scuttling towards me.

'Reve,' he said finally, clip-clipping short, quick steps through the nave. He was waggling his fingers for me to rise. 'Enough, Reve. If I can't go to the archdeacon by tomorrow morning with some information about Newman's death, we will all suffer for it. You've taken confession all day for the last two days – you have one more day of confession to discover something. Tell me you'll discover something.'

I raised my head from prayer. 'Well,' I said, 'haven't we already this morning discovered something?'

'A vanishing corpse and a stinking shirt?'

'Thomas Newman's shirt. And where was that shirt found? In the bulrushes. The *bulrushes*. Signifying the arms of God, as

17

you know – Newman's safe delivery to him. How did it end up there? And yet there it is, and I don't know about you, but there are few enough signs from God for me to take heart from this one.'

His mouth opened to argue, then closed. His posture eased, his lips moved to the faintest of smiles, and someone pleasant appeared in his expression, the boy his mother must have once loved. I wondered what had softened him. I saw him for a moment as I'd seen him on Saturday when he'd first ridden into Oakham on his sad and soulful mare. How unknowable men are, full of corners. Old and mean sometimes, and suddenly young and kind. But to no end, I thought; he was never kind for long.

Sure enough, he looked upwards, raised his arms. 'A shirt in some rushes, hallelujah!' Then dropped his arms. 'Not enough, Reve, sadly. Discover something else.'

I stood with my armful of cloth and the spindle of dogwood still in my hand, and nothing to say.

'As for that shirt, Carter gave it to me.' He affected pleasure at a good, clean idea, his hands brought together, a brow lifted. 'I'll hoist it up on the maypole at Old Cross, shall I, to remind us all of the shortness of these dear little lives we live?'

I bowed, because he was the rural dean and I only a priest, and for no other reason under the sun. 'Excuse me,' I said.

I went home, ate a slab of not-freshest bread, slept briefly, changed clothes, returned. By then the bell had long since rung out ten o'clock. In the village, children were outside playing catch-me with a dead chick, and running three-legged, and forming castles from mud. The churchwarden, Janet Grant, informed me she'd done her morning rounds, had knocked on doors to make sure nobody had overslept, or was newly ill or dead; door after door had opened, thankfully. I was relieved to hear that Sarah Spenser's was one of them; the way she'd been the evening before, I'd wondered if she'd endure the night. Townshend's fields were dotted with stoopers coercing the earth with spades, rakes and harrows in hand, trying to make the acres of mud ready for seed. It couldn't be called soil any more, this earth of ours, only an unfurrowable sludge, which met a rake as a fork meets melted fat.

I knelt in the chancel with the easterly light pale and flat on my hands. Heal Carter's wound, I asked, give Sarah Spenser back her health. Help with our soil, give our seeds something to grip to. Accept my prayer for Terce, which I'm late for, and Sext, which I'm early for. Forgive that I missed Matins and Lauds entirely.

The wind blew apart eleven strikes of the bell. Janet Grant went after that with the shriving bell to tell the workers to down their tools, and to urge them towards confession. I picked myself up from my knees and settled in this little booth that is just a triangle, this box-that-is-not-a-box, a box with no roof, a box made hastily and out of a sense of trial. Booth, box; both dignify it with a structure it doesn't have. Myself in a tight triangular space behind an oak screen, on which hung three rosaries to signify that I was there to take confession. There were three sessions in the day, and after each I'd take a rosary away. Creates a sense of urgency, a little drama, so I was told in my training. A little drama! As if we needed more of that. I gathered myself on a low stool with the amice pulled up over my head, staring towards the wall.

This was the south-west corner of the church, near the entrance. All the light it had plummeted from above and died at my feet. In the early morning the stone, though whitewashed, was a deep greyish-brown; as the morning wore on, it lightened to a flat wool-white, as it was then. I'd stared for many hours at this stone until it had seemed to turn into fabric that was being woven in front of my eyes. On a sunny day a strap of

19

light would fall across it eventually and change its substance. At this time of year that light would come at around two o'clock and the wall would wear it diagonally like a silken stole. If the sun stayed clear of clouds, I could tell the time by its progress, its changing width and slant.

I squatted with my legs gathered up awkwardly in a space made almost entirely of angles too acute for comfort, back pressed into one of them, knees into another, a cup of beer by my right foot. I pictured myself: *the roosting priest*. One day perhaps I'll give up on the ample discomfort of this home-made not-booth-not-box, or else finally get a real one made by skilled men with good tools, or one shipped over from Italy (which would involve sums of money way beyond this parish, if what I know about Italians is true).

Despite the morning's adventures, despite the death of Newman and the grief of Carter, I had a feeling of pure, divine waiting. Maybe the feeling was all the more for the morning's adventures. The year had tipped again towards spring and in a few short hours we'd be back in Lent. When I was a boy of eight and learning to swim underwater, I'd take in a last greedy breath so that it was as if my head had bulged bigger, and everything around took extra colour and shape just for one second before I plunged under. It was like that now; we hovered on the verge of deprivation, and forty days of feeling hungry. During those four days of Shrovetide before Lent began, we filled ourselves with air and we smelt and tasted and touched, we ate, we danced, we confessed. Or anyway, *they* ate and danced and confessed. I felt only apprehension and something eager stirring, a violent jarring of my senses.

I closed my eyes; there, the river bank and the mud calf-deep welled with hoof marks, and there some longer, narrower, shallower tracks that could have been made – had they? – by the slipping of a human foot as its owner tried to access the river edge near the bridge – probably to see better how the bridge had

20

recently fallen. Those narrow tracks perturbed me; they told of Newman's frailty. It was hard, still, three days later, to reconcile this clumsy fate with a man as self-possessed as Thomas Newman – and yet, with these rains of late, anybody standing too close to the river's edge would be giddied by its swirl and its stormy roar. Entranced as if dealt a hex. Even a sure-footed goat could've taken a slide down. Even the most self-possessed man in the world could suffer the consequences of worn shoe-sole on rain-slick mud.

Find something, the dean said, and by that he meant: find me the murderer. I'd assured him I would. What I'd neglected to tell him was this: the murderer isn't who you think. Who is it that invariably takes life? Death, of course. Death itself is the murderer, and birth its accomplice. Men die because they're born to die. By drowning, by disease, by mishap, by all God's assassins. What was either of us going to do to change that?

As I waited in silence I felt the universe fall about me in timeless cycles, I heard the planets roll and the hawthorn come to bud; the church's stone smelt of a vast deep lake, and the oak panel smelt of autumn woodland, and the pain in my bruised knees was a surge of sweet, hard life.

'Benedicite,' she said.

And I: 'Dominus.'

And she, young and harassed: 'Confiteor.' A quivering pause and fluttered breath and the fussy shifting of the fretful. There may have been a screen between us but my vision no longer relied on what my eyes could see. She gave a short cough.

I was about to ask her to recite her Creed, but she spoke before I could. 'Father, a man is dead.'

I asked calmly: 'Which man?' But the muscle running up the inside of my left foot shortened and the toes curled with cramp.

'I don't know, but he's drowned, just like the other one,' she whispered through the grille, and I could hardly hear, with the cloth shrouding my ear. I had to bend my back to draw myself closer. 'Word's going round faster than the wind.'

'Who did you hear this from?'

'Oh, others, all. I was on my way here and I heard it – '

'On the wind.'

'But it's true, Father, they say it's true.'

Wild with chance though this life is, there are things that seem impossible – such as two drowned men in one morning. So I thought: she must mean Newman. At the same time I thought this new drowned man must be Herry. I didn't know how these opposite instincts could live together so easily, but they did, and I saw Herry throwing himself in the river after Newman in his sorrow, while I napped soundly with a square of fustian over my head.

I reached down into darkness for the beer, for something to hold on to, and remembered then the small iron box I'd put under the stool the day before. I fumbled, anxious, to make sure it was still there. My fingers met it, spanned its length at a stretch and pushed it backwards. I fumbled next for the beer, but left it there on the floor after all, since my cold hands baulked at the pewter cup. The smell was warming though, the smell of hops and honey like the hilt of a summer afternoon.

'But you don't know who the dead man is?' I asked evenly, since this was the seventeen-year-old wife of Lewys, a little stalk of a thing, always so watchful and nervous.

'That's what I was hoping you might know.' Her fingers at the grille, picking. 'All that's left of him is a shirt – torn shreds of a shirt, they say, covered in blood – '

'A shirt?'

'Herry Carter found it by the river.'

'Herry Carter? Did you see him on your way here?'

'I saw him, he and his wife Cat were sweeping water out of their door; we're all swimming in our sleep these nights.'

'Was it a green shirt?'

'How did you know?' Her voice was incredulous and thin.
'Did you see it for yourself?'

'No, Father. It's just what they say.'

She sounded upset and close to tears. My fingers touched hers, I gave my reassurances. 'Please, settle, it's alright.'

'The second man to drown in our river,' she said, no longer whispering but speaking low into the grille with what sounded like a terrified calm. 'Never a dead person in there for as many years as I know, and now two in a few days, and I fear it, all this rain, the river is filthy and mad, Father – angry, like God doesn't want that bridge we're trying to build. He's not half-hearted with his signs.'

Not God who doesn't want it, I might have said. God has no gripe with a bridge. No, all the anger is from the livid little demons of the river itself. And yet if only what she said were true; if only God were sometimes a little clearer with his signs. Until that morning it'd been my life's thwarted wish to have a plain instruction from him, just one. I brought my hand back into my lap.

'If God has given a sign to that effect, it hasn't been known by me,' I said.

Her hand, too, withdrew, and fell away into darkness. 'He wants us to knock the remains of the bridge down, don't you see? He doesn't want us to make a profit from it at the cost of people who might be poor, he doesn't want men to die building it. Like those two other men from last summer.' She paused for a moment before taking up again, and I didn't know if she wanted me to say something about those other men. 'The thing is, those two men, and then Thomas Newman who gave his money to that bridge – look at them all now. Gone and dead and forgotten as if they never were. And the man found today, I don't know who he is, but I bet he'll have been one of them who helped build it or pay for it.'

'The men who died last summer died of a fever, not of drowning.'

'Because they drank the river water, you see? Tom Newman gave his money to building the bridge,' she said again, as if this fact were a threat to her safety. 'And my own husband helped with the stone-laying efforts too – he might be next, Father.'

I could hear the stiffness of her jaw as she spoke, and see the cold, unblinking blue of her eyes. I sat up. 'The body found today was not a second man,' I said, 'it was the same man – Newman. Thomas Newman himself. It's taken three days for him to be washed a mile down the river. It's not a second man. There's no sign from God. In fact there is a sign from God, but not the one you think. His shirt was found in the bulrushes, a holy place. He is safe in God's arms.'

She said nothing, and then she sobbed.

'It's mere superstition to think that God is punishing us. Do you think he hates bridges? Have you heard of the great bridges at Rome and – Wade – they've built a bridge there, the town is like new.' There I stopped; I didn't know any others.

A quiet I remembered hearing underwater. One that flooded the ears. There was a piece of oak a hand-span wide between me and the woman, but still I heard her loose hair brush against her cheek, loud as the broom in the yard.

'He's safe in God's arms,' she whispered. Then in a louder, sharper whisper, 'Are *we* safe, Father?'

'Yes.'

'Are we?'

'Are you afraid of God?'

She gave no answer.

'You should only be afraid of all that is not God,' I said.

A sniff. 'There's no second man who drowned today?'

'There's no second man.'

She breathed out. I'd have asked her now to say her Creed, Paternoster, Ave Maria, but I knew she knew them so there was little point, and a queue would soon be forming out in the nave.

'Do you have a confession to make?'

24

A shake of her head. 'I only came yesterday,' she said. Yes, she'd come then and confessed to taking the last spoonful of honey without sharing it with her husband, which I duly, quickly forgave.

'You said that you were already on your way here when you heard about the drowned man – '

'But I had nothing to confess, Father, I just – it's been an unsettling few days. I just wanted your comfort. I feel all at sea, sickly. Maybe it's this one.'

With that, I imagined she ran her little pale hand over her middle.

'Are you comforted now?' I asked.

'Yes, thank you, Father.'

'So then, that's all?'

'I think it is.'

At the very edge of my vision was the white flash of that little hand as it rushed through the sign of the cross. Out she went then, slowly and sighing, and the great orb of her pregnant middle filled the latticed window, like one of those planets up above rolling heavily past.

Desire

Day lifting, moment by moment. My heart beat, and beat again, and I thought: one day it will beat and not beat again. Then what's in store for me? And the light undid itself, separating out the grain of the stone into a dull, disparate yellowish-grey, the texture of cloth before fulling. I'd forgotten to eat and was hungry.

You see, my people are superstitious and have always been. They live in wariness at the whims and punishments of God and take everything as a warning. They quake too often at his will. He's made the river angry, they think. He's thwarted so-and-so for doing such-and-such. He'll send wolf-men from the northern forests to eat our children, and he'll multiply the grotesque creatures who swim in oceans that never lap a second shore.

I tell them: No, no, those aren't the things to fear, we've come too far for superstition. We know there are no wolf-men and no sea creatures of that kind; it's children who believe in those. There are only spirits – ill-meaning spirits, who live as we all do on God's earth but aren't made by God. This is no secret to us, and men much sharper than me have proven it. The spirits are here on earth to test and strengthen us; when things die and decay, the decaying matter that has no home in heaven emits a fetid cloud of minuscule spirited matter that brings illness of all kinds – of the body, of our fates. They're small and lumish and barely seen, specks and flecks suspended in the air or in water which, if only our hands could catch and our eyes could see, would show themselves as black, fast, lithe and slick, but made noxious by their swarming numbers.

They live among and under God's things, like our shadows live among and under us. They're what we wrongly call luck, ill or otherwise – because luck has nothing to do with God, who decrees with certainty and reason and whose will can't be fought; we're born already conquered by him. But the spirits, we can conquer. They're *our* battleground. Perhaps the river is bringing us poor luck, but Lewys's wife is wrong to think the fate of her husband is set. The river is the host of those spirits, who've found a home there, since God only knows what's rotting in its waters. Men, cows, sheep, offal, entrails, dung. The corrupted hopes of our broken bridge. If our two men last summer drank the spirits and died, and if Newman was pulled under by them and died, then what are we to do? Cower? Pray? Pray to *them* for mercy, as if they have such power?

Well, I've prayed, not to them, but to the Lord. Two prayers, at least one of them delivered. On Saturday, when a body had first been seen in the current, and Newman had disappeared and not come home, I'd prayed for a sign that he was on his way through purgatory and safe to heaven. A shirt in the rushes might mean nothing to our godless dean, but it meant much to me, and I gave my thanks.

I prayed too for wind to come from the west and blow afield this surging of the spirits eastwards, towards God. Overnight the wind came, though it was from the east, and sharp, and wintry. Maybe he hadn't heard the whole prayer, busy as he was; and maybe I hadn't asked clearly enough, or maybe I'd been over-clear and asked for too much. Still, I reassure my parish: in his grace all superstition dies and all need and desire are met by him, through me. And there was time yet, today, for that wind to change its course.

Father, came voices through the grille. I sinned, forgive me, Father. My left ear listened. It had grown strong with listening as a shoulder grows strong by the mattock. As the day forged inch-wise into brightness, they came thickly, my parish, because they wanted the hefty pardon I'd offered. Benedicite, Dominus, Confiteor. May I be blessed, may I confess.

Benedicite, Dominus, Confiteor.

Benedicite,

Dominus,

Confiteor.

Father, I forgot to come to Mass, I forgot to say my prayers, I forgot to feed my pig, I was rough with my child, I was sick with drink, I pissed in the churchyard, I woke up angry, I lost hope, I was too full of pride, I was too weak, a voice told me to pull my rotted teeth out, is the voice demon or God? I masturbated, but I thought of God as I masturbated, I thought of Mary Magdalene, I thought of John the Baptist, forgive me.

I fell, at some point, asleep, with my head drooping like ripe fruit from a spindly branch. I woke up to hear a voice whispering of masturbation, and above that the music of lutes, which fell as spring rain out in the chancel but came from nowhere. I sat up straight as a strut so that the sleep would fall off me. 'Try not to masturbate,' I said, 'or your hands may shrivel and fall off. At the very least try not to think of John the Baptist.' But lutes? Newman was the only person in this parish to play the lute, just as he was the only person to have worshipped at the shrines in Compostela and Jerusalem, and to have seen a man hack silver ore from its seam, and to have picked an orange from a branch in Spain and eaten one of their olives – sour in both cases, he'd said. He tried to teach me more than once to play the lute but I was cold-fingered and went about the plucking stiffly. Where others used a quill for plucking, Newman used his fingers, and all of them were busy. Your fingers had to be feathers, he said, yet his weren't, they were as strong and agile as living creatures. They brought about a sound that worried people with its softness; it seemed too simple to sit among the jumbled pelfrie of life.

But as I sat I realised there was no lute playing, and that the sound I heard must have followed me out of a dream; a dream of Thomas Newman? I couldn't remember anything about it, and would have thought that brief cleft of stolen sleep hadn't been long enough to sustain a dream, but it left in me a deep foreboding, the sense that I must do something. Run to the dean, tell him once more about the miraculous appearance of Newman's shirt; curtail his suspicions of murder. For otherwise something untoward and irreversible was waiting to come.

Abruptly, though, the curtain slid open once again and then closed, and somebody came to kneel at the other side of the screen. Somebody who moved easily and languidly, and whose smell was as sharp as a spear and wronged my nose. A boy, or young man, with the presence of a wolf.

'Long for a woman,' he said, after an iffy Creed.

'Any woman, or one especially?'

'One especial woman.'

'A married woman?'

'A just-married woman.'

'Then you know you must stop your longing.'

'Can't quite so easily.'

His head was low to the grille, which meant one of two things – or both of two things. He was short, or he had a lazy kneel.

'What have you done to weaken it?'

'Weaken what?'

'The longing.'

'Everything they say to do. When I took myself in my hand I pictured her as an old, dead woman with worms crawling out of her and the flesh falling off her face.'

'Did that help?'

'Then I just longed for her worms as well.'

'It would be better if you didn't take yourself in your hand.' Or your hands will shrivel and fall off.

'Can't help it, Father. I have urges for putting my thighs over her thighs and running my hand down her lovely back, and I don't get things done for the aching and the wanting – '

'I tell you, think of other things.'

'And now she's married off to some limp old shite from a far place.'

Usually I knew who was on the other side of the screen, but the more he spoke, the less sure I was. He was one of the boys who worked down at east barns shovelling the muck, clearing the ditches, but there were plenty of those and they didn't confess often; I couldn't say which of them he was, without looking.

'This woman,' I said, 'who is she?'

He hesitated long and – if I'm not imagining it – awkwardly. 'Not someone from here,' he said.

'When did you have a chance to meet somebody who isn't from here?'

He shifted and burped. A billow of beery air.

'Where is she from, if not here?'

'From – ' a breathless pause, 'Bourne.'

'Bourne? Some fifteen miles away – you went there recently?'

'No, no.'

'Is she taken to lengthy walks, then, this woman?'

'Yes,' he said, 'yes.'

'Is that what you love about her?'

'I told you, I love her hair and her thighs and this part, here, where it does this.'

It didn't trouble him that I couldn't see whatever it was he was pointing to, and his imagination of that part – whatever part it was – must have consumed him, because he sank into a reverie, his breath quick and quiet.

'There's a difference between love and lure,' I said.

'I feel none.'

'There is, all the same.'

'Then I'm encountering both.'

This dull ache in my lower back – if only I'd had room to stand, or lean steeply to one side. I kneaded the muscle with my fist. 'What age is she?'

'I don't know,' he said, but he added suddenly, 'Not a child. A proper woman.'

'Have you ever had physical contact with her?'

'Touchings? No, Father.' He sniffed; I've heard enough sniffing to know it's the sign of a lie, or a truth not fully given. At least he recanted swiftly. 'Or – yes, Father. But it was as faint as anything, I'm not sure she even knew it.'

'When was this?

'Many months ago, last summer, at a dance.'

'A dance in Bourne?'

A pause. 'Yes, Father.'

A poor liar, this boy, since Oakhamers didn't go to dances in Bourne, nor did Bourne have any dances, surely, what with their pinched-mouth priest, Serle.

I asked, 'Was it an accidental touch?'

'I don't know what you'd call accidental – I didn't have any plan, just that I saw her chest and my hand flew at it before I knew what it was doing, and at that moment she swirled around – I don't think to avoid me, only to swirl – and my hand touched her nipple – ' the briefest pause, 'like a leaf tickling a bud on a branch.'

'A leaf tickling a bud on a branch?'

'Yes, Father.'

'Who gave you that ladylike phrase?'

'Myself, Father.'

'You meant to – clutch her?'

'Not clutch, just grab.'

'The difference?'

He sat forward and moved a hand close to the grille so that I could see it, and closed the other hand tightly around the hazel. 'Clutching,' he said. Then, relinquishing the hand and letting it hover, the other swooped in and snapped shut on it for a moment and let it drop. 'Grabbing.'

'You mean, clutching is for a longer time?'

'Right, Father. I mean, I wasn't trying to trap her and smuggle her away.'

'Only grab her chest?'

'But she swirled off into the corner.'

'And the woman? Has she ever made advances towards you?'

'In my dreams, always, I'd say every night, and she's fairly loose and ready in those, if I may say it. Then there's my daydreams too, though she's quieter then and has more clothes.'

'You must end the daydreams.'

He sighed and sounded impatient, frustrated. I asked again, in spite of myself, 'Are you sure this woman is from another place?'

'Very sure.' He seemed confident by then, because he'd done what people do so easily, and had begun to believe his own fabrication. I don't know what it is about lies; I've nothing to say in the wake of them. So we sat for a short while with nothing to say.

'Do you believe in the Father, Son and Holy Ghost?' I asked him finally; the question was abrupt and I thought caught him unawares, because his answer had all the volition of the wind he'd given earlier.

'Yes.'

'The incarnation?'

'Yes.'

'The resurrection?'

'Yes.'

'The judgment?'

'Yes.'

'Have you honoured your mother and father?'

'Yes.'

'Been overly proud of your wit?'

'No.'

'Repeat your Creed once more.'

'*I believe in God, the Almighty Father, and Jesus –*'

'*The Father Almighty, Creator of Heaven and Earth, and in Jesus Christ –* '

He took up again and stumbled through. If he could get this right, and exercise discipline and piety, nothing else would matter, certainly not his desire. Nothing could be done about that – there was no cure for a young man's desire except to become an old man, and even that wasn't a cure that could be guaranteed.

When he ended his chaotic recital I exhaled and leant forward to rest my elbows on my knees. 'You need to learn your Creed,' I said. 'Word for word, and when the longing comes you can use its words to break the spell of the longing. Instead, you learn to long for the beauty of Christ. Repeat the Creed and Ave five times a day for a month, and whenever you feel the desire most strongly. You need to control the dreams and daydreams. If there's nothing you can do about the dreams, you must at least control the daydreams, in the same way, using the Creed. Do you understand?'

'I understand.'

'And don't think of your hand as a leaf brushing against a bud. Your hand is your hand, at the service of your heart.' And other parts, I thought. 'Not a blameless leaf.'

'I'll never think of it like that again.'

'And avoid this woman at all costs. The punishment for coveting a married woman is far greater than an unmarried one.'

33

He offered a mumbled 'Yes.'

'For touching her chest, you need to come each day for a fortnight and light a candle beneath the Pietà – *our* Pietà – and say your Ave.'

Our Pietà being quite different from Newman's, which hung audacious and bright as a kingfisher at Newman's own altar. He wouldn't like this, the boys from the barns never liked fiddling with lights and pictures of the Pietà any more than they liked joining the chorus of 'I sing of a maiden'; these were women's things.

'And you can do something for me – take wood, bread, milk and eggs to Sarah Spenser's house, she's unwell. Bacon too, if you can. Take some candles from the vestry. Ask for clean bedclothes to go there, and make sure the fire's lit. If there's water in the house, sweep it out.' I thought, uneasily, of the vomit I'd swept up there the day before. 'Clean up – anything that needs cleaning. See that she has water. I'll have Janet Grant pay for it all later.'

'Yes, Father.'

'Be comforted that you're given a pardon of another forty days for coming to confession before Lent. You did right to confess. Come back to me if the desire builds and you need to confess it again.'

I didn't expect to hear gratitude when he replied, 'Thank you, Father.' He wasn't one of those boys who came to confession more than he was obliged, and not one who was likely to rush back with a heavy conscience. But when he thanked me it was as if with relief that he knew he could return. He brought his face to the grille to get sight of me or meet my eye. Yes, a wolfish face, lean and dark and sharp-eyed. Ralf Drake. When he stood and pulled back the curtain he lingered strangely. If I hadn't known better, I'd have thought he was having an epiphany or a moment of ecstasy, as men and women do before an image of Mary or the saints. Then he gave an odd, short laugh, and he left.

* * *

Why did he linger, why did he laugh? Because he was awkward, I'm sure of it – because the married woman he was in love with was my sister. He meant for me to know, since she was the only one in the village to be recently married – she'd married on Friday, as he said, to *a limp old shite from a far place*. (And, well, there were some things in that assessment I agreed with.) She now lived in Bourne with this husband, John Endall, whose surname I could only think of as describing her fate, and who owned twenty acres of grazing meadow there. Our boy from the barns might never see her again except in passing, if she were to visit. He won't dance with her again.

What is it to be in love with a woman? Is it just to love her hair, her thighs, her *this part*? Or to worship her unduly – her hair comb, her footprint, her spoon, her smell, her shadow, the water she washes in? If a drop of rain touches her neck, is it love to worship not only her neck but the raindrop? Is it a spell, a trick, mere lust trussed up? Is it love if it drives you to act, or if it drives you to resist? I was told in my ordination that love can be a test that feels like a gift, and sometimes a gift that feels like a test, and only a priest can know the difference. But what did I know? Perhaps in love the hand does become a leaf; my sister's chest, to that possessed hand, a bud. Perhaps I was asking Ralf Drake to rid himself of the trickery of lust when really what he experienced was the transformation of love. Maybe his dung-darkened hands did become a leaf in her presence. Yes, there are transformations in the work of the heart. I wanted to call Ralf Drake back and ask him: Is love salvation or witchery? For I don't know.

Little dark box

Robert Tunley. Nobody else filled the small gap between screen and curtain as bulkily, with the breath whooshing out as the body went down. The bell chimed one. I strained to hear sounds from outside – a citole perhaps, nakers, John Green's pipe calling the worms from the ground, that cheery chirrup of the fiddle like a drunken songthrush, and the notion of quick-footed dancing that goes with it. But I heard nothing except the single wind-swollen chime of the bell.

'What's happening out there?' I asked, before Tunley could begin offloading his sins. 'Are there celebrations yet?'

'Is that how you open confession these days, Reve?'

'Well, I didn't know you were a man for convention.'

'You're the first priest I've met who admits he didn't know something.'

I looked down into my lap and smiled; Tunley gave a muffled laugh that didn't get further up than his throat, which was a shame because he has a laugh so thick and warm you could rug a horse with it. 'To answer you, I'd say there's some celebrating,' he said. 'Up at New Cross. Some drinking and senseless shouting at sparrows anyway, if that's what you call celebrations.'

'I don't know what sensible shouting at sparrows would be like.'

'Then that's *two* things you don't know today.'

Tunley made a sound somewhere between a yawn and a groan. I knew how he was kneeling, heavy and round-backed with his hands linked in the fold between his thighs and belly. His eyes would be dancing in his heavy, pale face.

'Will you join them, at New Cross?' I asked.

'Ah, no,' he said. 'The leg's sore. I'll sit at home and curse the Lord for giving us another Lent to endure.'

He reeled off the Ave spontaneously and silver-tongued. *Hail Mary, full of grace, the Lord is with thee; blessed art thou amongst women, and blessed is the fruit of thy womb, Jesus.* Just the sound of it drove me deep within myself to somewhere at once dark and light – Tunley should have found work in the church, the way his voice could do that. Then, without even a clearing of the throat, he said, 'You know Mary Grant's dog, the black one, I killed it. Last night.'

Even this was songlike, and the words rose from the enormity of his belly. Nobody knew how he managed to be fat. Envy the man who's fat in autumn, and distrust the one who's fat in spring, so they say. Well, Tunley was fat and envied and distrusted all year.

'Mary Grant's dog?' was my pointless query, given that he'd said it plainly already.

'That's right, Reve, Mary Grant's dog.'

The dog, of course, the one Carter and I saw on the track that morning. Was it? When I thought about it, I didn't know what Mary Grant's dog was – or had been – like. I hadn't seen it for years. It was a surprise I remembered how Mary herself looked, given how often she came to Mass – something like her daughter, I suppose, who I see every day. Though Janet Grant is sweeter-looking, that I do know.

'How did you kill it?' I asked. You started with the easy question, and that softened the path to the harder one: the why, the what for.

'A bit of monkshood in its food.'

'Monkshood?' Then I murmured, 'That's no good way to die.'

'I've yet to find a way that is.'

That poor dog. I considered its last moments, back arched and retching, its ribs opening and closing like a dying butterfly.

'You do know that Mary Grant's dog was her sole companion?'

'Not any more.'

'Tell me why you did it.'

'It barked and yowled and I could never sleep.'

'It's in a dog's nature to bark and yowl – '

'It's in a man's nature to sleep.'

I said, looking up into the rafters as I did when frustrated, 'We can't kill a creature for doing what's in its nature.'

That dog lying there with its tongue a dry pink petal, and Mary an old woman. Utterly friendless, if you discounted her daughter, who seemed more driven by duty than love.

'I'll tell you what's not in a dog's nature,' Tunley replied, over-brimming. 'To be tied outside in all weathers without freedom and left to yowl like a bloodthirsty beast all day and night while its master – or mistress, in this case – sits on her bony arse and whinges. While her only neighbour – her good neighbour, who brings wood and starts her fires and mends her roof – is sent into tension as tight as a flail and starts yowling in his own head and losing sleep to madness. Killing the dog was a mercy to us all. If it hadn't been the dog, it would have been Mary herself. So I don't come asking for forgiveness so much as thanks.'

'You're ripe, to come to confession and ask for thanks.'

'Ripe I am, Reve – all the women say so.'

'And cruel. You've left an old woman desperate.'

'She was desperate anyway, the brash old sow.'

Typical Tunley; for him, confession wasn't about forgiveness so much as the avoidance of any need to be forgiven. You tell it and it's out, it's finished. He's a big man and he says the devil

38

has plenty of room in him to hide. So he shows everything he does to the daylight before the devil finds it. It means that I know more about him than I might need – his trips to Bourne for all-night loving and sweating with the two women he seems to have impressed there: one married, one widowed. No other man in the village has better success with women than him. Is it his musical voice, the songs he sings them, the long, plump kisses on their necks? (He's described these to me in such detail I might as well have been kissed by him myself.) His over-generous endowment between the legs? (This, too, he's helped me envisage.) I once asked my sister if she knew what it was about Tunley, if women liked a man who carried the fat of two – did it feel like a bargain? She had nothing to say, only a smile.

'Poison was better than a knife,' Tunley said, as if something had moved him to defend himself. 'I'm not so canny at stabbing and I would have been sorry to look the creature in the eye and do that.'

It struck me that I saw that dog in the first hours of its life, a small, wet thing that smelt of malt, its eyes barely open. It was lowered into my palms, this breathing bag of meat.

I tried to share this with Tunley. 'The day Mary Grant found that dog, up on the track to Oak Hill, she brought it to me – not a day old and the only one alive of its litter. She came to ask me if I could smother it, with the Lord's blessing. I persuaded her to keep it – that must have been six or seven years ago.'

'And it's been howling ever since.'

'And now it's stopped.'

'And for this we thank the Lord,' he said.

I asked him then, 'Did it die where it ate?'

'They take themselves off somewhere.' There was distinct uninterest in his tone, and a hint of impatience now that he'd said what he needed to. 'I poisoned it where it was tied, then untied it and let it die where it wanted.'

'Do you know where it died?'

'Can't say that I do.'

'Could it have made it to the birch copse, down on the way to West Fields?'

'Could have – monkshood takes a few hours to kill you. And it had seven years of bounding to catch up on, wretched beast. Probably the best few hours of its life.'

'Well, there's a dead dog down at the copse.'

'Then you wouldn't need to be much good at arithmetic to put those two things together.'

If I'd told him that I thought I'd seen something running down the road the night before, it would have only been to think with my mouth. Tunley didn't need to know and he wouldn't have cared. But til that moment I hadn't thought of the black thing that had flickered past me through the night rain. I'd been spooked, had designated it a ghost and had run. To think it was only Mary Grant's dog with a bit of monkshood in its gut.

'You're quiet, Reve, have you died?'

'If I have,' I said, 'it's much like life.' He laughed, and I said, 'It's a long way down to the copse, from you out at the brook.'

'Tell me about it. It's a long way to anywhere from the brook.'

A long way, a wet way, since the brook fills and spills after rain and the people in the only two houses on the other side of it, Robert Tunley and Mary Grant, have that to wade through. Tunley does it even with his bad leg, but we don't see Mary Grant for weeks on end. Being kept busy by Tunley, people say with a wink, though the idea – his pillowy lips on her rack of ribs – is enough to make most wish they hadn't.

'Well,' he said, 'and now I'll be off. I've a lot to do today, Reve, much as I'd love to keep talking about the what and where and how long of a dying dog.'

He tells a priest at Shrovetide that *he* has a lot to do. The wonder of Tunley is his boundless self-regard. I too had things

40

to do, and to establish – the what and the where and the how long. Absolution isn't a throwaway thing to be aimed at a vague target. It needs all the precision of shooting a bird out of the sky. His penance depended on increments of intent – whether the killing was mainly to put himself out of his misery, and only slightly to put the dog out of its misery, or vice versa; and whether, and how much, it was to harm or punish Mary Grant, and if it was, how long that intent had been brewing, how thought-out and with how much malice, how the poison was chosen – for speed or drama of death. Whether, how much, how long, why. I went to draw these questions out as an archer his bow and arrow. But Tunley had already stood up with heaving breath and was parting the curtain. He hadn't even waited for forgiveness; it's occurred to me more than once that he uses me like a privy – comes in, sheds what corrupts him and goes.

'Confess and apologise to Mary Grant,' I said. 'Chop her wood for the rest of the year. Bury the dog and say three Hail Marys where it died.'

I said it all for my own benefit. Tunley had gone.

I stared at a thumb-sized scuff in the stone of the wall in front of me, the one that looked unavoidably like a man's upright organ. With a crude scratching I once tried to make it look like the hump of a camel, the creature of temperance, but I'd never seen a camel and my drawing was no better than a child's, and offered no disguise.

I had to go and see it again, the dog. At least to make sure it was carried off and buried and not left to the hawks or hobbies. I stood and kicked my feet against the wall to wake them to action, but then there were voices, some sort of agitation in the nave, and footsteps that ushered a quick scuffle-flutter towards me.

'Reve.'

41

I sat. Lord, I said silently. You made this man; help me with him.

And there he was through the grille, our loud whisperer from abroad, our travelling naysayer, our passing pedant. Our little rural dean doing his sheriff duty, his Oakham prowl. Without a rush I slid the amice from my head and shunted the screen aside.

'A word, Reve.' He smiled as he said it, and he gave a courteous, shallow bow. 'If I'm not disturbing you.'

'No, no,' I said, looking towards my lengthening queue. 'I've absolutely nothing to do.'

That urge of earlier to rush to him, to speak to him, was nowhere to be found now that he was here. Instead its opposite: to be done with him, to see his back and the back of his mare disappear out past New Cross and away. He scurried up the aisle and across the nave to the north door of the church. My queue looked away from me and I from them; I hoped they knew where my loyalties were – that is, not with him, who was conniving and meddling in our business, but with them, our parish, of which I was one. As we stepped outside, the wind whipped about with all the hostility of late winter, a last swish of the tail. Music wafted in from the direction of New Cross and I saw plumes of smoke from the vicinity of our sullen reeve's house, Robert Guy; quite looping and dancerly plumes that carried the smell of mutton fat and bacon.

The dean was a few paces ahead and had adopted – what was it? A little trot? I'd never seen a grown man do that. Did he have a problem with his body, something irritating his undercarriage? Otherwise I could only think it was his way of pretending to be relaxed and at ease with whatever untranquil thing it was he wanted to say. I didn't quicken my pace to catch him, in fact I dragged my feet on purpose, and eventually he waited.

'I was hoping for some privacy,' he said.

'We've only the church walls to hear us.'

He looked up at those fresh, soft, yellowy walls as if for assurance, which, by his frown, he didn't get. 'This has been a difficult few days for your parish, John,' he said with his conspiratorial whisper. John! Just before I was Reve – people always became friendly when they wanted something and weren't sure they'd get it. His little etched face had become lively with slander. 'How is today's confession?'

'One laugh after another,' I said.

And he continued, 'I saw one of those boys from the barns came. What did he have to say?'

'That he was in love.'

'Oh? Who's the lucky woman?'

'It hardly matters.'

'Love always matters when there's an unsolved death. Love is always,' he paused, 'an accomplice.'

I sniffed. I sometimes felt that if I could do something suddenly enough – make a noise, a motion – a dream might be broken and the dean gone.

'It was Annie, as a matter of fact. My sister. The boy Ralf Drake. Just a fleeting infatuation.'

He let out a short *Hff*. Meaning what? I'd have rather told him nothing about anybody, breathed not a word of what passed in confession, but there it was, we'd agreed that I would, back when I trusted him and thought he was here to help.

The dean had slowed to an excruciating dawdle and kept looking at me with something intense and needing. He took my wrist. 'A word of warning,' he said. 'You know that if the ones with something to hide *do* come, they'll tell you a fine, tall tale about something else. Which is why it falls on you to be subtle and cunning and hear what it is they've neglected to say.' He inclined his neat head, and it was as though the air, shrill and pure, rushed away from him. 'And – has Oliver Townshend been to confession?'

43

He was holding my wrist as I'd held the dogwood earlier – not knowing what to do with it, but trying to make it look meaningful now he'd started. I answered, 'No, I haven't seen Townshend.'

'So then,' he said, '*has* anything – murderous – come to light?'

I worked my wrist free and walked on. 'Robert Tunley killed a dog.'

'Oh.' He collected his hands in front of him. 'Did he sit on it?' A rare moment of humour from the dean.

'He poisoned it.'

The word 'poison' lifted him – a momentary stalling of stride, a small triumphant smile forming at the corners of his mouth. 'Poisoned with what?'

'Monkshood.'

'Monkshood? I see. Monkshood – so. But, I have to ask, where did he get it from?' He marvelled at his question as if it were a gold coin he'd unearthed. 'Monkshood grows in the last days of summer, and it's the middle of February.'

'It flowers in the last days of summer, I believe its root exists all year.'

He asked then, with his face especially pinched, 'How did he know where to find it?'

'It grows a few fields along from the brook where Tunley and Mary Grant live, at the foot of the ridge where it's damp and shady, in the warrens. Anybody in this village will tell you that, we lost too many sheep to it before we stopped grazing them there.'

I was irritated by him and made no effort to hide it. What did he know about our village? His questions were the wrong ones; it was no mystery how you'd kill a dog with monkshood any time of year, a piece of root the size of a child's fingernail would kill even a full-grown man, you only had to slice a scrib of root and drop it, as if sowing a seed, into the mush of old entrails the dog had for dinner. His questions were salacious

44

and gossiping; he hadn't even thought to ask whose dog it was, or why it had been wanted dead. He just heard the word 'poison' and the serpent in him uncoiled.

'So we know Tunley had poison at around the time Thomas Newman died,' he was saying to my back, and I replied, 'We could all have poison any time we wanted, it grows everywhere we look.'

Monkshood, henbane, belladonna, hellebore, which isn't even to begin on the mushrooms whose warty caps and pearly milk can have you delirious and very soon dead. Any man, woman or child who'd grown up using the land and had so much as a speck of soil under their nails would know any number of ways to kill or be killed by the duplicitous things that grow around us – it fell into the ilk of things we called common sense, an instinct the dean lacked.

Begrudgingly, realising the topic had come to a close, he said, 'I'd hoped you'd have something to tell me about the murder of a man, not a dog.' And he fell quiet.

He might have had reason to be suspicious of Tunley, given that it was he who first reported a sighting of a man in the river on Saturday morning, and he who'd been away all Friday night, and no one to account for what he was doing. But Tunley was a man beyond reproach; it interested me that even the dean detected that. A man so frank and guileless that no suspicion could rest on him. Or just a man so feisty you didn't risk an accusation.

As we rounded the top of the church my restless stride warred with the dean's nervous shuffle. I had in me the remains of the impulse to go and see the dead dog, a coursing in my legs and arms. I couldn't help but notice anew that my companion had the most unlikeable face – I'd tried to like it but it kept ducking clear of my respect, something about its greyish colour and its thinness, and the dour downturn of the lips.

'Do you know,' he said, 'that in Italy last year on Shrove Tuesday a man died having oranges thrown at him in a so-called

45

carnival? He was trampled in the street and at night when the revellers left, the wolves came, enticed by the sweetness of the oranges, and ripped his body to pieces, leaving only his two eyes on the cobbles.'

The wind hit us as we rounded the corner to the east side of the church. 'What do wolves have against eyes?'

He looked at me, then jutted his chin upwards so as better to persist in his pointless story. 'As for the French, the things they do at Mardi Gras – God himself has to look away.' On cue, he looked away, a theatrical little gesture. 'It's important,' he went on, 'that we here, in our gentler land, remember our own customs and the solemn piety of the occasion. Of course we may enjoy ourselves. But we're not to behave like savages.'

Did the dean know what savagery was? It was taking up in a man's house the very day he dies, washing with his soap, shaving with his blade, curling up on his mattress of down.

'I noticed as I came into the village that the revelry at New Cross was already quite boisterous. Drunken. A little too much guzzling of the *lift-leg,* uh? Isn't that what they call it? *Angel's food, dragon's milk*. And we're only at noon.' *Piss-quick*, I thought; that's what they call it, not that it's your business. He looked up at me with what I thought was his attempt at sympathy and complicity. 'Yes, John, a difficult few days for your parish, but let's not allow that to excuse wrong behaviour.'

He'd asked me nothing, so I said nothing.

'I trust you'll make sure your parish doesn't start behaving like those Italians I mentioned. Worse still, those French.'

We'd reached the south door and I stood in front of it. 'I think we'll be saved from that, most of us here have never even seen an orange,' I said.

I took his hands in mine and squeezed them gently, then let them go. He assessed me with alarm; I hadn't done or said whatever he wanted me to do or say. Then he cradled my face with his hands, one hand cupped lovingly under each jawbone, and said, 'Look at you, those splayed cheeks, that handsome haughty nose, those eyes grey-brown as a gibbet iron, smoky as an old pyre. There's a bit of the Frenchman in *you*, I'd say. We have to watch out for that.'

His look was one of weak malice; the look of a man new to the nastiness of power and not sure about it. I stayed mute and he pressed his thumbs into the hollow pockets behind my jaw. Almost my throat, not quite. A soft place that even my own thumbs had never visited. It was a half-hearted violence and his hands dropped.

'I suppose I think about things too much, Reve,' he said, kneading between his eyes to demonstrate the burden of all that thinking. 'Some of the thoughts are to be ignored, some not, and some – well, some I don't know. For instance, if Newman's body is found in the crook of a tree at West Fields three days after he drowned, and his shirt is found just beyond him in some rushes, why did the shirt get further than the man? How did the shirt come off, for that matter? Did it arrive at that place at the same time as the body, *attached* to the body? Or did one arrive a day, two days, three, earlier than the other? In which case, a coincidence that they washed up within a stone's throw of each other. Though, of course, coincidences happen.'

He walked away from me at the end of this speech, hands linked behind his back, bumping gently on his narrow-robed rear. The dagger of his suspicion once again drawn, then resheathed.

'Newman had been buying up Townshend's land, hadn't he?' he said, turning back to me.

'As I recall, we've spoken about this many times before and you know full well the answer.'

'I know, I know. I'm trying your patience. But the more we speak of it, the less I can get it from my thoughts. Newman bought – what? Two-thirds of Townshend's land? Newman getting richer, Townshend getting poorer. Townshend had every reason to wish him dead.'

He shrugged and looked askance for a moment, then turned, swaddled and shuffling, flapping his arms angrily at a crow that wasn't even in his path.

The dean is a man who's outgrown his own shoes and is feeling the pinch. We've no bishop, no archdeacon, not for now, and he finds himself, bewilderingly, at the top of the heap.

First of all things, Oakham is eyed greedily by the monks at the abbey in Bruton. The dean has warned me, and is worried. As they grow in numbers they need more land, so they cast their gaze about them and see place after place filled with sheep, and no arable land in sight. Then their gaze stops at us, with thousands of sheepless, croppable furlongs (more than anywhere for a hundred miles), and they see that our parish abuts theirs, and that they could live well if they took us over and made Oakham their grange.

Second of all things, our bishop is in prison for trying to put a pretender on the throne, and is dying there – the dean says he won't last long. The archdeacon is preoccupied by worry, and by doing all the work the bishop would do if he weren't in prison. In this turmoil who's watching out for us down here in our little parish, oak- and river-bound, with our church that matters only as much as any other, our hundred little lives with their little thrills and pitfalls, our pigs, cows, hens, our barley and wood? Our bridge-that-never-was? Who'll keep the monks from our door, and the proverbial wolves? The reply is nobody, nobody but the rural dean. And how much does he care? He has his own skin to save. He runs about trying to please the archdeacon in a bid to gain – what? Favour? Power? He yearns to lay a murderer at the archdeacon's feet, as a cat – quivering with pride – brings in a bird to his master.

48

Two years ago I had a conversation with Newman; he told me that in Rome they have purpose-made boxes for confession. They don't kneel at the feet of the priest in the flat light of the nave, but enter a divided box with the penitent in one side, the priest in the other. A *little dark box*. The idea had, to me, beauty and mystery. I thought of this box as a church in miniature, a church within a church – the priest's side being the chancel, the penitent's the nave, and the screen between not so much that which divides the two as that which unites them, through which the two speak to one another. The ordinary man, freed by the discretion of the screen, tells the priest the things of his soul, so the priest can tell them to God and bring him closer to heaven. The screen no barrier, but a surface on which the holy mystery plays itself out.

There'd have been no hope of us having a box like this, all things being equal. Had our bishop not been punished for trying to disrupt the line of the throne, had our archdeacon not been too busy, had our rural dean not been inappropriately in charge and precisely the man he is: no, then this box wouldn't exist. When he, the dean, visited over a year ago, at the start of that winter, I put the idea to him. The church within a church, the screen that unites-not-divides, the play of holy mystery, et cetera. He was uninterested at best; at worst he was offended. He muttered about Italians and sidled greyly across my hope like the cloud he so often is. A cloud that had lately found itself capable of producing rain.

But the winter progressed. Winters can be savage things that persuade by force. We lost a lot that season – crops to flood, animals to snow, men, women and children to illness and hunger. I did my best and so did we all, but in desperate times people do desperate things: they steal, they lie, they cheat, they despair, they forsake Mass, they seek refuge in forbidden beds.

When people are desperate, they do desperate things that they'd rather not tell their priest, who is a neighbour. Maybe it was the priest's bread they stole. Maybe the priest's friend's wife they went to bed with. The priest's sister, even. That Lent – which was the one before this – only half the village came to confess. I petitioned them every day in Mass: You must confess, you cannot take the host unconfessed. Still they didn't come. Then I began to notice increased comings-and-goings at Four Ways where the roads go out to Oak Hill, Bourne, Bruton and Fox Hole, and when I followed someone (as if on a casual walk) I found what I'd already begun to know, that they were going a mile out of the village to meet a travelling friar who took their confessions there by the side of the road, with his hood heavy over his head. He could see them but didn't know them, and they never once had to meet his eye, not even to pass the coins into his purse.

I told this to the dean; the money that should be staying in the village for tithes and donations is going out of it into a friar's purse, for the sake of a confession given incognito. We're a small village with a river that may as well be a wall, for all it keeps the world out. We'd be ruined as a parish if this custom of paying a friar continued, I told him, and it was the truth. Money is a notion the dean can follow, not because he's shrewd or particularly opportunistic, but because he too is desperate, more and more as time goes on. The parishes he's been given charge of suffered that winter, and whose were these sufferings now, if not in part his? If there aren't enough people to see to the land and animals, and if half the animals have died, the village starves, and if the village starves it looks to me, and I look to him, and he looks to the archdeacon who looks to the bishop and finds nobody there. And people lose faith because their protectors have not protected them, and the Lord loses faith in the protectors, whom he appointed to keep him in the hearts of all. Once the Lord has lost his faith in you, you're upriver with no raft and one leg.

And, so, there we were, two men who had little time for each other, one having been lucky enough to stumble on the other's knottiest hate – to him, travelling friars were little but salesmen or frippers, with as much spiritual authority; they were thieves and thugs; one had been found that was half-beast, he said, with the body of a bear. I gave the dean ale and lamb by the fire, it was shortly after Easter, and I listened to his views. It was like having dank water seep over my feet to hear such passionless hate. But at the end of it we joined hands weakly and made our concessions – he to a period of trial for a confession box, and me to installing it without more expense.

Last winter the wide oak door at the north entrance was replaced with a new one; we propped this old door against the south-west corner of the church to improvise a triangle of space for me to sit in. Philip down at Old Cross cut a hole in it and his wife, Avvy, wove a very passable hazel lattice to serve as a grille through which sins could be spoken. A curtain on the other side of it shields the penitent, who kneels between curtain and door. It's crude and childish. I don't know what the Italians would think – it probably looks like an animal den to them, not fit for the workings of God – more a little place for the workings of the bowel and bladder.

Oakham, small and unknown Oakham penned between river and ridge, has the only confession box in England – at least as far as we know. Maybe there are other Oakhams. We've never heard of another. Any bishop in the country would order the box to be torn out – any bishop, that is, but one in prison who hasn't had a thought for years about anything that wasn't his own life, and how to prolong it.

There are advantages to being forgotten. The confession box has drawn the parish inwards towards itself as tight as a clump of primroses. The church is now stuffed with donations: two new chalices to add to the one we had, three extra sets of vestments, a new processional cross, a deep purple Lenten veil, a holy-water pot, four great branched candlesticks and countless simpler ones, incense, a fine carved wooden cover for the font, embroidered banners, a spare rosary for the church porch, a cushion for kneeling in the box, a lantern, paintings of St Katherine, St Erasmus and St Barbara to fend off death, a crudely illustrated Jesu Psalter, and every image and prayer to Mary it's possible to have: a copy of the sweetest prayer to her, the Obsecro Te, and of the meditation 'I sing of a maiden'; an engraving of the Mother of Mercy and a woodcut of the Mother of Mercy and an unaccomplished wall painting of the Mother of Mercy and an ivory figurine of the Mother of Mercy; we've the painting of the Pietà, the Virgin's eyes hooded and doleful, the Christ on her lap rigid with death. Then the strange and dubious Pietà at Newman's altar, the Virgin's eyes turned to us searchingly, and Christ splayed shocking and wounded and tender as fresh meat. The painting glows with pigments only the Italians know how to make. And there at the chancel arch the carving of the Mater Dolorosa, where she stands at the foot of the cross in her most blood-curdling grief. And for every image or prayer donated, we have enough lights to illuminate her for months or perhaps years to come.

The dean's always been doubtful; he says a confession box won't stop them going back to a passing thuggish friar; after all I know who most of my parish are, even with a screen between us, and they know I know, and I know they know. What privacy is this? I think this is where the dean most shows his lack of subtlety. It isn't about me not being able to see them, but them not being able to see me – does he understand this? I've laid the most terrible of burdens at God's feet because I can't see him; why else would one so great keep himself invisible? If I'd been able to look the Lord in the eye, maybe I'd have confided just one or two and kept the worst for myself. My heart would have closed in defence of itself. In other words, a placid dog looked directly in the eyes will snarl and show its hackles. No, our souls are handed over best in blindness, and if the dean needs to be convinced of this, he need only to come to confession here himself and let me, invisible to him, take his darkest and his worst.

The dean isn't a man who has anywhere to rest his troubles. I saw he was getting worried about Oakham, that we were becoming rebellious and falling into bad habits like drinking at noon and drowning by foul play – that the priest in his little dark box was himself a maverick, too loose and daring with the commands of God. I knew he envisaged an army of monks proceeding towards us, come to take our land, which was supposed to be under his guard. He moved into Newman's house even while we scattered the floor with preserved and faded violets. We scattered violets in case Newman's corpse was found and could come home and rest; we had to scatter them around the dean's feet.

From there he watched us; it was a terrible accident that befell Thomas Newman, he'd said; an accident that threatens the future of our village. He said he'd protect us all. But he's a weak man, and weak men go for easy power; he saw a flock in grief and turmoil, and decided to prod it into the pen. Maybe he liked the sport of it, of catching us off-guard, and suddenly there he was gently, solicitously proffering notions of murder so that he could find and hang the murderer, thus fulfilling the cycle of sin and recompense that gives order to this cryptic world and would show him to be in control of his parishes. He feared the ship would sink. I don't blame him for that; it's the fear of anybody who's found himself, mistakenly, at the helm. At several helms at once, and he not a captain. I dare to add, not even a sailor.

Eat we must

We must, and I was past hunger. But for another hour I went back to confession because I didn't want my parish to think the dean had turned my mind against them – that, while they were waiting in line to confess, I was going around their houses furtively looking to incriminate them.

At some time past three I gave my mid-afternoon prayers and took one rosary from the nail on the wall to show the first confession was finished. The second and third would be short, there being other entertainment; once it got dark, my competitors were beer and carolling and shadowy groping, which I was no match for.

I emptied the pillar sconces of Annie's wedding flowers, which were anyway dying. The small witch-hazel frills had wilted and some had fallen. Lent tomorrow – the church must change from bride to widow. From the vestry I took the purple Lenten altar cloths, and the plain cross, which I propped in place. I took the darkest of the cloths, which was the deep hue of blackberry juice, and draped it over the cross.

Next, the wedding gifts and trinkets – a poorly tied bow of straw, two painted stones, which must have been there to designate bride and groom, another stone with a faint glint of tin running through it, and a square of green velvet initialled with an embroidered red *A & J*. Slightly apart from those, a child's wooden doll, which could only have been left by Newman: a wish for healthy children. I folded them into an old altar cloth and put them in the vestry.

I went outside; it was bright to the brink of blindness, the light so sheer, new, cold and fresh. I dropped the wedding flowers around the side of the church. Townshend's fields were empty now – the three behind the church, the three sloping up to the manor, the two just north of New Cross. Nobody was working. Those, and the grazing meadows at West Fields, were all Townshend had left – and admittedly they were the best, but they weren't much; the rest was Newman's. The arable fields spreading out for hundreds of furlongs, then the rough meadows that went beyond our gaze, right up to the parish boundary three miles away. Acre by acre, year by year, Newman had bought the land from Townshend; if it hadn't been for that, Townshend and his wife would have had to leave the manor. They were clinging on. In the empty, white light their little fields looked like boats becalmed at sea.

Some boys were climbing the oak in the churchyard; I walked to the lychgate where I could see the road. The village games and processions. There was otherliness; the sun was stealing colour and the wind was stealing sound, and I thought I was seeing a hundred unearthly things kicking balls. Then came the smell of food frying – eggs, meat, old winter cabbage and trenches of fried bread. The smell of spiced beer, cups of metheglin giving out the sweetness of honey, the hot lushness of pancakes.

And then sound: the tinkling of tambourines, a pipe, drumming on goat-hide, clapping, singing, shouting, cheering, the frantic squawks of fighting cocks. Colour came back to the world. I could just see the crowd where the road bent at New Cross. The main revelry was always at New Cross, which they garlanded with winter ivy. They picked Our Lady's Bells, if they were still blooming in the woods, or Star of Bethlehem, or whatever new spring flowers had grown, and made a garland also for Christ's head. They tied a block of wood to his feet, which he might rest his weight on, and wrapped a shawl of wool around his shoulders for warmth and comfort. Smoke rose from there, the communal pancake fire they'd made.

The four boys in the churchyard by the young oak were raucous with laughter over something. At first I thought they were climbing the tree, or preparing to climb it, but they had their backs to it – not climbing at all, but lolling around it. One of them, I was sure, was Ralf Drake. The game of campball was shifting fitfully up and down the road outside the church, the one stretch of road that was cobbled, and slimed enough with winter wet so as to be as good as ice underfoot. All the young men of the parish were out, some of the older, some girls too, trying to test their small feet against that lifeless, reluctant bag of pig bladder. I didn't know how they kicked it anywhere – it was always the labourers who could, the ploughmen especially, who spent their days moving and turning and lifting waterlogged earth. When I walked past and through their game to the other side of the road I saw the dean, standing at a short distance, watching those boys at the oak. Watching Ralf Drake.

The campballers scuffed that bulging bladder towards me and whistled and bantered. I did try to kick it back; it got lost under my skirts and it came to little Sal Prye to get it out, who was always quick and plucky. Too plucky perhaps, the way he went straight in without much in the way of asking.

From there, and paying no heed to the dean, who paid no heed to me, I set off for Old Cross, which admittedly had no cross. Newman's first gift to Oakham had been a new stone cross at the village's northerly end, and since then the old rotted wooden one had been weathered to a stump. Now there was just the maypole, rising skewed from the rutted road.

I saw nobody but the miller Piers Kemp, hobbling his pained way back from Newman's house with his shoes filled with stones. It didn't often please me to see my Oakhamers do their penance, to know the stones in their shoes were there on my command, to know they hobbled at my will. Mercy seemed a strange thing to me, taking as it did such outwardly unmerciful forms. All the same, he raised a hand in jaunty greeting, said he'd just delivered bread for the dean.

And there it was, the maypole with Newman's shirt atop, tied by a sleeve. In the brisk wind it had dried damp and was flapping without elegance, banging open and closed as if there were a man convulsing inside. If the villagers had seen it, they'd said nothing. It seemed to me an unnecessary cruelty to fly Newman's torn shirt. There was something in the way the loose sleeve kept extending as if the arm were pointing to the west, to all things evil, unlucky, ungodly. As if to say, Newman has gone that way.

A brash prayer, hastily assembled: Lord, turn the wind to blow from the west. I know it isn't for me to ask. But I ask. Let that sleeve unfurl eastwards to all that's good, lucky, godly. Let the wind open and fill it and (like a heart full of love, like a flower bending lightwards) direct it, Lord, to you.

A warm day in summer, four years gone. Newman and I were walking by the river when a man and two women on foot, with a lopsided and shambly cart, passed along the opposite bank. *Farsiders*, we called those travellers we saw on the other bank – and the man had called to us, 'What is this place?'

Newman had called back, 'Oakham!' And then, 'Where are you going?'

'Rome first, Santiago de Compostela after, France then, on the way home.'

'A long way.'

'Shorter if your place had a bridge.'

They were gone soon enough, beyond the oaks that gave us our name, upriver with no trace but the briefly trampled grass, which would soon spring back. Newman bent to pick up a weighty old knot of yew from the bank and hurled it in the river. And I saw that yew roll away downstream, clumsy in the shallows, but inexorable, and I said a thing that came from old thoughts and conversations, and maybe from our languid mood that hot day, and from the sight of those travellers here and gone.

'That wood isn't coming back,' is what I said.

Newman stood hand on hip, one foot kicked forward, squinting.

'But the seasons come back, don't they,' I pressed, 'they come back every year. We're flooded, we're parched, we're thirsty, we've enough, we've nothing, it's winter then spring, it's Lent and Holy Week, it's the summer bonfires, Rogation, Embertide, Corpus Christi. The sun is high, the sun is low, the wheat is green, then gold, then gone. And no year is more tired than the last – have you noticed that? No year is old or tired.'

He looked at me; at the river; at the clouds; at me. 'No,' he said, 'that's true. No year is old or tired.'

'The river of time, isn't that what they call it?' I said. 'But it's no river at all. Time comes back on itself always new. That piece of yew in the river will never come back.'

Newman was upright and firm as a birch at the edge of the bank, and he looked outwards with a private gaze. 'Time's more a circle than a river,' he said, though I couldn't tell if he'd just come to that point of understanding or if he'd had it for years.

'Yes – yes.'

And it was; this endless watermill of days, these rounds of seasons, so clear to me then that it felt as if the world itself – the river, the ham, the woods and skies – were gently curved and motherly, and that we were all healthily round with the recurrence of time.

It occurred to me to say to him then, If time's more a circle than a river, what stops it going back? Can't wheels go this-wise and that-wise? I didn't say it, because I knew already his response, for which I had no response: if time can go that-wise as well as this-wise, why couldn't God bring back his wife and child? And there was nothing I wanted to say or do to provoke in Newman a fresh feeling of loss; it was something to do with the way he'd called across the river to those pilgrims that single word, so emphatic and loyal: Oakham! Something in that word had made him fiercely brotherly – it was us together, the guardians and champions of this village.

It was coming towards lunchtime, and we'd taken to pensive standing, so I tried to nudge him out of thought and into appetite (for he was a man who saw food as a tedious necessity, a man who was prone to sighing *Eat we must* when a bowl of stew was set before him, and eating with enough gratitude, but no zeal). 'Back,' I said. 'Annie's doing us lunch.' Bread and buttermilk, curds, honey, quince, a first ripe fig or two.

But Newman stood his ground and scrutinised the river as though there were a spectacle to see, so I looked too, into the scene of his imagination, and knew full well what he saw, because in that moment I saw with his eyes. He bent again and this time collected a stone, which he sent with a great windmilling hurl beyond the far bank, whipping at the top leaves of an oak and landing invisibly.

'That stone's been further than most of this village,' he said, and in that close brotherliness he turned to me and asked the very thing I'd been about to ask him. 'Do you think those folks who just passed through were right, John, about a bridge?'

'I think – '

'We could build one.'

'Across this river.'

'Across this very river.'

'Why not – it seems high time.'

59

'Gone high time.'

'Why not?'

Indoors was chillier and darker than out, and it stank of cooked goose. The fire pit was a mound of cold ash. Goose-fat bespattered. They think Annie and I are peculiar for throwing water on the fire each night before sleep, but I tend to think they're peculiar for preferring to burn in their beds. Once you've lost your mother to fire, you never feel the same way about going to bed with a flame still live.

I lit two candles at the table for cheer, and to see what I had. The last time I'd eaten was the evening before, when I'd finished the goose. Nineteen hours without food, and now ravenousness that had grown in the wake of yesterday's rare feast – the highest waves make the deepest barrels, after all. My bones felt hollow. There was a piece of bread, one last apple, some milk – I ate and drank it all, and an egg, which I broke into the dregs of the milk and gulped down. Not a meal that inflamed me, I must say. To think what that egg might have been capable of. A fritter, beaten with the milk and flour with some apple chopped in; a simple feast, fried and eaten with bread and fat; or a pancake with the fried apple on top with honey, or a soft scrambled cloud of it with butter and bacon, and the milk warmed. Sorry fantasies, and short. There was no time to light a fire. And there was no bacon, and even if there had been, my fasting from meat had begun that morning – and eat we must.

No time either, now, to go down to the birch copse and see Mary Grant's dog. I didn't even know what I'd do with it if I went. But that copse had always been a strange place to us in Oakham, the winds talkative through the trees and the shadows especially quick and flitting. In the summer we'd hang the birch branches with swatches of horse tails and coloured festoons – some dyed plaits of hemp and linen, some velvet offcuts from

Cecily Townshend's marigold dress. The festoons would see off the spirits, so some said, though I wasn't sure myself of that kind of magic, and now I felt for Mary Grant's hapless dog and wanted it buried in more wholesome ground.

If my sister had still been there I'd have asked her, What shall we do with that dog? And she'd have said straight away, Do this thing, do that. Strange not to have her at hand any more to share things with or ask things of. To do those tasks she'd always done. My discarded cassock in the corner awaited her expert hands and warm water. The pot awaited our two spoons that always came to friendly blows in the stew; quibbles over a piece of grayling or dace, more spirited battles over a piece of precious trout. How could it be that four days before I'd had both her and Newman, and now I had neither? A grief redoubled within my ribs. Annie, my sister and only blood. Her new husband called her Anne, and though she never said so herself, I think that was the reason she married him (none of us could find any other). It made her feel womanly, I suppose; no longer a child.

I cleared away the crumbs and broken eggshell. Then a clack at the door, which made me crush the eggshell in my hand, a rapid hail of clacks – when I opened the door there were a few stones at the step and five or six boys running down towards the west track, away from the village. One of them stopped and turned round, and he looked at me for a few breaths as if he wanted to leave his group and come back this way.

It was Ralf Drake again. Tall and strong and angled leanly. His pose reminded me I'd seen him at my sister's wedding; he'd stood just that way, intent and staring, watching Annie dance. I closed the door on him and stood this side of it, and I thought he was probably still watching.

Shrovetide pranks. Even when my father was a child they hurled stones and mud and bits of pots at doors on Shrove

Tuesday; nothing changes. Egg-rolling, mud-throwing, clothes-swapping – a man in his wife's tunic, a woman in her husband's belt and boots. Let them run loose and untormented for a while, I couldn't imagine any angel in heaven who'd begrudge them that. We carried so many torments, and winter was the most tormented of times – too much thinking in too much time in too much darkness.

Before I left I rinsed the milk cup in the bucket outside and cleared away the stones. By the door there was a patch of warmth away from the wind and a pool of sun warmer than any so far this year. My feet throbbed with gratitude for it. Inside, I put the cup on the table by my knife and spoon, which I kept wedged upright in a gash in the wood made by careless sawing.

My father once shut me outside in the rain for arranging knife and spoon upright in a similar way, as if they were bride and groom at the altar – men must be men, he said, and not play make-believe with knives and spoons. There was ploughing, sowing, dunging, marling, harvesting to do. Ewes to lamb, pigs to butcher. I stayed outside til late and then my mother brought me in. The next day I sang before breakfast, which was bad luck and also shameful whimsy. That night I didn't go indoors at all, but spent the night in the barn. These weren't tendencies I could stop; I spent three dozen or more nights in the barn when I was young, and the darkness moved with demons that slid up and down my skin and slurred tales of death into my ears, and left my skin raw and red, so that in the morning it was as if I'd been cooked by a heat not provided by any earthly process.

I spat into the rinsed cup. Man of Sorrows; blessed image of Christ that I kept on the stool by the bed. I kissed the wood it was carved into and could taste his blood; I brought it to my chest and pressed his hooded eyes and dark lids against me until I could feel his hair, his lips, his swollen veins, as if his hands, which hung down overflowing and empty at once, had been given my life to hold and found it small and wanting.

Now that Annie was gone, it occurred to me that I might never have really known what happened in her thoughts, behind that high, spacious forehead, between those two small ears – she might have had a fondness for that man, who carried with him the stench of sewers. Her chamber was perfectly deserted, much better for me to sleep there now that she was gone, but I couldn't bring myself to move into it. Her bowl was still on the table, scratched and dented, and her vial of ambergris on the shelf.

The door had swelled with the rain and I couldn't close it, only wedge it ajar. A frenzied drumming and calling came strong on the wind, a drinking chant, and the campball game in the street outside my door had grown in number and noise and violence; men fought on the ground to get hold of that pig's bladder. I'd never known anything so illogical as that game, which had spread west, where the road became the westerly track. Fifty or sixty men were part of it by now, hurling and burling, fist over foot, leg over neck, grunting from guts. And the music! Unsweet and out of tune, where the pipes and drums were rain-warped. It was then, hurrying across the road to the church – longing to be back within it – that I saw Tunley at the far side of the haphazard throng of players; he was walking away towards New Cross and slung across his shoulders, like the heaviest of winter collars, was the dog. Its legs hung and bobbed and swung, its body seemed flat as a dead eel; I'd never seen anything more unlively, unlivelier even than something that had never been alive.

Was it a trick of vision, or a premonition (a lurching forward on that wheel of time), that delivered to me, in a lightning strike, the notion that it was Townshend slung dead over Tunley's shoulders – Townshend heavy and lifeless. By pure instinct I looked around for the dean, whose presence had begun to feel persistent and bitter; murderous in its bid to find a murderer. If Townshend is executed, I thought for a moment, Oakham is finished, and in the scope of that thought all sound and vim drained away and the air was cold as iron. But he was nowhere, the dean, and when I looked back at Tunley, it was only a dead dog on his shoulders, and it was towards some meadow that he was doubtless going, to give it a burial.

As I went through the lychgate, as I noticed that the boys who'd been around the oak tree were gone, I understood something only barely related, but connected by anxious associations – I understood what those boys at the old oak were doing. They weren't trying to climb the tree but pretending to be Newman, trying to arrange themselves to appear the way his body had against the fallen tree that morning. They were aping his second death.

Silence.

'Please speak.'

'You first, Father.'

'Don't you know what you want to confess?'

'I know my Ten Commandments by heart, and the Seven Corporal Works of Mercy. Aren't you going to ask me?'

'If you know them, I needn't ask.'

'Aren't you supposed to be testing us, Father?'

I tucked the amice clear of my left ear. I heard the pout of her lips and the tightening of her brow and the sulky twitch of a muscle in the roundness of her cheek. Townshend's servant girl from the manor, Marjory Smith, Mippy they call her for some reason around the village; twelve or thirteen and will probably be married in another winter's time.

'Not testing you, no. But you can tell me which of the Seven Works of Mercy you've practised lately.'

'None of them,' she said.

'That's worse than I feared.'

'So I need your forgiveness,' she whispered through the grille, 'since I could die on my next breath.' She exhaled a faint laugh;

I felt unnecessarily grateful – there was her next breath and she was safely past it. 'He up there could snatch me away.'

'He could – but only when the time is right.'

'Ah,' she said with a hoarse voice. Yet so young, her parents both dead of the sweating sickness when she was nothing more than a baby.

'And that's not my only sin, Father, I also stole. The cheese-makers were quarrelling in their chamber and there was a shoulder of ham on the block in the kitchen, so I helped myself.'

'You should give them their proper names.'

'*Lord* and *Lady* Cheese-maker,' she said.

'Townshend.'

She made a sound. *Hna*, it went, or something like it. She was childish, impish, coarse, I think well loved – even by her cheese-makers, who'd taken her on reluctantly at Newman's goading and were bound to her – I'd learnt – by contract. The lady didn't like female house servants, for reasons I suppose she never needed to state; but still, they seemed to show love of sorts to this one. A child to replace their ambitious four, who'd long ago left Oakham.

'How much ham did you steal?'

'A mountain. But I took it from different places on the joint, so they might not notice.'

'How much is a mountain?'

'It filled my tunic.'

'Why did you fill your tunic with ham?'

'I hid it in my room for eating later, I ate it in bed in the dark and chewed like a lamb. Although I might as well have chomped it in the kitchen, they were arguing long and loud enough.'

'Do you know what they were arguing about?'

'Thick doors at their place.'

'So you heard nothing?'

'They were quarrelling like this,' at which she began lisping in fast, spiked whispers, from which occasionally rose a distinguishable word or phrase. *Well-horsed. Remnant. Sheep and cows. Monday. Venison again.*

'We can't glean much from that,' I said.

'And if you wanted to, that would make you an eavesdropper, Father.'

'Ah,' I said.

She was a little wild thing, a rabbit, pelting about as she always did. But I've heard there are men queuing to marry her, orphan or no. Maybe it was that slight surprising plumpness and petulance, as if she were brought up with privilege and not the hard, parentless shoddiness that had been her childhood that far.

'He ties his wife up – Mr Townshend. He ties her up to the bed and leaves her for hours. She calls to me for help.' Again her mouth was to the grille, her lips a small gasping O, puffing words as a dandelion gives out its seeds.

I lowered my head. 'Do you – help?'

'Would get a flogging if I did.'

These sorry lives people live inside their own walls. Money makes them no better; but then nobody's ever quite trusted Mr Townshend, with his strange cheese fascinations which transcend sense, and sometimes belief.

I closed my eyes. I thought of her mouth at the grille, lips so full of blood and shapely sounds; and of Cecily Townshend, old now and tired from childbearing, but dignified and still beautiful around the eyes. Tied to a bed, like Mary Grant's dog tied howling to a post. I'd thought better of her husband, who'd always seemed good enough, if erratic and a fool in business – and so I found I was asking this child, though I knew it was the wrong question, 'Why does he do that? Tie her up, I mean. Do you know why?'

'The man who's an animal always tries to make an animal of his wife, Father.'

66

That's a deep wisdom for a shallow number of years, I didn't say – and I didn't say it because her years might not be many but they weren't shallow. All that suffering, losing her parents. That can deepen you. I let go of a breath I hadn't known I'd been holding; I felt suddenly, unspeakably low. No words came.

Her voice fell quieter and contrite for the first time. 'I shouldn't have said that,' she said. 'It was ungrateful to those that feed and warm me. And I shouldn't have stolen their ham.'

I drew my head back because she'd made me remember, with shame, that she was the one confessing, she was the one to be forgiven, not Townshend, whose sins were his own. It was as if the dean had passed a seed of suspicion into my hand and the ripe hopefulness of her little voice had made me think of sowing it.

'There are certain sins that we look on lightly and forgive easily,' I said, 'since they come from a wish to be well fed and healthy, which is what the Lord wants for us. But you must learn to take without stealing, and to take only what you need.'

'Yes, Father.'

'I won't ask you to go to your masters and admit to them what you did. Maybe they won't be fair in their response.' Cecily Townshend tied to the bed – Mr Townshend with his rope, frustrated by the failure of his cheese-making empire, a small man who never did well with the wealth he was given. 'But the sin lives on you in smells and fat, which might have got under your skin. Scrub your hands with warm water three times a day to scour it off.'

'I will, Father. Thank you.'

'Tell me,' I said, 'what's the second of the Works of Mercy?'

'Giving drink to the thirsty.'

'And the fifth?'

She said without a pause, 'Caring for the sick.'

'So, next time Mr Townshend is rough with his wife, will you go to her later, when she's untied, and offer her a drink, and help her out?'

'Do I get my forty days' pardon, then,' she asked. 'For confessing, and for doing all that?'

'Yes.'

'Good, because I want to get to heaven quickly. That's where they are and I want to meet them.'

'Who?'

She stood and her hands were in front of the grille, in small fists.

'Your father and mother?'

Her fists eased. Those strong, small hands dropping open. And Thomas Newman? I wanted to ask. Do you miss him too? Thomas Newman who saved you as an orphan and brought you here, and made the Townshends take you on. Will you miss him? The back of my foot found the iron money box under the stool – Thomas Newman's box, with the deeds to his lands and house scrolled and folded inside. It wasn't yet time for the second rosary to come down, but I took it down anyway. I noticed, by the bittersweet smell of hops, that my cup of beer had been knocked over at some interval and had puddled on the floor, as if blown down. But I kept my gaze to the corner, where the stone had a dark, dirty, rough weft. The weft of wet wool and faded day.

Burning

Night comes early to our church. The three windows at the west wall are small and narrow, since glaziers couldn't be found to work at a price this parish could pay. The world has filled with windows, windows the height of four men, the colours of jewels, telling the news that Jesus is born, the magi have come, Lazarus is raised. England rises tall with wondrous cathedrals, as if it has grown at last into an adult, handsome and curious. A land of rich glaziers who, if they trouble themselves with work at all, don't trouble themselves any more with the likes of Oakham.

I've told Townshend, if you want to make money, the world needs glass. But he says glass needs sand and more wood than we have or could afford to buy – glass-makers have flattened the forests of Europe to heat their furnaces, wood is the price of silver. Whereas we have cows, and cows eat grass, which we also have, and breed by themselves and grow faster than trees. Better than sheep, who give all their strength to growing wool – cow's milk is richer and fattier and thicker and more plentiful than any other, an abundant luxury. Cheese, he says. Cheese is what we'll make.

What about wheat, I've said. We can grow hundreds of acres of good wheat. But Townshend says we need our land for sustenance, not for profit. If we devote most of it to wheat and the crop fails, what'll we live on? Sugar, then, I tried. If you want luxury, put your money into sugar – cargoes have started sailing straight into our westerly ports, no need to go to London any more, and if we had our bridge it would be easy to bring it from there to here in cartloads and sell it in portions, or make those little cakes of caffetin the rich like so much, and sweeter, stronger beer. A single pound of it is three times the cost of a whole pig. The rich have a taste for it – they think their tongues are made different from tongues of the poor, who can't taste it. It sets them apart and above. For their tea, for their cakes, for their wine and preserves, they suck it while bathing, they sprinkle it on plums, it keeps their children from crying – sugar has come, sugar would buy us a large west window for the evening light.

Cheese, he's decided. It's cheese will make our fortunes. But only the poor eat cheese, cow's milk or no, and the poor will never make our fortunes. So each afternoon, when the sky is still offering a fair amount of day, the church falls prematurely dark and I or Janet Grant bring a rush-dip to the church lights til there are a hundred or more circles of grainy orange glow around which the darkness deepens. In February the light fades early, and this day I was late to light them. The silken stole of light that slings itself across the wall in the booth had been fading and narrowing to nothing, even as little Mippy had been kneeling there.

Those left waiting in the nave were vague and grey, loose dirty wool, briefly glinting eyes, shifting feet. One man became another, one woman another. Their rosaries clinked; they whispered and laughed. They'd come in from revelry and were giving off a reek of beer. Two of them wore masks, that mush of leaves, mud, twigs, grass, whatever could be found, bound with sheep or goat or goose-fat into a paste and moulded into shapes often too crude to recognise, but always animals, real or supposed. These two were crude – one a dog's head, the other not obvious.

A bird? It seemed to have more a horn than a beak, but I could think of nothing horned that looked like that.

I was tired but restless; Newman's lute, once again, picked its way among the shadows. Or had it been there all the time? None of them in the line could hear it, they showed no sign as they stood and watched me wind my way around the walls making light. The sound followed me and was loudest wherever I was, a gentle but not timid plucking that quivered each new flame into a strong, still, upright petal.

Singing, music, dancing, in the churchyard. The whole village gathering around us, pressing at us. Their torches sent light thrusting and jutting outside the windows as they danced past – all the boys from the barns, the children, the weary mothers, the spinners and ploughmen and yeomen and shepherds, the milkers and cheese girls, the butcher, the carpenter, the blacksmith, the baker – we have only one of each – Lewys's wife with her pregnant load, Tunley perhaps, Janet Grant even, Herry and Cat Carter. They were carolling around the church, giving a repeated rendition of the same song, louder and louder with each round.

> *Broad and beauty, do your duty*
> *Chupader, woah*
> *Time and reason, work for season*
> *Chupader, woah*
> *Young and old, work when you're told*
> *Chupader, woah.*

Soon they'd form a ring around the church as they did every Shrove Tuesday before the curfew bell rang, before they were asked to go indoors and put out their fires and grit their teeth for forty days of Lent. They reached a fever in their masks, dressed in one another's clothes. I took the last confessions with a candle by my feet, whose short well of light served only to make the darkness darker. Their tongues were loosened by drink

71

and they came with more than one sin to hand over, some several. The sky darkened to perse, then to coal, and the noise outside the church lifted and toppled and lifted in waves that hit the church walls like the incoming sea.

Father, I used all the torches (I was scared of the dark), I'm drunk, I poached a rabbit from Townshend's warren, I gave Joan Morris's bottom a playful pinch at the end of dancing 'Hawthorn', I laughed at Jesus in his shawl at New Cross we called him a baby baby-Jesus we fed him some milk, I'm drunk as a lion drunk as a monkey bowsy as a sow, I killed Thomas Newman, Father, I killed Thomas Newman.

'With these hands,' he said, and I said nothing. 'Don't you hear me?'

His breath stale and insistent, and his fingers at the grille like the fingers of Lewys's wife earlier in the day.

'You did not kill anyone.'

'I killed Newman.'

'You did not.'

'I need your forgiveness.'

His fingers of both hands were tugging at the brittle criss-cross of hazel. '*Forgive* me. *Forgive* me.'

'Herry Carter,' I said, 'I can forgive anything you've done, but nothing you haven't. Tell me: what have you done that torments you so much?'

But Carter and I had been there before, and he wasn't going to tell me anything other than that: I killed Newman, with my hands. He thought I wasn't listening. He pressed the crown of his head against the hazel, pressed hard like he himself was the offered ram, and for the first time I felt something other than pity and concern; I felt fear. I didn't know if it was fear of him, or for him.

I took the light from the floor and held it near the grille. The cut in front of his right ear was worse than I'd perceived it to be that morning, deeper and angrier, and was beginning to ooze a sickly greenish-yellow. Was his false confession a form of raving? The pain of these sorts of cuts could drive a man to rave and rail; the pain was a fire that burnt and deranged him. Perhaps if his wife could get him some clean cold water?

'Go home and ask your wife to bathe your head,' I told him.

'If you won't forgive me, I'll go to hell.' His voice was steady and slow and part-buried under the chanting outside. *Chupader, woah, chupader, woah,* the chant beating rhythmically as a drum, and senseless. 'As sure as anything, I'll go to hell.'

'I forgive your confusion and despair; these are forgiven. Go home, get Cat to bathe your wound.'

In a pause from anger, a haze of sorts, he touched his fingers to that wound and, when he drew them away to look, his expression distant and dreamlike, their tips glistened with the wound's yellowy weep. He stood and as he did, he snatched at a strand of hazel, which snapped. I pulled the candle away.

'Benedicite,' she said, and her rotting breath made me lean away.

'Dominus.'

'Confiteor,' she whispered. 'Confiteor, *confiteor*.' This last word was hurled from her lips and I heard only *teor*, which ripped like a bat through the new break in the grille and landed in the cup of my joined hands. At which my palms turned downwards on my thighs to empty themselves.

'He said he did it, I know he confessed, he said he was coming to confess, we spoke just now in the nave and he said it, he said he did it but he's lying, he said it but I did it and he lies. Don't you know about the way Carter lies?'

This whispered rush of words, like trying to hear a voice in the wind, and I wouldn't have been able to, if I hadn't known her voice well and if I didn't know already the kind of thing she'd say. In fact Carter's never been a liar; her saying this made the fact of his honesty strike me. The most plain and honest of men, who'd chosen something so harmful to lie about. By now they outside were throwing small stones at the windows and walls, a few clipped at the door.

'I did it,' she said, and already I was weary of those particular words; weary of the dean's suspicion, of death itself. 'I killed Tom Newman and I want you to tell it and I want to be punished, I can pay with my life, I have what I must to pay, you see?' She stretched her hands out for my attention, both as hooked and rigid as scythes. 'You see?' These hands clutched at her clothes and pulled them away from her skin, as if to show me the life she intended to pay with. 'You see?'

The flat, ridged chest, and then the first swelling that hinted at breast. I turned away. Would that she'd keep these milky places of herself private, for herself only. Poor child – or woman. Before the disease she was a child, round and whole and strong. Only a month before, she went away on a pilgrimage – she went round and whole and hopeful; she walked a hundred miles at least to a shrine in a far church to see a strand of St Katherine of Alexandria's hair, and maybe St Katherine's tooth. In a fortnight she came back – she'd seen the hair and the tooth (which surprised her by being half-rotted), but she didn't seem better for it. She was tired. Then full of fever, then bouts of delirium. Then convulsions, then she wasted.

Maybe it was God's rebuke for her worship of a fraudulent shrine, for praying to the tooth of some old butcher or brewer. Though an overstated rebuke for a small sin, I couldn't help but think. Or maybe she'd done something there about which God was truly enraged. Now what was she – a child still? The shrivelling of her body had turned her into something else at once uglier and more seductive, something gruesome and dangerous that men long for in their loins, though their hearts are repelled. The devil in us all wants death. I prayed for myself quickly and silently.

'Bring your hand here,' I said, gesturing to the hole Carter had made in the grille when he snapped the hazel. She did so without question. The hole was just big enough for me to reach my fingers through and hold her fingers, to stop her tugging at herself. 'Were you brought food today, and bedding? Did the boy come and sweep out the rain?'

'Yes,' she sighed, 'yes', as if all that were of no use to her.

'Did you manage to eat some bacon?'

A hiss: 'The bacon ate me, Father. From the inside, to punish.'

Her hand was cold, yet apparently she yelled at night as if on fire. It's the most spiteful of diseases that says one thing and does another. I squeezed her fingers, which were bent as old branches; I was sure they were more bent than they'd been the day before. Her whole condition seemed sorrier, madder, altogether deathlier.

'Sarah,' I murmured.

She came to me, or I to her, each day of Shrovetide, as Carter had, and confessed to a death she had no part in – perhaps out of lunacy, perhaps because being hanged for a murder was better than rotting slowly in agony. I had nothing else to say. It was as good as being bound in rope – the one thing I could do was forgive, but I couldn't forgive what hadn't been done, and she and Carter wouldn't confess to anything else. So they went away still burdened and troubled while I sat here in the dark, burdened myself by forgiveness that Jesus had entrusted to me to give out to those who needed it, while those who needed it walked away. It made me heavy and helpless. It caused my back to buckle.

'You did not kill anyone,' I said. Words rushed from her, Killedhimkilledhim, ownhands, rippedhim, bithim, me death me yes. Clawed him, stabbed him, axed him. Outside, that chanting. I didn't know how they could repeat the same chant for so long, so loudly, so keenly, and the stupidity of it angered me. The more she muttered, the faster and wilder, the more I repeated myself slowly. 'You did not kill anyone.'

75

With my free hand I crossed myself once and twice. It felt like death wasn't far from her but I couldn't say why; some survived this burning disease, and she was young – but she stank of death. The air around her was musty and thick. I didn't know what to say to save her, and no confession manual would help. Jesus gave his life and, in doing so, the Treasury of Merit overflowed with forgiveness, overflowed. We're men standing at an endless heap of gold while the poorest walk away.

'You are forgiven,' I said at last, since it no longer mattered what she'd done or not done, or what reprisal God sought in riddling her body with disease; in a day or two or three she'd probably be in her grave, soil in her mouth and eyes and her skin at last cool and sallow. At the knowledge, my hand tightened around hers and gripped, and the hands no longer knew which way the comfort went. 'You are forgiven,' I repeated, this time loudly, since the church, but for us two, was at last empty.

Or so I thought – and yet when I'd drunk the last of the beer and closed my eyes and rested the candle on my lap to hurry through Vespers prayers, a voice at the other side of the screen startled my heart to my mouth.

'Father.'

'Who's there?'

'It is very difficult to do the right thing in this life. I once had a friend – or should I say, an ally – who did something I knew was wrong, and for days I pretended not to know, and resolved to defend him if asked.'

'Is that you?' I said.

But he didn't answer, and I didn't need him to. This wretched dean. I'd heard enough of his voice these last few days, and he brought with him the smell of Newman's soap, which he'd washed with that day, after sleeping in Newman's bed. The expensive white soap from Venice, not the black soap we had here. The good feather-bed that wasn't his to sleep in.

'Have you come to confess something?'

'Yes, Father,' he said, 'I eavesdropped. But I understand that eavesdropping is a sin that's easier to forgive than others, coming as it does from curiosity, which is the beginning of faith.'

'All sins depend on intention.'

'Ah, well then, that's even better. All I intended to do was stand in line waiting for confession, but,' he knocked on the oak screen, 'not such thick doors at this place.'

I looked down at the candle flame, which seemed to rush up at me, infernal and infinite, no longer a single flame but a world of fire, dreadful and beautiful.

'You see, I overheard the servant girl's confession earlier,' the dean said. 'Which was diverting, wasn't it? Townshend arguing with his wife, tying her up? I wonder what they argued about? They say Cecily Townshend is very upset about Newman's death. More upset than most.'

'You're forgiven your sin. Say five Our Fathers. Please, go. I'm tired.'

'Be brief, be brutal, be gone. Isn't that how it goes at confession? Bring them in, send them out. No need to listen to what they say.'

'What do you want?' I said.

'Tell me about Ralf Drake.'

'What about Ralf Drake?'

'He was in love with your sister, your sister and Newman were close, so I'm told. A rivalry, I wonder?'

'Your aim is wild,' I said, entirely embittered by now. He was a man flinging stones at birds with his eyes closed.

'Yes.' He let out a breath into the darkness and his *yes* sat as a hush in the air; the silence curdled around it. Then his face came to the grille, a glint of eye and not much else, that smell of soap. 'At least I'm trying to take aim, unlike you. Until today

I was merely confused – today I'm suspicious. Nothing adds up: a man drowned but we don't know why or how, his torn shirt on the rushes, his body, apparently, in the crook of a fallen tree, yet seen by nobody who can prove it, and then strangely gone. Your parish all sinful and superstitious and muttery. And you, the one person who might show guidance? You turn away as if it's not happening.'

'Don't you see there's nothing to be suspicious of? And Ralf Drake. Ralf Drake! Suspicion is corrupting your better sense.'

'Townshend, then,' the dean said, his mouth still at the grille. 'We're back to that.'

He disappeared from the grille and sat deep into the shadow of the booth. I could see nothing of him. 'You want to protect Townshend, because you feel sorry for him, but in my opinion a priest needs higher motives than pity.'

'I feel neither way about Townshend, he's just a man.'

'Can't you accept that nobody in this parish has more reason to see Newman dead?'

For the first time in this exchange the dean's voice rose and thinned. I leant back against the wall. My pity was almost with him, desperate foolish man, building and rebuilding accusations from the same bent truths, just as the stoopers were trying to build furrows out of sludge.

'Newman came here a freeman with one field to his name,' the dean said, 'and ended up with two-thirds of the parish. Do you think Townshend liked him for that?'

If we killed those we disliked, I wanted to say – but I let the rest of the thought alone.

'And then there's the fact of Mrs Townshend – ' he said, his voice more languorous and cunning. 'What could she have done to drive her husband to such unkindness and anger?'

I sat up. 'Perhaps you'd be better to give up with this,' I said. 'After all, some could say that the man who takes up in a dead man's house the very day he dies, and who gains respect from

78

finding the murderer, might be the murderer himself. Who's to say your hand didn't push Newman under? It's no secret you were wary of him.'

He gave a laugh that was falser than any I'd heard. It extinguished his candle, so that the only light he had was the little of mine that made it through the grille. He flapped and fluttered, and the tin candle-holder clattered on the stone. Then quiet.

But how could I be at any peace myself when I knew that he must also have been lingering outside while Sarah confessed, and heard what she'd said? And perhaps – worse still – what Carter had said. If he had, I knew he'd be unable to refrain from telling me, so I waited. I didn't have to wait long; I heard the excitement of his silence, his breath cupping at the back of his throat til finally it spilt.

'That diseased girl says she killed him.'

'Sarah.'

'Sarah.'

'Anybody can see she's mad with sickness,' I said. '*Furore detentus*. And weak. Too weak to stand up most of the time, let alone grapple with a man in a river.'

'I agree, but she did confess.'

My eyes closed briefly against what he might say next. If he'd heard Carter's confession, it would be much harder to argue it away as empty ranting; Carter wasn't mad, though grief-stricken, and was there this very morning to find the shirt, and could have killed another man – though Newman was as good as his father, and was loved as one.

'It seems to me,' said the dean, from whatever composure he'd gathered in the darkness, 'that we need a murderer by tomorrow, and if you won't back me up in offering Townshend, then my only choice is to accuse the one person who has confessed to it. What else can I do?'

The one person. Only the one. So he hadn't heard Carter's confession? My relief was such that I didn't notice at first what he was saying. Then, alas, I noticed. Someone had to be offered by the morning, Townshend or Sarah, and the choice in that was mine. Townshend, the lord of our parish, even if no great man. A bad man of business, a worse husband, but not a murderer. Even if he was, Newman wouldn't have been one of his victims, Newman was the only thing keeping a roof over his and Cecily's heads.

But Sarah, dear Sarah, my sister's closest friend. The noise outside filled the silence within; the beating and singing and chanting, the pelting of stones against the fragile, barely paid-for glass.

As if he'd been privy to my thoughts he added, 'I could throw in Ralf Drake if you'd like a wider choice. Less scandalous if a dung-slinging boy's found guilty, the whole thing could be cleared up quicker.'

'Cleared up? You mean one of my parish tied to a stake and burnt.'

'Tomorrow's Ash Wednesday, what better day to do it?'

I didn't know chills travelled down spines except in sayings, but one found my spine and snaked down, and met an outbreak of sweat at the base.

'Ralf Drake has no part in this.'

I'd gone forward, my own face to the grille now, and was met swiftly by the dean's eyes, a glint of candlelight catching the sheened skin on his nose. '*This* being what?'

'Forgive me,' I said, and put my hand to the lattice, 'but we don't have to persist. What if you tell the archdeacon that Newman's death was self-murder? And if self-murder, nobody else can be blamed.'

'What a credulous man you must think the archdeacon is, if you change your story at the last moment from accident to suicide and expect to be believed.'

'Those who knew Newman would be able to see he was his own murderer, I'm sure of it; he – he was a – a man of dark moods. He wasn't a happy man.'

'If every unhappy man jumped in a river, this village would have very few living men, and no dry ones.'

I curled my fingers around that lattice. But swallowed my words, and made ready to reason, to pacify, to flatter.

'In your wisdom,' I said, 'on Saturday, you issued a pardon, in the hope half the parish would come for confession before Lent, so that we could confirm nothing suspicious was to be found. They're a good parish, good penitents, you could tell the archdeacon. And here we are, with Lent on us, and about seventy of this parish have confessed, well over half. Aren't you pleased?'

'I was wrong, perhaps their eagerness to confess only speaks of being riddled with sin.'

So you change the rules of the game! I went to say, then heard how risible this was, to even think of the dean's scheming as a game. Yet he had. He'd told me to bring the parish to confession to show how faithful and repentant they were, then when they'd come, he'd said they must be guilty – and so I sat, stunned, in this cleft stick he'd whittled, and felt each heartbeat imprint against my chest those two names: Sarah, Townshend, Sarah, Townshend. Sarah. Sarah? Townshend. While the dean sat cool and firm.

'You're a fair man – ' I said, and he curbed me by pressing his palm against the grille. My nose and lips almost touching it. I backed away.

'You've failed to keep a grip on this parish, Reve. You have a village of people who are no better than livestock. You should thank me for helping you bring them under control.' He rose from kneeling, if he'd ever been kneeling, and I heard him scratch about, taking the remaining rosary from the nail, which he pushed through the grille. 'Confession's over,' he said; he fumbled with the curtain, the dropped candleholder finding his foot, skittering across the stone. 'Make your choice and let me know what it is in the morning.'

* * *

Sarah had been cowering all that time in the porch, in the corner, her neck twisted in pain. I took her at first, by lamplight, for an old woman. The dean had gone, perhaps by the north door. She said, 'Not safe out there, Father.'

'You must get out of Oakham,' I told her. It was a rough whisper, and instantly regretted. For in telling her to escape, and if only one of the dean's chosen pair was left in the morning, wasn't I now making my decision? Hadn't I just condemned Townshend to death? She only nodded as if she'd do anything I asked without question, and I, disturbed by this trust, stood.

I let her wait in the darkness while the stones assailed the door. The wind that flung at the east window was the punishment of failure, since I'd asked for it from the west and it was not from the west; what hope of saving my parish, if I attracted that much scorn from him up above – that he should go to the trouble of sending a wind, and send the wrong one?

When I unlatched and pushed the church's outer door a little, the raining stones stopped and a new chant punched the air – *JohnReve, JohnReve* – and as I emerged to them a cheer went up. A continuous circle of shadows holding wind-thrashed torches, and a mass of shapes that bloated and narrowed. Masks that reared into impossible shapes of griffins and dragons and leafless trees, in the woozy lurch of flame. Leviathan one moment, then demon, then friend. A child lengthening into the fleeting form of a hare. I had just enough wits to see Sarah, who'd broken free of the porch, running out through the circle, under joined hands, and away. Barely a human, no more than a spectre. And then it seemed that another body came from the spot Sarah had vanished into, a shifting shape running towards me with the large head of a pig. I cried out with a sound that came from a pit in my gut, a place I'd not even known existed. Then the circle disbanded and they rushed inwards with a hollering that was possessed and joyful. My shoulders were clasped, my head gripped by blind fingers, and a mask placed over it whose weight jarred my head forward. I knew it was a mask by its stench of animal-gut and mud and the slenderest sweetness of grass – the pig's head, the hare, a unicorn, an owl? It was heavy enough to be the head of a real bear. I saw, through the ill-placed eyeholes, only the flashing of darkness and flame. I thought I saw the great laughing mouth of Townshend, and beyond him, watching him, the dean – his small, sober face half-hidden by his hood, a cold, pale waning moon. They began to spin me round to a feverish clapping, and I stumbled over my feet. Blind inside my own disguise, baffled and frantic. They were chanting my name as if they wanted me to do something, but I couldn't act – we behave according to the creatures we are, and I had no notion of what creature they'd made me become.

Day 3
The previous day, Shrove (also Collop) Monday

Goose, cooked

The day started rainless and tender. When I got up and went outside to empty my bowel and fetch in water, the horizon wasn't entirely dark and was forming a streak of distinct and kindest pink; a sun rising to greet us. It was more comforting to me than the blood-red stain of a usual winter sunrise, and the sky was spacious enough to make way for the inrush of a cleansing wind, much needed, long absent. Today, perhaps? I took a bowlful of water from the flooded bucket.

There'd been so much rain that I'd failed to notice the coming on of things, things that were now, even in this frail light, speaking out. I noticed how the stark branches of the rowan and hazel that shielded my toilet were pocked with new buds. How the birds were venturing song into the half-darkness, and how hopeful and strident they were in their preparations to make families. How newly, secretly fertile might be the ground, though it sloshed in places ankle-deep with water. How adventurous the air seemed. I wanted to walk for miles. There were clouds, but not threatening or many, and the stars were dimming.

My shoulder forced the swollen door. Inside I drenched a piece of wash lint with water and showed it a scrape of soap, then, still cassocked, scrubbed what was reachable. I was famished, the brief famishment I always had when I woke up.

As if, each dawn, my body was petulant about rising again and threw a newborn's rage – feed me! It was a feeling that was always eased quickly with a mouthful or two of bread.

But there was a thing to do. A thing that had pressed on me so much in the night that I'd found a way to forget it. I went outside again, to the back of the house, where it waited near the wall. A goose, hacked clean of head and legs but otherwise just as it had been in life. It'd performed the miracle of being outside all night wrapped only in sackcloth, without being devoured by fox or dog. Sometimes you're given a gift you don't want, or you can't use, one that's too much. I was grateful to the Townshends, it was a good gift; a young small goose – but not a good gift when Lent fasting was one day off. As a rule I ate only as much meat as could be afforded, and even then only as much as God allowed, which was never as much as I wanted. But Cecily Townshend had asked that I shared it with nobody, and how could I eat a whole goose myself in one day? It would've been easier if a fox had helped me out; I'd fully expected that one would.

At the table I plucked it roughly. The room was scattered with feathers and smelt of thin blood. Its skin puckered sore and ugly. Then I rolled my sleeves and went in for the viscera. I cut it into pieces, and though I tried to find the natural contours of its parts, I wasn't a butcher and I hacked and tore across muscles. In the end I had a slick pink pile of flesh that had no resemblance to a goose, but which seemed to throb with injured life like something hit by a speeding cart. The bones, gristle and viscera went in a bucket for burying later. I swilled the table down with water left in the washing bowl and mopped up the watery blood with rags.

I started the fire from the one guarded candle I kept burning inside the door, which I lit before bed, replaced at Matins in the blackness of midnight, then again at Lauds, then at Prime. We weren't short of candles in Oakham, no: women spent their evenings basting rope in sheep-fat and cutting it into lengths, they could do it with one hand and cook or spin or darn or dandle with the other. They claimed that they could baste while coupling, and that their husbands didn't notice. Candles were stacked high in the vestry, and more in the porch, hoarded as donations and offerings for the safe traverse of the soul past death. If the church caught fire, there'd be so much tallow it would burn for days.

You want too much, the goose said, as I lifted a skewer to it. I showed it the fire, which had taken smokily at first, then unfolded well into flames. *You want, you want, you want. You want candles, then you complain: too many candles.* I hushed it by pushing a skewered piece of it into the flame. Had I complained? I'd only said that we have a lot of candles. *Hoarded, you said.* And I realised this voice of the goose was that of Townshend, since it was Townshend's goose, raised and fed on his attitudes. Townshend wanted too little; he'd helped not at all with the building of the bridge, would rather we all lived stooped and poor. He feared the colours and scents of wealth. I ate the morsel of goose. I'd no idea which bit of its body it was from, but it was oily and sapid and rich.

Then I cooked it two pieces at a time on the skewer, so it could say nothing more. I ate as I cooked, as much as I could, and fried pieces in both the skillet and cooking pot to speed the task. The vacant happiness of eating filled me; the meat was tastier than any lifetime of bread. One mouthful of it scythed a whole field of summer wheat to stalk and husk. There was no choice but to open the door a narrow crack, and then a larger crack, for want of air to carry away the smoke from the fire and spitting fat. I cared that someone would see, but cared more that smoke would make me cough, and coughing would keep that soft flesh from my mouth.

Yes, the people of this parish are hoarders, I found myself arguing to nobody, in defence of nothing but an imagined reproach. Do they want their loose change to go into a pot to build a bridge or a road, or start an industry that would make them tenfold richer? Or to make the church itself more sturdy and magnificent a vessel in which to reach heaven? No, none of these; they want to spend their money on candles, and they want to get to heaven by filling the church with trinkets and offerings as a finch brings grubs for its brood – so that while we have insufficient windows and too few carvings, we have more lights, I suspect, than the whole world combined, and buds and nuts and beetles, so that a visitor to our church might think the wind has blown the forest floor in and left it at the altars. And I wonder at times if that ship, our church, will sink under its own weight before it can sail us anywhere. I would rather it floated than sank; is this me wanting too much?

Carracks of sugar sail into ports only thirty miles away, square-rigged and fearless ploughs of the sea. And Newman saw silver dripping from seams – *dripping*, as water from a sluice. The new cathedral at York has its Great East Window that tells the story of mankind, beginning to end, foresees our apocalypse even while it's triumphant with sunrise. We have a ruined bridge and a church full of holy clutter. Do I want too much?

I feared the goose wasn't listening. Even with the door open, the room filled with smoke and my eyes swelled and reddened and my stomach began to ache as though I'd swallowed a rock that was stuck at the lower end of my ribs. A few pieces more, and then I should stop, a few pieces. The villagers might eat some last flesh on the Tuesday if they had any left, but my fast began this Monday night. There could be no goose in this house after that; any I didn't eat would be wasted, and a sign of disregard for the abundant grace of God. I couldn't bear to not have it. So I speared one piece after another onto the skewer and shielded my eyes. Wouldn't you have done the same, even if it seems greedy in the telling? Then I cooked more to pile into muslin, thinking I might offer it to Carter. Cecily Townshend wouldn't mind, or know. That fleeting appetite I'd woken with had lasted me well, everything after that was pleasure and greed, and that too was finally gone.

By eight o'clock that morning I was more stuffed with food than I'd been for months or years, though a third of the goose still remained in its pile of glistening pink. I washed my hands outside and splashed my face. No rumour of wind yet. In the village at this time of year we had only one way of telling the weather: if you can see the ridge, you know it's going to rain; if you can't, it's already raining. I could see the ridge, the sun glowing low across its slumbering spine. But the promise of the day was already half-broken. Clouds were fattening, some from the north, some from the east.

Golden hook

For what was left of the morning, while the villagers were at their jobs, I saw to my garden. Where nothing grew I turned over the soil to work in manure, and I tried to drain water away from those things that did still grow – some colewort, beets, turnips, parsnips, smallage, leeks, rosemary, radish. You'll have to grow gills, I told them. They hadn't a lot to say back. Oh for the days of sweet peas and vetch and beans and plums and gourds and peaches. Figs!

I knocked the wattle fence deeper into the ground, else rabbits would be in there, and deer, sheep, cows, anything with a stomach. Robert Tunley, no doubt. Rotundley, as some privately called him. I made five shallow waterlogged trenches and scattered in broad beans. A little late – plant them on the first day of February's new moon, they said, which was a week before. Still, what did the beans know, they couldn't see the moon. All this cloud – nobody could see the moon. I covered them with soil that wouldn't be coaxed anywhere near a crumble, in spite of trying. Ten o'clock had come by the time I'd finished.

Out on the road, a patch of sun raced away the moment my foot met it, and the clouds had come down weighty. You could almost see the spirits aloft in these sudden shifts between light and gloom. They were marauding minutely between light shafts.

Churning the air up into rain to make more river to curse bridge and crush hope.

People passed on their way home from their plots, weary for lunch, with some weak sun glinting off the edge of their newly sharpened spades, and a sparkling rain beginning to tap at their coats and at the headscarves they were hurriedly tying. The weasel-faced hustler David Hikson, our seedy brewer, but today dragging a mangled harrow; ploughman and piper Morris Hall and his wife Joan; young Sal Prye; little Mippy; labourer John Hadlo and his sweet boy Tom; Marion and Jane Tunley, daughters of Robert, who spun, fulled, sowed, gleaned, made hay, kept house, tended animals; three of the barn boys, John Mersh, Ralf Drake, Mickey Brackley; Piers Kemp, miller, on his way back from Townshend's; Adam Lewys, also ploughman, not with his pregnant wife. I nodded at them without speaking, and only some of them nodded back. Morris Hall grinned to show how unmurderous he was. The dean's skulking and house-searching were beginning to unnerve them; all of you are suspects, the dean's twitching lip said. If they thought I suspected them they were wrong, but I couldn't stop to speak and maybe that made me look vexed. The truth was, I was more worried by my own gluttonous secret than theirs. I was stuffed to the seams with goose, my cassock greasy and my smell betraying.

I followed the road towards New Cross. Here, our short stretch of cobbles, and on it the broken axle from the cart that had tipped the day before, which John Hadlo and Paul Brackley were preparing to carry away. Though the dogs and the rain had dealt with the six churns of milk that had spilt, the water between the cobbles still ran greyish. Then the far sound of girls' voices in song. The whiff of fire smoke and fresh ploughed earth, the cawing of hens, the snuffling of breath from bodies that had overwintered and grown wet and soft like wood. The yews clumped on the boundary of the churchyard were purple-barked and busy with hawfinches.

There was Townshend up at the manor, a distant figure strutting around among his churns and pails like a man who'd lost something. His cows were tethered in a row along the fence of the pastureland, a paddock watered by hand in dry weather, drained by hand in wet, zealously surveyed from the manor rooms. The sweet song came from his milking girls who sang at their stools to make the milk flow thicker and faster – or so Townshend had heard. Next he'd be making them sing to the grass by moonlight, bare-chested; and if it would help his woeful cheese empire, maybe he should.

I had two chunks of bread and three apples. One chunk of bread for John Fisker just past New Cross, who was down with a gash in the leg from the harrow; the other to Sarah, whose suffering was both less and more – no unseemly bone-baring gash through a calf muscle, but this burning from inside, and a growing madness. I'd had five apples, I'd eaten one. The last was at home. Three were in my hand. How was I to divide three apples by two? If I cut one in half, both halves would only go brown, and both brown halves would speak less of apple and more of lack of apple. Not such a loving God, they'd think, if this is all he can do. I should have brought all four and not saved one for myself; four doesn't force the dilemma of three when divided by two, four is equally abundant, or else equally mean. I held the apples at my side uselessly, all three in one hand. I stood without movement under the strain of the decision, my eyes going this way and that: Fisker, Sarah, Fisker.

When I reached Fisker's door, which came first, I found myself knocking and leaving the bread and only one apple. When I reached Sarah's door thirty yards down and knocked, and left the bread and two apples, and walked away before I'd have to see her wasted, grateful figure, I was glad at my decision. An apple in February is a treat, and an aid to thriving. I'd go again later, I thought, and bring her a blanket from the pile in the vestry.

* * *

I called, 'Hello?' and nothing called back. Yet something or someone had moved in the church when I walked in, I was sure I'd seen a shadow fall across the chancel. I thought it must have been the churchwarden, Janet Grant, daughter of Mary, because she'd been that morning – the church was unlocked and the candles and incense lit. So I called again, 'Janet?' and I stood for a while for the church to prove itself empty. It was bright with morning. Awash with sudden sun, painted and lovely and shadowless. I smelt the sweetness of Newman's soap, and almost muttered, Tom? Then remembered the dean; he must have been through.

I hung the three rosaries on the nail and went into the little dark box; I waited for confession; I gave my prayer: 'Thank you, Lord, for the bewildering spectacle of days that fall like water from a mill, one day after another, one beginning where the other vanishes. For the eternity of this.'

'I've succumbed to envy, Father.'

'Of what, or whom?'

'Of you.'

'Why?'

'Because you'll always have enough to eat. You'll be the last person to starve in this parish.'

Why did she say this? I turned my head away from the grille because my breath and skin and cassock smelt pungently of goose-meat. I waited for her to say something else – *I saw you filling your mouth with a goose, Father; explain that.* But she said nothing.

'I wouldn't readily let my parish starve,' I said, and it wasn't a lie. 'I have never. And if you did starve, I would too – I'm only a man myself.'

'Well, if you are, then you surely will,' she said. 'Without Tom Newman, what do you think is going to happen to us all? Half this village has been renting his land for ten years, always good land, and if we're late paying he gives us time, and if crops do badly he lowers the rent. Do you know how many good landlords there are in the world? None, now that Newman's gone.'

I knew her brusque and raspy voice – Agnes Prye, grandmother to young Sal, a widow who lived a stretch out of Oakham on the east edge of the parish, where Newman had a belt of grazing land and a dozen or so acres of tenanted arable in plots marked out neatly by doles. She was barn-ish in her build, hair the colour of cold ash, a firm face eased by a small, sweet nose.

'It's true he was a good man,' I said.

A rich man, too, who was two days dead – at some point soon the question would arise about his property and land. It would dawn on some of his tenants to take an opportunistic view: with their landlord dead and no known relatives in sight, wasn't the land, by proxy, theirs, at least until somebody said otherwise? His cows, his sheep, his goats and pigs, his horses and his hens were property of the parish, in some opinions at least. A few were likely eyeing up his house, which was small but – as the dean was finding – no less comfortable than the manor, and had a chimney, and a mattress of duck down.

As if she knew my thoughts, she said, 'None of us know which relative from afar will turn up and claim his land, and there's nothing worse than a distant relative. They never mean well.'

The last time I saw Agnes Prye, except at Mass, had been about two weeks before, with Newman, when they'd brought his horses to be shod. Newman had hired her to manage the three mares that grazed the paddock behind his house, probably in exchange for some land – but maybe not. Maybe he paid her, he was shrewd like that. If you paid someone, they had money. If they had money, they could rent more land, and who would they rent it from? A man like Townshend who never paid a penny, or the man who gave them the money in the first place?

'Envy is the saddest of sins,' I said, 'the one God would most like men to conquer.' I laid my hands on my thighs and turned my face towards her, though she might not have known. 'Laziness is a man wasting time, greed is him wasting food or money, anger is him wasting his peace. But envy – envy is him wasting his fellow man. Wasting the solace of other men.'

She breathed with an old rhythm that had worn a track across her heart. I could hear the tired progress of it.

'Why did God give us one another?' I said. 'Why did he make us love and need one another? Why do animals huddle together in the field, when the field is big enough for them to stand alone?'

'Life is lonely enough, Father, that's why.'

'And so we're given each other for company on earth before we reach God in heaven. To envy your fellow man anything is to waste his love, to forget what a comfort he is to you.'

Then she said tentatively, 'But you aren't a fellow man. You are – the Ghostly Father, him between us and the Lord. The golden hook, didn't you say? The golden hook that the fisherman must use to catch the fish. Well, lucky you, to catch all the fish. Do you know what it is to be ignored by our God? No, because you've his ear constant at your mouth.'

'And you've my ear at your mouth.'

'But the Lord grants the final mercy, doesn't he? I envy you because whatever you do, he'll listen and forgive and protect you from hell. Whatever you do, even the most dire of all things, your neck will never have to get familiar with a noose.'

I wanted to ask her, What is it I do? What dire things? I saw her vividly then in the street, some months before when the sun beat hot, with a horse's tether in her chapped fist, thick strong calves emerging from the russet tunic, her hair hidden by a wimple as though to declare she remained married, though her husband was dead. She was waiting with an expression that didn't dare be anything but blank and unknowing. The horse was dozing in the sun, resting lax-lipped on her chest.

'I am *primus inter pares*,' I told her, 'chief parishioner. *Parishioner*, you see, which makes me one of you.'

'Our Ghostly Father, higher than the angels.'

'And also one of you.'

'But you'll never go hungry.'

'I've often been hungry.'

'And you will never be punished.'

'I'm punished like all the rest.'

She shifted on the cushion; kneeling wasn't comfortable for those with stiff joints and wide legs made for work. 'What shall I do, Father?'

'Declare what you're grateful for, every day for seven days declare it to an image of Mary and, when you don't have an image of Mary to hand, declare it, if only to the air.'

I remembered how she'd looked fixedly downwards at nothing that hot day, with the warmth of the sun on her. Was she thinking, *The angels are above me, I must not look up*? Perhaps she, tied to the earth by filth and horse flank and low hope, didn't wish to hear that her priest was similarly tied, didn't want to be cured of her envy of him, didn't even care if he did dire things – only wanted his holy neck to be safe so that it could be capable one day of saving hers.

'May God give you a good day,' I said at length, and she seemed to jump, as though she'd forgotten I was there.

'And you, Father, a good day.'

Cheesechurn

Father, I slept all day, I cut a hole in a wall to spy on a woman, I shovelled some of my no-good-clay onto my neighbour's plot, I stole the last spoonful of honey instead of offering it to my husband, I ate the lucky egg, I cursed my father, I swore, I snored, I farted, I doubted.

'Benedicite,' Piers Kemp announced.

'Dominus.'

'A woman, Father, labouring in childbirth. The midwife says, Let me inspect your private downbelow to see if the child is coming. To which the woman replies, Best to check the other side too, my husband has often used that road.'

'Confiteor,' I said with a sigh.

'Pardon?'

'I say Dominus, and you say Confiteor.'

'That you do, that I do.'

When I saw Kemp that morning on his way up to Townshend's, I'd wondered when he might appear; he was never one to miss out on a pardon. A wiry bachelor with a bent grin and fast-disappearing hair. He'd worked for Townshend longer than my time in this parish, since he was a boy, grinding the corn down at Townshend's mill. Every day he did that; every day his hairline retreated further from his forehead.

'Do you have a confession?'

'I have quite a confession,' he whispered, his loose, wide mouth suddenly at the grille.

'Then please.'

'Have you ever heard of a woman with the head of a pig?'

'Not – '

'But with the body of a sleek young girl, as fuckable as they come.'

Words crowded at the top of my chest but didn't organise themselves into anything worth saying, so I slouched in silence, back aching, elbows burrowed into knees.

'Then again,' he said, 'I suppose lovely young girls with pigs' heads aren't really your speciality, Father.'

'I'm not sure they're anyone's,' I said.

'Ha!' A single eruption of laughter – and then without laughter and once more low and lascivious, 'They're my speciality now.'

I felt for Piers Kemp. Some said he was the most cheerful man in England, with a quick smile that could cheat the devil, but I'd seen the other side of that smile and it was disappointed, wary and tired. He had only two she-goats for company and he liked to amuse children by lifting the goats onto their hind legs and causing them to dance. And it did amuse children, though the goats' cold lizard-eyes always held a look of startled dismay.

'This pig-girl I know was born to a good family, believe it or not,' he said. 'Father with a human head and mother with a human head, with not a snout between them. They said her mother died of disappointment when that little piglet snuffled forth between her legs. Her father was trying to sell her off in marriage, so he didn't have to bear the sight of her any more – and she'd been around many a man before she reached me, my poor girl. She was sold to a captain first, and the captain took one look at her and asked for her to be sent away. Then she was presented to a doctor, this time with a sack on her head, and the doctor became glinty-eyed and interested and got ready with his money – but when the sack came off, he was disgusted and put it back on. Another, this time a poet, who had no money, took it on himself to try her out for free. He undressed her and laid her down with the sack still on her head and was happy with what he saw, because her body was milk and honey, with long, round thighs and an enticing deep cavern, but when he went to take her she squealed, as pigs do when they haven't been paid for. And what do you think this poet did?'

I sighed again.

'This squeamish poet jumped up from the bed and claimed a poem had come upon him, which he had to go and write down. You'll guess, Father, that he left and never went back.'

And I put my head in my hands and wondered what it was like to be Piers Kemp. Did he find a still pond, and tell these stories to the audience of his own face?

'Word got round that there was a little village called Oakham,' he was saying, 'where anybody could go, no matter how unwanted in life. A village of scrags and outcasts. So they took this foul beauty there – though nobody seemed to know where Oakham was, and they ended up in Wales before they found it after two weeks of looking. When they got there and asked if any men were keen to marry, they were told there was a miller, a poor miller who hadn't yet found time in all his milling to have a wife and was handsome enough, but not that picky – and her father was desperate to sell her by now. So the miller – who you'll have judged as being me – paid five shillings for her, which is the price of a pig with a bit added on, probably with the money his priest – that's you – gave him to mill his corn, Father. When the miller took the sack from her head she was, yes, as vile as a January morning. But he shrugged and thought to himself, Well, never mind, I don't mind a bit of grunting.' He leant in once more to the grille, his wide chin and long

101

hairless jaw bright against the shadow. 'And besides, all are alike in the night.'

Still slouched forward, I found I was tapping my top teeth. I turned my thoughts to his absolution. It would take a lot of Hail Marys for him to repent his lust and lies – a higher number than he could count to. But my imagination wasn't with his absolution, it was with his lover sitting in the corner of his house with her hands resting primly on the fine silk dress her father had sold her in, looking down at the white moons of her rounded nails, smelling, with her great snout, the violet scent she wore, the smell of sweet humility, and glimpsing – in longing? in dread? – the mess of straw and blankets that Kemp called a bed. Later, she would lie on that bed and her inhuman squeal would rend the quiet of the village. Pain or pleasure, we couldn't know. People would come to know us by her; Oakham, home of the squealing pig-woman.

'Go before you tell more lies,' I said. 'And fill your shoes with stones from now til the start of Lent, to persuade you to think twice about lying again. Pray the Rosary morning and night.'

Piers Kemp sprung from his knees with a Yes, Father, gladly, Father, thank you, Father; a woodpecker cackled past the south window.

A village of scrags and outcasts. Oakham: Beastville, Pigtown, Nobridge. The village that came to no good; the only village for tens of miles around that doesn't trade wool, doesn't make cloth, doesn't have the skill to build a bridge.

Here's the village we pass by, with its singing milkmaids; we call it Cheesechurn, Milkpasture, Cowudder. Its lord is as pudgy and spineless as the cheese he makes. Its people are vagrants who were ousted from their own villages and are in most respects desperate. Its richest man was whisked off down the river and drowned. And here is its priest: young John Reve, roosting in the dark. For all that he's overseen by Christ, he's led his people to no further illumination. And he stinks of goose and burps goose, no matter how he tries not to.

Was ridicule the cost of kindness? Because we'd been kind in Oakham, so much so that God made note. In these recent decades of ours, when endless furlongs of cropland have been taken from villagers and given over to sheep pasture or rabbit warren, and crops pulled up and grass sown, a man might have gone staggering dispossessed from his home, suddenly landless, and where would he stagger? He'd stagger our way, because he'd followed roadside rumours of a place that would have him. Here he'd come with nothing but a brass pot, a horsehair rope, a plough chase (no plough, no horse), a packet of peas, a hen, a wife and four children, and this village would take him in, and give him land.

Townshend's grandfather – who'd no belief in sheep – took in as many of these families as wanted to come. Wasteland was shown the plough, heath and woodland too; all of the parish was ploughed up for crops. He gave incomers six months free tenancy, then six months half-rent, while they got themselves going. By the end of that, Oakham had more land for crops than anywhere around, and good land too, I'm told. The Townshends became richer by it, but that wasn't to say there was no kind motive; there was more welcome here, for anyone, no matter, than anywhere else in the world. There were no folk less offput by a man's bad breath or a woman's limp or a child's filth than those in Oakham. God saw the truth of that, because he gave fifteen good harvests in a row, and he gave us places where wheat would grow where we'd once only been able to grow rye or maslin. We built this bigger church for him, and dedicated it to the Virgin, and let the timber one in the woods go.

Harvests fail eventually, though. Always they do. We had nothing else to fall back on – little pasture, little wool, no fulling mills, our only watermill was all for corn, and the little wool we had was still fulled by foot. Foreigners had come to like an

English shirt on their backs, but we had no skills at making those – we had no specialist spinners, weavers, tenterers, teasers, dyers, they were busy elsewhere. Even if we'd started, it was too late; our neighbours had already dressed the whole of Europe. Oakham was all crop, and balanced on the fates of the weather. By the time the manor came to Oliver Townshend the weather had done its worst too many times. He tried to warren some of the land for rabbits; trees downed for bracken and pillow mounds – I remember that the first time I saw him he was sending his dog at the rabbits, and singing 'Blow Thy Horn, Hunter!' with false optimism. Rabbits were not going to save us then any more than cheese does now; Townshend knew it too. He sung anyway, and loud enough that all rabbits in these isles would hear and scarper.

But is kindness enough? Open-heartedness? Tolerance? *The meek shall eat and be satisfied* – and yet I sometimes wonder if, for all that, God favours brightness, a spark, an aliveness that could be turned to cruelty, but which worships him instead. Does he tire of Townshend's dimmed wits? Of mine too, for that matter, as I roost slumpily in the dark? Does God prefer a man or woman who comes with a hundred ideas, each one a sharpened arrowhead, who peers – as the eagle does – into the heart of the sun? Do those people who pass on the other side of the river, with their cartloads bound for Europe, look across the ham and say, Woe to Cheesechurn, for its one bright man has died and left a village of fools?

Resurrection

A rap on the screen, and the dean's voice: 'Reve.' A throat roughly cleared.

I came out of the booth to find him disappearing into the vestry. I took one of the rosaries from the nail, left it on the floor and followed him. Except for us, the church was an empty hush, a pewter light. No lustre, no shadow. I closed the vestry door behind me. The dean sat on a pile of blankets, a greyish shape on grey. I wished he wouldn't, it made him half my height and difficult to do business with, but he seemed to think it gave him the authority of the relaxed; he smiled like a man stepping into a tub of warm water – feigned, I supposed, but what could I really judge of this man. Each day he became more unknown to me.

'Purgatory,' he said, softly enough. 'What is it, do you think? A cattle market? Everyone trying to avoid being prodded into a pen by the devil? Everyone looking for the gate the angels have left open?'

An unexpected question, with some humility, some searching in it.

'I sometimes daren't think,' I said. 'But perhaps it's a more subtle place than that. A place of quiet reckoning.'

He nodded – that too unexpected – and ran his fingertips over the piles of blankets. He continued with this stroking of the wool, and in the dimness he was woolly too, his edges picked at. I was enticed by this picture of humility, this shepherd-turned-sheep.

'Hell is surely the cattle market,' I ventured, 'where you're prodded, rounded up, and cry out in protest against a fate already decided. Purgatory is – a womb. If we visit a womb when we're born, then don't we visit another when we die? One the gateway to life, the other the gateway to the afterlife. Purgatory is the second womb. So I'm inclined to think.'

'A warm rosy cloister, a hushed chamber.'

Was he mocking me? 'Yes,' I answered, 'in which we gestate, quietly, wrapped in the life we've lived, all its sins, all its kindnesses. Then we're born into the afterlife, hell or heaven, and God must decide which.'

The dean pursed his lips into contemplation. The vestry's smell – damp wool and candle tallow, soapwort and marjoram – gave our dialogue a homely, ambling air, though I had to suspect it wasn't ambling at all, but steering towards a point just beyond my seeing.

'A very charming picture,' he said, with a face that had lost its tightening of scheming and threat. 'Mine's more prosaic – though I agree, a cattle market isn't right, no. A quiet reckoning, like you said. What is purgatory for me? A room full of men and women who've silently emptied their purses so the Lord can assess. Have they got enough to go to heaven, or will they need to go to hell? The purses, I mean of course, are their souls.'

'Your picture has its own charm.'

'I think not. But it has more – flexibility than yours. If the men and women in my room don't have enough in their purses for heaven, it might not be too late. Some others outside that room – their loved ones still living – might send gifts and offerings to compensate. To top up the fund. A nice set-up, I think, that allows for charity and a bit of last-moment making good – whereas your womb, for all its charm, is a very closed-off place.'

I crouched on the floor, against the wall, and managed a vague nod. We rounded the bends of conversation softly, but the dean had his direction set. Exhausting for him, surely, to be always arrow in hand and out for the hunt. This talk of purgatory was, of course, to say: If Newman's still there, in purgatory, why? When he emptied his purse in front of the Lord, why was there not enough in it? Why have Oakham's offerings and prayers not been sufficient to help him through? Are their purses half-empty too? What shall I tell the archdeacon? (For this was his favourite line.) Must I tell him that the good man Newman seems too heavy with secret sin to get to heaven alone? That the good people of Oakham seem too impoverished of soul to help him? If Newman's in purgatory, what are you all hiding?

'Reve, tell, me, what shall I do? What shall I tell the archdeacon?'

Ah, there it was, so soon. I dropped my head.

'Do I go back and tell the archdeacon that Newman's death was an accident?' he said.

Without lifting my head, I told him, since he'd asked me to tell him, 'I think you do.'

'And then the archdeacon says to me: Why was this man Thomas Newman by the river that morning? And I say – what?'

'I don't know – do we need permits now, to be by our own river? Writs from the king?'

'You knew the man. Why don't you hazard a guess?'

I pressed my hands to the floor and brought myself to my feet. 'Perhaps he was down there wondering what to do with the bridge.'

'He wanted to rebuild the bridge, a third time?'

'He was an adventurer, it pained him to see the world pass by on the far bank, as if the far bank were as unreachable to us as – another country. Just as it still pains me.'

'So he was there, by the river, doing what? Dreaming? Dreaming of a wondrous bridge and a hundred pairs of feet boldly crossing it? And then, what, he – toppled in?'

'No, of course no.' The word 'topple' sat strangely against a thought of Newman. He was always lean and strong as a hazel; a bull couldn't topple him. 'How can we know what he was doing, when he was doing it alone? He might have waded into the water.'

'Waded in?'

'There's no other way of seeing the bridge from underneath, and without seeing it from underneath, no way of seeing exactly what fell, what still stands or what it would take to rebuild it.'

The dean pointed a finger into the air. 'Ah yes – because it'd become his life's work to build that bridge, so his mind must have been on rebuilding it.'

'You keep asking me about Newman as if I had some clairvoyance with him. I don't know what was on his mind.'

'He gave a lot of money to the bridge, I understand.'

'Yes.'

'All of which I should surely tell the archdeacon?'

He was watching me with what I could only call triumph, his chin thrust up and his lips forming, almost, a smile, though one restrained by inexperience.

'Well, now. And yet, according to the church records, Newman's last donation to the church for the bridge-building efforts was last June, some eight months ago.'

At this, he pulled a scroll from his ever-giving sleeve. I could think of nothing but the deeds Newman had had written up, which were scrolled in a money box beneath his floor. The dean's nose would've gone straight to that, his little hands with a little knife making short work of the seam in the mud floor, loosening the slab, prising it free – and there, a cavity with a scroll in it. Aha, the arrow flies straight to the target! *Deeds?* he'd say? *I wonder what they say?* Knowing, of course, what they said, and knowing what they said made Oliver Townshend so suspicious he was already half-dead.

Of course, these weren't the deeds, they were the church records; the dean had said it himself. And they were a cheap paper, where Newman's deeds were parchment – but still, my heart gave way like a weak knee and seemed to tumble gutwards. He unrolled the document and made a theatre of reading it, as if to check a fact he plainly knew. 'Yes, here it is, every month a donation of a crown for a year and a month, and suddenly, as of June last year, nothing.'

He handed them to me and, nonchalant with relief that they weren't what I'd first perceived them to be, even though I knew all along they weren't what I perceived them to be (because the fearful heart is often lagging behind the clear-sighted eyes), I rolled them up and gave them back.

He unrolled them, cocked a brow at me as if to say, Whatever you do, I can undo, and looked at them affectionately. 'Your churchwarden kindly supplied them,' he said.

'As she should, there's nothing secret.'

'You're not going to read them?'

'I read them every week. It's Janet Grant and I who keep them.'

'So you know, then, that Newman hasn't been giving money for the bridge for a long time – that he lost all interest in it.'

'I know the first half. The second isn't true.'

'No? Janet Grant said it was true. Newman himself told her – he'd lost hope in the bridge, it was built in the wrong place and would keep falling down. He said he might as well throw his money directly in the river and save everyone's efforts.'

'Well, maybe *that's* what he was doing then, on the morning of his death. Throwing his money in the river.'

I stooped to collect the blankets from the floor, folded them without care and made a new pile of them. He might come to Oakham and act the sheriff and make scandal, but it was too much that he also knocked our blankets to the floor, blankets hand-spun with ancient distaff and spindle, maybe the last distaff and spindle in the whole country, and woven and foot-fulled by women with stiff ankles and bad backs and a bit of charity in their hearts.

'And therefore,' the dean continued, prodding the roll of papers inquisitively at the air, 'if Newman wasn't at the river for love of the bridge, and if he isn't one for toppling, and if he wasn't likely to be in the river looking – what did you say? – at the underside of the bridge, then won't the archdeacon, if he has half a wit, consider that an accident seems less likely, and still want to know why the man was there? At that time of the morning too. These aren't my questions, Reve, they're the arch-deacon's, which I will have to answer. So grant me patience. The archdeacon could ask me, for example, if Newman could have been meeting someone there, at the river. What will I say? I'll have to say I don't know, and then he'll ask me what I *do* know. Well, I – we – do know that Townshend holds those good grazing lands at West Fields, don't we, and we know Newman would have seized the chance to buy them. So,' he shrugged, his upturned face lucid and almost beatific with self-love, 'who knows? Maybe Townshend invited him down at that early, clandestine hour to take a look, to walk out some bound-aries, to talk costs and yields. And, well, brought Newman to the edge of that rushing river and – you know what I mean to say. We do also know, after all, that Newman and Townshend had their disputes.'

'Which exist largely in your head,' I said.

'If you wish.'

The dean's bravado fell in a strange motion in which he tucked the records back up his sleeve, turned and took again to pressing his hands along the blankets behind him with an absorbed motherliness. Peculiar man. As if his nastiness had made him downhearted. His small, smooth hands folded and pressed and folded the topmost blanket. Without turning to me he asked, 'What do you say, Reve?'

'That you've made some great leaps of logic.'

'Better for logic to leap than stumble.'

'Have you asked Townshend where he was that morning?'

'He says he was tucked up in bed. His wife agrees.'

'Then we must believe them.'

'Must we?'

I watched him without moving, then said, 'Are you entering into a courtship with those blankets?'

He looked up. His hands stilled, then lay flat. 'You seem tired and in need of some company,' I said, and he did, in that moment, look paper-skinned and forlorn, all lucidity gone. 'Why don't I drop by to see you later, we could sit by the fire a while. We've had no time to be friends.'

He jerked his head towards me as if in shock at that word, friend. 'I don't have much fireside time, I'm here to investigate – '

'A death, I know, but if you tell me when you'll be done with the day's investigations, I could bring a bit of goose, some wine?'

He laughed – one short *Ha*. 'Goose,' he sneered. 'No, I wouldn't like to deprive you.'

'Then tell me when you'll be back and I'll leave some wine inside your door, waiting for you.'

He looked up towards the narrow window. 'As long as I have light I'll be out, and maybe beyond. I don't need wine.'

I smiled at him mildly as if in admiration of his tireless, futile, dawn-til-dusk efforts to save Oakham from itself. 'Then I'll come as long as it's light, leave the unneeded wine, and I'll be gone before you're back. You won't even have to see me.'

He stood in front of me with his hands awkwardly on his thighs and gave a dismal, short nod. Was it the wine that lured him, or could even he not resist an act of kindness? When he opened the door and went out, he had a good look at who might be in the nave. Carter was the only one. The dean shuffled past him and away. I was barely across the nave and in the booth before Carter entered and knelt with all the hurry of youthful anguish.

'Benedicite.'

'Dominus.'

'Confiteor.'

And Carter was away: 'Father, Father, Father. I killed Thomas Newman, hear me, forgive me – '

'Cannot forgive what you haven't done – '

'Hear me, forgive me.'

His voice was churned and soft with grief. He spoke of the neighbourly favours he'd done since Newman's death on Shrove Saturday, to try to atone for his guilty stake in that death, a guilt that was entirely imagined. *How can you know it's imagined?* came the dean's insinuation. How? Because I know Herry Carter as if he were my own son, and he loved Newman as if Newman were his own father: that's how. A man cannot do something that's completely outside his own nature any more than a horse can fly.

There was nothing I was more sure of in all this world than Carter's innocence – yet he believed he was guilty, because love is like that. When my own mother died in a fire that I couldn't have stopped, I blamed myself for not stopping it; I blamed myself for the world not being entirely otherwise. If I'd not failed her that time as a child, and that time and that time, and not angered my father, not done this thing or that thing, life might have been different and the fire might never have happened. Love thinks like that. Love in the face of death is a torment.

Carter reeled off his list of good works: he'd filled a hole in old Norys's wall, swept out others' houses for Lent, laid new slate on the porch roof (and fallen, and received a worrying gash in front of his ear for his efforts), finished Fisker's harrowing, given the few eggs he had to his neighbour, paid for miserable Mary Grant to have her corn milled, helped mend the milk cart that had come to blows with the road the day before, and lugged the churns back up to the manor, and helped fill them once more with milk, and delivered the milk to those who needed it.

'Too much, Herry Carter, first help your family.'

I could find no other way to explain: you didn't kill Newman, though you suppose it. 'Can we always save those we love?' I asked.

'I disappointed him.'

'Disappointing a man isn't the same as killing him.'

'I wasn't good enough.'

'You mean, you didn't replace the child he lost.'

'Though I *tried*.'

'But failing to be a replacement for his dead child isn't an act of murder.'

Perhaps he didn't hear me; he began on his good deeds once more – Norys's hole, Fisker's harrowing, Mary Grant's corn, the milk churn, the porch roof.

'All men and women stand for themselves,' I said, over the top of him, 'and reckon with God.'

And God decides, I thought, and the airborne spirits do their cunning worst with whatever's decided. If God decides a man's life is ready to end, the spirits – if numberly enough – arrange for it to end horribly. Where in this crowded field of force and influence is there an opening for boys like Carter to sway fate?

'There's no *body*,' he said. 'What if he's still alive?'

'You wonder if he's alive, while insisting that it was you who killed him.'

'But there's no body.'

What a dextrous thing was a man's mind, straddling two opposite truths at once, as if flitting between dreams. It wasn't like Carter to flit and confound himself; he was a simple man whose thoughts went in short, straight lines. I worried about the gash in front of his ear and that he was shivering – though that stopped suddenly; both of us had gone mute. A lull, the rain hushing against the window.

'Tomorrow,' he whispered, defeated, 'I'll go and see about what we'd do to clear that tree from the river.'

I nodded to myself, closed my eyes. He meant the tree that had fallen at West Fields. This was the one penance I'd asked of him, he thought a penance for murdering Newman, I meant only penance for falsely confessing to his murder. What did it matter, so long as it was a penance he found sufficiently dangerous, cold, bleak and thankless; one he could do at the river, which was the almost certain scene of Newman's death; something that could make him feel he was punishing himself, until he'd punished himself enough.

'Very well,' I said, though anxious now at the notion of him cold and bleak. 'But be careful, will you?'

When he got up to leave I asked if he'd made this false confession to anyone else – his wife? Our friend John Hadlo? He said no. I told him he mustn't. Mustn't. And that I'd left some goose-meat for him, wrapped in muslin on my table, he should go and help himself – the flesh would speed the healing of his head wound. He muttered that he wouldn't take it, didn't want it, wanted forgiveness, not goose. Wanted to die of his wound, if it was punishment from God. That would be some recompense for Newman's life. At that he left.

'Confiteor?' I said, because although I hadn't heard another person enter, somebody was there – the presence of breath and the unmistakable filling of space, where flesh took over from stone.

There was no reply, so I said it again, and then once more. 'Newman?' I said, before I had time to consider it. No reply, but something shifted; I wouldn't say I heard as much as felt the shift, as though something unseen had moved closer to me. I insisted, 'Newman?'

Then his voice came at half-strength, not a whisper but a full voice that had scant force, as if coming from behind several screens. 'Help me to move through. Pray for me.'

What reply could I give? This was no plea, no order, nothing but a fair request, as if he were asking me to help lift a pail. I smelt the odour that was all his own – a sharp blossomy soap, a hint of horse, a tinge of mint which he liked to chew. Wine, too, in that smell. The slight wheeze in his breath from a defect of the lungs he said he'd had since birth. I jolted forward to look through the grille and found the space empty.

On the Lord's Prudent and Timely Use of the Wind

'**D**o you remember a wetter winter, or a winter that left more things to decay and die? Do you remember more animals washed into the river? More men, women and children sick and dead? More food wasted to damp and mould? You know that the vapour from these decaying things causes air rife with malicious spirits.

'You ask why our good God has let our earth become so decayed. You ask: why hasn't he protected us? I'll tell you as best I can: *the Lord tests us*. When he sorts the pure from the impure, he might leave some of the impure on earth in his great mercy, to punish and strengthen us. The tiny remaining sinews of a rotted pig, the residue of sin in the souls of dead men, a trace of blood from the entrails of a diseased lamb, the cord of an unbaptised newborn, the urine of a woman with bilious fever, the airborne fleck of poison from a man dead of chin-cough.

'Our Lord, the great sweeper and clearer, swerves his broom around these impurities and is careful to leave some dust. After all, if he left the earth always clean and perfect for us, what responsibility would we have for our own lives? Wouldn't we become lethargic and overly dependent on his goodwill, like lazy children on their parents? So he sweeps, but not in every corner. These impurities left out from heaven or hell are no longer of his creation but instead become unearthly spiritual vapour, enemy of our earthly flesh.

'This vapour hangs upon us heavy and corrupted, and gets populated with spirits that are far from well-willing, and so it becomes the terrible Night Air: vapours and spirits mixed. Organic and spiritual at once. It enters our lungs and hearts and souls, and causes more death, disease, decay, degradation, despondency and despair, and so the cycle continues until we, us small men and women, find our own human strength to banish it.

'How many ways can I tell you this truth: *the Lord tests us.* What will you do, he asks, about this spiritual vapour, these vaporous spirits, this Night Air? Will you choke, or rise up? Will we rise? How will we rise? If we come, all of us, during Lent, to confession. If we sweep our floors and sluice them with water, if we wash our bodies, if we cut our hair, if we tend our creatures, if we come to Mass and take the host and pay our tithes and offer our prayers and do no wrong, then the Lord will deem it that we're ripe for his love and have earnt salvation. He needs to see us make some effort. Perhaps then he'll match our efforts with his own, and set the sun ablaze to dry up decay, or send in a fast wind to blow the spirits to sea.

'A fast wind? you ask. The last thing we need is a north-easterly bashing at our roofs and blowing our brassicas diagonal and downcasting our animals. But listen: I have here a treatise, *On the Lord's Prudent and Timely Use of the Wind.* It divulges how wind can be sent by the Lord not to punish, but to save us from corrupted vapours and reward us for our good work. Think how the locust plague came in on an easterly wind and, at God's fitful command, was blown out on a westerly – for the wind is God's breath, and through it he speaks to us. I am praying to him to ask if he'll send a sign to show that better days are coming, and I'll suggest a wind to see off the foul Night Air, and though it's not right to be pedantic with God, I'll ask if this once it might be a wind from the west, as per the locusts. That's my prayer, which I ask you to join me in.

'Be faithful! If the wind is the breath of God, what can it not do? A good westerly would help blow Thomas Newman's soul through, clean out of this world and safely into the next. We must all show the Lord, now and during Lent, that we're worthy of his favours. We must keep our bodies clean and our floors sluiced and our animals tended and our hair cut and our tithes paid and our sins trivial and quickly confessed. We must remember Newman in our hearts and do good deeds in his name. No meat to pass our lips, and our prayers should come often. We must love each other; we must draw close. We must show our esteemed dean that we're a courageous and virtuous parish, us in Oakham. That we'll do our best to please God, that we'll worship at his feet. Gloria Patri, et Filio, et Spiritui Sancto. Sicut erat in principio, et nunc, et semper, et in saecula saeculorum.'

Amen, they said to this sermon, and obligingly an unseen and sourceless wind caused the flames of the two candles at the altar to bow dangerously deep. Some low, muffled flatulence issued somewhere from the crowd of bodies in the nave. Then they moved restless to the door, and against their motion the dean progressed salmon-ish upstream.

'*On the Lord's Prudent and Timely Use of the Wind*,' he said, and took from the pulpit the pamphlet I'd held up, which didn't, as he knew, have that title. It was only my priest's manual, over-thumbed and with faded Latin. 'This is your treatise?' he smirked and, when I didn't reply, smirked some more. 'Quite the holy crook, aren't you?'

'I know what I said was true, about the wind, the vapours, even if it's not written in a treatise.'

'You'll have to hope none of them learn to read Latin and catch you out.'

I took the manual under my arm. 'It's our job to give them hope.'

'They need more than hope,' he said, watching the retreating huddle of hemp and jute and matted hair. 'They need a miracle. And a wash. They stink of ale.'

He shrugged and wandered away through the nave, which now held only a few who'd stayed behind for confession. It had been a full congregation, even if it had shuffled and whispered and chattered; at least nobody had slept. In other parishes they did. The dean reached the door. 'Into that salving wind I go!' he called, and he opened the door to the same wet and motionless air that had been stagnating about us for days.

Night Air

I stood in the middle of the church. Its emptiness was rare. There was no confession queue, nobody muttering a prayer in the nave, nobody gossiping in the porch. The displays of wedding flowers on the chancel pillars were beginning to die, and even as I stood a witch-hazel frond fell, and its entirely soundless meeting with the ground added a new depth to the silence. I locked the door from within, crossed myself and lit candles.

I'd abandon the last sitting for confession; who'd come now in the rain? And besides, I had no strength left to be encouraging, and a terrible fear of what would appear at the other side of the screen. I took the last of the rosaries from the nail and left it on the floor with the others, then stood in the tawdry light of the west windows.

Thomas Newman had been in this church, alive and as well as any of us can be, only three days before. Friday late evening, when the church air was thick with the smell of wintersweet. He'd come, as he always did, to pray before the painting of Mary and her crucified son, which he'd brought back from Italy and placed at his own altar next to the Townshends'. Every day he'd light candles for his lost family and for the sick of the parish, and leave one or two shillings. Always he'd pray and sing from his gilt-clasped primer that lay open in his hands.

On Friday he was wearing his green shirt, I remembered that. A special shirt unfit for the fields. A plain tunic, an old fur collar, plain dark gores over his shoes. Only the shirt and gores suggested he'd been to a wedding that day. He looked tired as we all did, because we'd spent a cold day in the barns with a wedding feast while the rain fell, and it was an effort to keep warm. Then, when the bride and groom had gone to Bourne, we'd been left with the carcasses of chickens and bowls of stew to clear up, the milk puddings, the honey strewn from its dishes into cups of ale, everything sticky, everything damp. That's what Newman had come from, and so he looked tired and like he needed a fire to sit by.

That Friday, then, what had he done precisely after Annie's wedding, when he came into the church? I went to the south entrance to tread his path. He'd walked there, across the nave, and knelt in front of the Virgin; I knew that, not only because he always did, but because I'd joked with him: 'You make a handsome couple, you and Mary.' Which in that moment they did – his devoted weariness, her rested strength. And he replied something like, 'But she settled for that browbeaten old cuckold Joseph instead.' And I: 'The prerogative of women, to always choose the lesser man', to which he smiled, and bowed his head.

Before that, though. Before he knelt, when he came into the church at the south entrance and walked across the nave, did he look up and see the wall painting of St Christopher? Or did he stride in with his head down? I stood again at the door and imagined I was him, wet and tired, with his rangy, guarded bearing, carrying his primer. The wet and tired don't stride, they're too beaten; he must have ambled, and when we amble we tend to look up and around more, wasn't that true? If he'd looked up and around, he must have seen St Christopher, because it was impossible not to. St Christopher would have been in front of him on the wall, unmissable to any eye that wasn't intent on the floor. His wasn't intent on the floor. He'd seen me at the altar preparing for Mass and said, 'The porch roof's leaking, John.' So he must have seen St Christopher, even if only a glimpse.

But was a glimpse enough? *He who looks upon the image of St Christopher within a day of his death will be carried to heaven.* Looks upon, not sees. Just happening to see wasn't enough. Do these words matter? Is there latitude? Looking, seeing – is it all the same to you, Lord? The rule of St Christopher only said *he* who looks, but it was meant for women and girls too. So if *he* included *she*, *look* included *see*. I repeated this to myself; for some time it did console.

Yet if he came straight to me at the altar, his attention would have been there, not on the wall opposite – he wouldn't even have seen the wall opposite, not even glimpsed it. 'The porch roof's leaking, John,' he said, and I said, 'I know it, Herry Carter said he'd come and fix it tomorrow.' 'Herry Carter does too much, he'll drop dead before he's thirty,' was something like his reply, and he seemed wearier for the claim. In that give and take, he'd have gone to his altar blind to any wall painting, and lit candles and knelt, and opened his primer at the Little Office. He'd have read from Luke and sung the Hymn of Adoration as he did each Friday.

As for his exit, it was hurried. I copied it, with my skirts gathered in a fist. I strode – because this time it was a stride – from Newman's side altar to the door where Sarah had been standing, shivering and clutching at her skin as if it were cloth she could pull off. She'd come in while Newman had been singing and I'd seen her and gone to her, and she'd made a grotesque cry of pain, muffled, but otherwise like the sound of a woman in childbirth. 'Father!' she'd said, 'I'm cold as hell', and I'd gone straight to the vestry to get her blankets. Newman had run over, put his coat around her, wrapped her in the blankets and carried her home, probably lit her a fire and warmed her some water. He neither looked at nor saw nor glimpsed St

Christopher then. After that, he hadn't come back to the church. The next morning he was drowned.

If he didn't see St Christopher then – that night before his death – if he didn't, and since he went to his death abrupt and unshriven, with no help from a priest, his soul would be in torment now. It would be trapped between this world and the next, rapping its knuckles at the gates of heaven, which wouldn't open. Those river spirits and airborne spirits that somersaulted so invisible and free through our midst would be having their sport with him. Hell would beckon, and what else could this tormented soul do but go back to the world it knew and creep about at dawn playing the lute, or sit in the church waiting for somebody to pray for it and do good works in its name, until heaven's gates cracked open enough, just enough, and hell's fires glowed more distant.

'Newman?' I said. 'Tom Newman?' St Christopher shifted on the opposite wall, a short lurch, as if about to trip and spill the babe from his hands.

I went home, wanting to run, but from what, to where? So I walked as if calm, and at home I saw that the goose I'd wrapped in muslin for Carter was gone. Carter had taken it after all, despite his protest, and he'd wasted no time in it. I took a bottle of wine – my only, and it wasn't full – from the shelf. A knife. A taper, too; it'd be dark in Newman's house down there in the woods.

Yet out on the road it was daylight still, with familiar rain and familiar Lazy Dog, behind which dusk gathered in fistfuls. I was anxious not to see the dean. I surely wouldn't; he was going north, I was going south. He'd been making his way from door to door, starting south from Newman's and working north, towards Tunley's at the brook, which was the most northerly of all houses in our village. After a day and half at it, he'd be past New Cross now, maybe sniffing about at Robert Guy's place, the reeve's house – praise the Lord, he'd be thinking, at last a house worth searching. A house with more in it than a hen, a wood pile, some bed boards and an unemptied piss-pot. At last, a ewer and a chest and a pear-wood mazer and perhaps three pairs of leather shoes and a nice old coat and any number of ordinary things made newly suspicious under his crabbed scrutiny. I could see him, tiny dean, tapping eggs with his neat, clean nails as if the shells might surrender a confidence, and it made me all the more satisfied to have duped him: it was a pretence to say I wanted wine with him; of course I didn't want wine with him, and I knew he wouldn't want it with me – but the bit of theatre yielded a useful fact. He'd be out of Newman's house as long as there was light, he'd said – and there was still almost an hour of light.

The door to Newman's place was a sleeker fit than my own. When Newman asked Philip, our carpenter, to make it, he must have asked for it to fit small, with room for rain-swelling. Fixer Philip, they say, but they say it with tongue in cheek. Bodger Philip is also his name when he's out of earshot. (It was him who, sawing me a piece of wood for a cutting board, sawed also through my table.)

I put the wine inside the door, and lit the taper from the fire that perpetually burnt, safe in its hearth. The luxury of a hearth! A chimney! By what divine calculation did the work of landlording pay so much better than the work of God? Immediately I went to the left side of the hearth, moved aside the straw, rushes and violets that were strewn there, found an indistinct square marking in the ground and let my knife follow it. The ground here, near the fire, was dry, and the square would lift out with enough shimmying of the knife, enough patience, gentle prising. I raised up a plate of compacted earth, a makeshift lid.

There was the unlocked iron box, a small, weighty thing just cuppable in both hands – and inside it, rolled, folded and lastly crammed, the deeds stating that in the event of his death, all Newman's goods and land should be left to Townshend, and his house to little Mippy, Townshend's housemaid, whom Newman had rescued as an orphan, and his animals to Carter. It wasn't legal to leave your goods to the church, as he'd have liked, and failing that Townshend was the better recipient of the bulk of Newman's worldly things because, for all the antagonism between the two, there wasn't another person who'd have the means to fairly divide, distribute and administer those goods and that land. But bequeathing your worldly goods to your worldly rival could raise brows, if the death was by some unclear cause (so many deaths are, on this mysterious earth).

So he'd hidden the deeds and told nobody about them but me; thus, on his deathbed he could reveal their existence and whereabouts so that his wishes could be honoured, and the recipient of his wealth could have no accusation of foul play levelled against him, since he knew nothing of standing to gain by the death. And if Newman died unexpectedly, there'd be one other person who knew where the deeds were – myself, who had nothing to gain.

All this I'd thought elaborate and overwrought when Newman told me about it. But circumstance had proven him not too careful. All very well, yes, if there was no dean prowling, and if the dean didn't already have his arrow aimed at Townshend's innocence. If the dean found these deeds – and he could, since the markings of their burial were there to see, if you were someone who liked to look – Townshend's coffin might as well prepare for its first nail.

I replaced the earthen lid, scuffed the markings with dirt and dust, muddled the straw and rushes over the top, and threw my lit taper on the fire. I put the box under my cassock, pinned between arm and hip. Must get out, I told myself. My heartbeat was so insistent it brought pain. *Thus we know we are alive.*

* * *

If what I've told conveys the actions of a directed man who moved with normal ease, I have to tell it otherwise – to say in truth I moved impeded through Night Air that was thick and temperamental.

I felt suddenly that God had sent an eternal rain to render everything water, to punish us, since we couldn't fight water – there we were, sluicing and washing with the very stuff that was most corrupted, since everything decaying ends up in the river. It wet our hair and decayed our sown seed. Our animals drank it, then we ate them. The river filled and overflowed with great pieces of our bridge on its bed. We couldn't stay clean, our clothes were filthy and our shoes rotten. Our wood begrudged burning. We were losing our fight. Was the dean right when he called Oakham lazy and lost? Was it God's anger to take Thomas Newman, then flaunt him before us in a painful haunting between worlds? Was Newman a hostage in purgatory, awaiting our payment in return for his release? Awaiting *my* payment, after all, mine.

A force pushed at both my front and back: at my front it urged me down towards the birch copse and the river, where, I imagined, an unearthly, infested darkness had dropped. At my back it pushed me the way I was going, church-wards, with a force that was cleaner. Prostrate yourself, worship, sacrifice, do enough right to compensate for all the wrongs, do good, better than good, be the Ghostly Father you are, and be quick about it.

I went – I fear, scampered dean-like – up the road, through the churchyard, up the nave, to the vestry; I put on a bright, white alb, slid the iron box under a pile of blankets, took a blanket from the top, took the sacramental oil, the host in its pyx and holy water from the tabernacle on the altar, put them in a burse that I hung around my neck, and left again. The bell tolled five.

* * *

'Father,' she said, extending one bony arm past the threshold of her door. 'Thank you for the bread and apples.'

'It's nothing.'

'I ate most of it.'

'I brought you a blanket.'

I put the blanket around her shoulders and went into the house. I hid the bag with the host and oil under her chair in the corner. Rain had puddled in the over-trodden hollow at the door; I took the broom and swept it out. 'I'll ask one of the men to come and do this for you morning and night,' I said.

Already she'd coiled herself in the far corner of the room, which was near dark once the door was closed. The sight of her room, even in the dark! And the smell; the smell of disease, of rooms that see no light and get no air, of places under beds, of fungus and damp. It had once been a lovingly kept room, plain but lit and dry. The floor had always been covered with clean straw, often flower-strewn for colour and scent, and the bed made, the wood neatly piled in the corner, the plate, cup, spoon and knife washed. Now the floor was almost bare and muddy in patches, and the fire was out, the wood disarrayed and running low. Food was left on the table: some broken bread, some furred cheese, a bowl of old and thickened porray which held up the spoon; when I went to it I saw there were mice droppings. On the floor, an apple and a core. The room was grimly cold. Next to her was vomit that she'd tried to slosh away with water.

'You need a fire,' I said.

I took the fire striker, quartz and char cloth from the basket by the wood and struck, struck. For a good while we had only the rain on the roof and the chink of rock on steel between us, until sparks finally took to the cloth and set it to glow. Then even the chinking stopped, and we had just the rain. I lit the tow with one hand, blew it to flame and put it in the fire pit.

'I think I remember more about how I killed Newman,' she said flatly; it wasn't the flatness of common sense and reason, but of madness. I glanced up but didn't answer. There was some sawdust, shavings and kindling at the bottom of the basket, not much but it was old and dry. I laid it in the fire pit on top of the tow. It took.

'You asked me yesterday how I killed him,' she said, 'and I remember now. I axed him; truth be told, I cut him down like an old branch. I need to be forgiven for pride, you see, because I loved him and he didn't love me. *Superbia*, Father, that's what it was, and God has punished me with this burning, crawling body, as he should. It's no small thing to axe a man to death. Forgive me, and then arrange quickly for my death.'

'If those were really your sins, I'd forgive them,' I said.

'And arrange quickly for my death. Tell the dean what I've done.'

'I will not.'

'But see what I did!'

'Even if your axe had come into contact with an old branch, you couldn't have cut it down. Look at you.'

Crouched, claw-fingered, bird-toed, twig-limbed, fog-eyed. Only her noble un-Oakham-ish nose gave away what she'd been – a proud young woman, strong as a boy, quick as a goat, with the laugh of a child. The grimace of her pain used the same lines laughter had once used, fanning across the top of her nose.

I stood from the fire; no logs yet, they might suffocate the new flame. With my arms under her armpits I lifted her to the bed and covered her with all the blankets I could find – her own, the one I'd brought and two that Newman had wrapped her in the night before his vanishing. 'Tomorrow I'll get clean bedclothes for you,' I said. Hers were grimed with a month of bad sleep.

'Do you hear me, Father?' She touched her hand to my neck. 'You heard what I confessed just now? That I killed him with an axe?'

128

'With what strength?' I asked, taking her hand in mine. 'With all respect, no man would tolerate being half-heartedly hacked to death by a sick woman.'

I moved away, took the broom again and the sweeping pan, and swept the vomit into it. Then collected some straw that had gathered in the corner and laid it where the vomit had been.

'Last night I dreamt I was tied to a stake and you were there to light the pyre, John, and I was so grateful to you for finishing my punishment when God is lingering over it.'

'I would never light that pyre,' I said.

Since Annie and I had come to Oakham, Annie only eleven, she and Sarah had been two hooked thumbs – if my hand would have any part in harming another soul, it wouldn't be that of my sister's childhood friend. I gave the fire some logs, since it was going well, and lit two candles. 'I'll have more bread brought to you tomorrow, some bacon. Tomorrow you'll be feeling better, there'll be feasts tomorrow, and dancing.'

I crouched near to the bed and rested the back of my hand on her brow.

'I don't feel my fingers,' she said, jaw juddering with cold. 'My feet neither.'

'You need to get warm.'

'I could scratch my thighs off.'

'Close your eyes.'

'I'm as wicked as a cat!'

'Sarah,' I said, my voice summoning, 'when you went away from Oakham last month – ' and my voice recoiled from its own question. 'Did you sin? Is there any sin that could have caused this suffering?'

Her look was drowsy and, yes, for a moment, wicked. But the wickedness was nothing but a trick of pain.

I goaded tenderly, 'If there's a sin you should confess to, it isn't too late.'

'I killed Thomas Newman.'

'While you were away, last month, did you sin?'

'I killed Thomas Newman.'

I closed my eyes and saw flames, then the rotted tooth she'd knelt to and worshipped on her ill-fated pilgrimage – as if its rot had caused her own. 'There now,' I quietly enthused. 'Imagine – Jesus on the cross! Imagine the sight of his boundless heart, and his head bent to kiss you.'

Her shoulders eased and her jaw stopped. She wasn't dying yet; when death approached her, there'd be rage in her eyes and she'd reject all touch, thinking it was the devil come for her. Her skin would be flushed with the wildness of her last fight – for she wouldn't be one to go meekly. The room would fill with angels and demons all vying for her in the afterlife. She was too calm and patient to have reached that crossing of the roads, but I was anxious. She mustn't die unconfessed, like Newman.

While she was falling into rest I brought the chair near, and the burse. Soft and hurried, I was. A makeshift altar – water, pyx, oil. I fetched the two candles. She wasn't to know I was giving her the host and the cross of holy oil as I do for the soon-dead; if she knew, she'd think I'd given up on her life, that I wished her away. Softly and hurriedly, I questioned her. Have you confessed all your sins? Are you truly sorry? Have you forgiven those who've wronged you? Do you trust fully in Christ? Do you choose heaven over all the things of this life? It was enough that she nodded. I dipped the host in the water and gave it to her mouth and she idly sucked, and muttered one of the rhymes they passed around. *O, Jesus, For your Holy Name, shield me today from sorrow and shame.* I pressed my hand more firmly to her head and put the water aside. Her mouth found words even when the rest of her body conceded to sleep. *When your lips blacken: momento. When your eyes mist: confessio. When your feet stiffen: contricio. When you want for breath: nosce te ipsum.*

When her mouth too fell still, and I'd prayed the Domine Sancte low and insistently to bring her to sleep, I dipped my finger into the holy oil, released my pressing hand and drew a cross on her head. *Holy Father, physician of our souls and bodies, heal your servant, Sarah Spenser, from every physical and emotional affliction.* I stood slowly and gathered my things. I took the sweeping pan outside to the pail and rinsed it clean, then propped it by the door. Night poured through the rain. I cleared the hem of my skirts from the ground and walked wetly home.

Farewell to the flesh

I must explain, briefly:

  I was born in a house at the end of a row, in a village at the edge of the forest, and in neither fact is there anything special. But I came into the world in a summer which happened to be enduringly dry and hot, the Yellow Summer they called it, because both sky and ground were that colour – the sky one perpetual bright haze from a sun that seemed bigger and closer and had about it a threat, and the ground crisp and dead like straw, the grass leached of green, the crops leached of nourishment, and all waterways except the sea low and sulky and inadequately wet.

One August afternoon the people in my village noticed a darkening and saw that the sun seemed to be in an eclipse, but not an orderly one, no gradual sharp bite taken from it, but a nebulous and sudden one, which other senses soon confirmed wasn't an eclipse but smoke. Fires are fugitives, as we know – quick and stealthy. By the time it was met with buckets of water, it was far too late for buckets of water. Spades smacked into dry earth in an attempt to dig a trench to break its path. It was far too late for that too, given the time needed to dig a trench in earth that had been slow-fired to brick, and given the wind, which was goading it village-wards. Some said the fire was two hours away at most, some said one, some said best just to run.

In all of this, I was being born. I was in a furious dark tunnel that wanted only to expel me; I didn't want to be expelled. My mother had been labouring since sunrise and had bouts of howling with bouts of insentience. Being the house at the end of the village that was closest to the forest, we were in danger, and my mother couldn't be moved. When she was lifted she shrieked like a pig being skinned and had to be put back down, and when I think of it now, I'm sorry it was me who brought her such squalid pain, since although I couldn't help being born, couldn't I have been swifter and less obstinate about it?

I could describe suspensefully the approach of that fire and the desertion of most who were at my mother's bed (including my father). They gave their prayers for a speedy birth, and followed them with hasty farewells, in case; my mother was given the sacrament. What could be done? Do you all die trying to save two, or all live and leave the two in God's hands? There were houses to empty and livestock to round up and lead or carry away; there was a river a mile south of the village which was low enough for a human to cross, but high enough to halt a fire. Off they mostly went and left just my mother, the village midwife who was also my mother's devoted friend, and my stubborn tiny self, striving backwards against a force that knew only forward.

I could describe all that suspensefully, but time's already revealed that I did survive, as did my mother, given the later coming of my sister. We survived by what my mother insisted was a miracle, which is to say that when the fire was close enough that flames, and not only smoke, could be seen in the forest, the wind direction abruptly changed. It doubled back from its easterly course to a westerly one, and returned the fire into a forest that was already charred and had not much left for a flame to feed on. The absconded villagers came back and put all hands to the spade. Through the evening and night a trench was dug, a vigil was kept, the fire retreated and, in the midst of a dirty, bloody sunset, I was born.

My mother told me that the priest told her that no such miracle had been performed with the wind since the Lord sent in a westerly to banish the plague of locusts. When the priest explained that it was Moses who'd been the instrument of God in this miracle, first spreading his hand to bring the east wind, then spreading it again to bring the west, my mother made associations between the newborn Moses who'd been left in a basket in rushes – which she'd heard about in a sermon on the monumental courage of faith – and her own newborn, and saw me as a Moses refashioned, and surmised I might be an instrument of God.

I grew up supposing there was only one way of testing the truth of her wildly leaping faith, which was to see if I could, after all, summon that wind again at will. The wind came plenty, but never at will. The ambition died with failure and adolescence, which left me with other ambitions that weren't as Moses-like. It was only when my mother died (in a fire) that grief led me to want to be what she'd wanted me to be, and I began my training for the clergy, and made it the ultimate standard of my closeness to God that he would, one day and perhaps only once, bring a wind from the west because I asked, and for no further reason.

That was a private barter that I'd never shared with another soul, for fear, I admit, that he wouldn't oblige. What thing in me had made me say it that day in front of my parish and the dean? My mother? Fear? A clutching at straws? Who was I to ask? And then, who was I not to ask? Who was I not to ask, when there'd never been a time that Oakham needed its priest more, and its priest needed God more, and the dean needed proof more, that this wasn't a place God had deserted? Who was I not to ask for my life's work to be affirmed by the very miracle that had made my life possible?

And yet in the asking, the chance of not being answered, and a whole parish waiting and wondering: where is it, then, this western wind? This life's work of yours? Is it coming?

* * *

Eat it. You must. Each last sinew, vein and slake of skin. Eat its feathers, if your gullet allows it. Goose yourself into a purged sleep, Ghostly Father, *primus inter pares*, Father John Reve, you who's Higher-than-the-Angels, you, God's faithful servant. Chew through the devil with your angel teeth; go on, eat your way to God.

I skewered and cooked the rest of the goose in the spitting flame. Eat it, Newman said. It's your punishment, your sacrifice; eat its flesh as if you're eating up sin. Eat it all, crunch its bones, chew its skin. You're eating the sins of your parish: Kemp's sickened mind, Tunley's lasciviousness, David Hikson's weasel-liness, Carter's mis-confession, Oliver Townshend's foolishness, Oakham's woollessness, the river's bridgelessness, the church's windowlessness, Sarah's sinful disease. And you, Father, you, John Reve, your sin that's greater than all of those: letting a man die in your parish without taking from him a last confession. Eat the poor man out of purgatory and into heaven, where he'd be, if not for you. Eat the goose, and maybe with it you can annul your guilt.

What happened after that, I can't say precisely. The day had been long and strange, that's all I knew. I wasn't a man for strangeness; I liked a life that was plain and sensible, where those dark things that live at our edges stay at our edges. But the dark things come. Some of them don't even seem dark at the time, but lit with perilous joy. I began to think – as I forced the goose into my mouth – of Piers Kemp's imaginary woman. I thought of what he'd said about her body of milk and honey, with long, round thighs, a deep cavern. Well, this is what you get when you fill yourself with flesh; you become flesh. Little else but hungry, wanting flesh. Your airy soul itself becomes a carnal lump of meat and gristle.

But when I banished the thought of Kemp's pig-woman, another shape loomed behind it, far more real. It was that of a woman I'd known, a married woman long ago, and in my thoughts I was entangled with her as in the moment of love itself; I saw a concoction of limbs that my mind tried to solve, puzzle-like, and couldn't. How that calf came to be under that knee and this hand came to grip that ankle. I saw her hair splay out across a floor of leaves, fresh and green at first and then, by the end of our season together, mulched and rotted. I saw her teasing, loving lips, the ridges of her upper back teeth, the hollow behind her ankle bone, anger flickering like sunlight in the cold blue ring of her eye. I was a boy in all respects when I knew her. How had I lost her? How had I ever allowed myself to have her?

'Forgive me,' I said aloud, because it was Piers Kemp's lewd fantasy that had brought her back to me after so long. That was precisely how the devil crept in – through our animal weakness and our perversity, not through tales of love, not through real tales at all, but through fantasy and magic and talk of unnatural things. Those are the things that bring on our lust. A woman with long, round thighs and the head of a pig! While my swallowing rejected the thought, so that I was close to running to the door and emptying my stomach of it, my head itself filled with blood and devilry, and a longing for the married woman, who might be dead now, for all I knew.

My room had darkened with smoke. The goose was shrunk to an exhausted handful. Eat it, Newman said, and his presence was so real that each time I turned to find him not there I scowled, perplexed at the place I thought he was. I chewed with listless despair. The smoke swirled, and the pile of uncooked goose quivered with rebuke, and seemed not to shrink, regardless of how much I chewed and how determinedly I swallowed against rising bile and stirrings of sickness.

When it was finished I dipped my forehead into goose-slick hands and smelt myself, the woody, smoky, filthy, sweet human smell of any man or woman, and I did now go to the door, open it into the darkness, run to the back of the house where the goose had been that morning and retch; an abundant offering to the soaked ground. With a spade I shovelled mud on top of it. I wiped my mouth with one sleeve, my eyes with the other. 'Well then,' I said to Newman when back indoors, 'is that what you want?' and knelt by the fire to pray.

I tidied away after the goose, doused the fire with two cups of water, kept a light by the door and put myself to bed. The village was silent around me. The bed was soft and warmer now my sister had gone, since I'd taken the mattress from the bed in her room and added it to mine, and taken her boards too so that mine stood higher from the ground. It was sumptuous by my own standards. But I couldn't sleep. The quiet innocence of the village scorned the tumult of my thoughts, of my deeds. Smoke got into bed with me. The cooking pot hung in the middle of the room. I kept thinking it was my father.

I got up, put on my shoes and went outside without a light. Rain bounced livid on the road; I almost tripped over a handcart on the roadside, almost stumbled into a sorry fence – such was the bombardment of the rain that it took my wherewithal. But I didn't need to see the village to know it; the surface of the millpond dented and black, and under it eels and pickerels that had stopped thrashing in nets; the rain trickling perpetually off the still wheel of the mill, and the cows' deep dreaming breath, and Sarah's oil-crossed forehead, and Carter's wound weeping into his pillow, and the dean drinking his wine wakefully by the fire, the reeve Robert Guy placid in sleep with all the untraversable distance of an accountant, and little Sal Prye splayed amid shirked covers, and that unborn child in Joanna Lewys's womb anxious for the world, and everyone with a belly full of bacon collops lying fearful of Lent.

Sometimes a man will look at a sack of earth and think it's too much for him to carry. And each person in this village had to be carried into Lent. I felt then the whole weight of Oakham on my shoulders, as if God had picked the village up and laid it there.

I hurried across the road towards the church and, as I did, something sleek and black ran past me southwards. I turned to see what it was and saw only broken flickers of black between the bars of rain, which were soon lost to the night. A were-creature, I thought, barely remembering that I had no time for those superstitions; or else a phantom, though a muscular one – for there'd been a glisten of haunches as it passed.

Then I ran. Places you know can seem like foreign lands when your mind's lost itself to the dark. I was a streak of startled white. The short path from the lychgate to the church door took me through Indian forests where satyrs lived, through gangrenous swamps of biting fish, and herds of claw-headed one-footed beasts hefting across dry plains beyond the safe shrines of Jerusalem. The welcoming last slope became the baked deserts of Incognita, roamed by headless people. Will-o'-the wisps were bold enough to swarm my hands as they found the latch. It was only when I was inside that peace came back to my heart. The walls were cold and calm to my palms. A few lights were lit along the south wall.

I brought the stool from the little dark box into the nave, poured some ale and lit a taper. Then I sat on the stool with the ale and the taper in the middle of the nave and gazed. I didn't have it in me to pray. I set the taper on the floor in a holder and passed my forefinger back and forth through its flame. So much is given up. So much. When those hands are laid, both at once, on your head and no word or chant or prayer is spoken, and the power of priesthood is given to you, you think the gift has been gentle, since so gently bestowed, and little do you know what thunder has been passed into you. What violence.

For evermore your blood will run fast, trying to do your duty by God. You're a man trying to do an angel's work. In time, you carry each and every soul in your parish across the breach, from death to the next world, like St Christopher carrying the child Jesus across the river. Well, I can carry most, but how do you carry a man like Newman? When a man like that asks you to help him, what sort of help can you offer that'll do any good? Thomas Newman helped every human he crossed paths with. The Townshends, Carter, little Mippy, Sarah, every man and woman he rented good cheap land to; me. He helped me. He gave more than four pounds to that bridge, a year's wage for most. For that I gave him a plenary pardon that should have helped him bypass purgatory altogether. Yet it didn't, so what help am I? What power after all?

I closed the church door and latched it firmly. I thought of the horse that had fallen the day before – slipped on the cobbles, they said, but what if she'd seen something, been spooked after all? Mares had a way, with their placid sliding gaze, of seeing into the spirit world. I took the iron box, with the deeds folded inside, from the vestry and held it to my front. The church wasn't a shelter but a darkness inside a bigger darkness, and wherever I went in it, I felt there was too much between my head and its roof. I was suspicious of all emptiness.

I picked up the stool eventually and, with the deeds still to my chest, shoved my way into the little dark box. A small darkness was better than a big one. I sat and leant back against the wall with the taper by my feet, and pushed the deeds under the faldstool; a small fortress for them, guarded by my feet Tomorrow was Shrove Tuesday, carnival, *carne levare*: farewell to the flesh. So much more confession to take, a sermon to give, the dean to answer to. Endless, thankless job, this one of serving God. I needed to sleep, but I couldn't. What if I were to hear a knock on the screen during the night, or a rustle of the curtain, or a shifting on the cushion?

My hands looked like a skeleton's on my lap, as if I'd met my dead self. What had I come to, spending a night in the booth? The roosting, cowering priest. What had that black thing been, running past? Really a were-creature? The devil? Most likely a dog, but so undoglike in its low, mendacious charge. I thought of my sister in her new life in Endall's house, of Sarah. In my fraught and head-pained state I thought dimly: the wind! I realised that the reason the church door had come open was because a gust of wind had come in – the rain had stopped and the wind had gusted. I'd closed and latched the door because of that wind and not even noticed why. A wind! Yet when I stood and listened, I heard it was coming not from the west, but at the east window, which rattled a little – the faintest ecstatic quiver of its panes. I'd go and stand in it, just to be sure – stand out there in the churchyard and feel it move my skirts.

I rocked forward to stand, but found myself too afraid to leave the safety of the booth. Never mind the direction for now, a wind is a wind, and a wind from the east can become one from the west easier than no wind at all. Feet tucked in under me, I made a pillow of my hand. My eyes closed. A whispered moan in the trees. I thought of Carter, the gash on his head, his intention to go down to the river first thing to see about that tree. I was too tired for night prayers or a thoughtful request. Tomorrow, I asked, please give us a better day. Thank you, Lord, I added. Thank you.

And I slept.

Day 2
The previous day, Shrove
(also Quinquagesima or, in
Oakham burr, King Can't
Guess It's Us, or Guessing
King, or more simply Guessing)
Sunday

Farewell to the flesh

The hysterical cry of a horse woke me, and at the same time a banging at the door, so that it seemed to me the two things were the same, or connected; in my sleepy state I thought at first it was the horse banging to come in. I rushed up.

'Reve,' was all I got when I unlatched the door, and an amused look from the dean at the sight of me in my night tunic. It was still dark outside, with the grain of dawn. 'If I may?'

He spread his hands to part the space between me and the doorframe. There he stood, inside my room, kicking at the cold fire. Something had happened; there were voices down the road towards Old Cross, and when I went out, John Hadlo was running past, saying that a milk cart had come down. Milk all over the road. He was off to tell Townshend. The horse was down too and needed freeing.

I went back indoors to see the dean still standing where he'd been, a dark shape in darkness, watching the door.

'A bit of light might not go amiss,' he said.

'A milk cart's down,' I said. 'I'm going to go and help out. You light as many candles as you want. Please.'

'No, stay here.'

I could tell by the dean's eager let's-get-started shuffling that he'd come to search my house. I could barely see him, but I could feel his keenness in the same way you could feel the open eyes of someone lying next to you in the dark.

'You know how it is,' he said. 'If I look around someone's house with them there as a witness, I can't be accused of stealing anything.'

'I have nothing worth taking.'

'So they all say.'

We stared at one another. I tried to see something friendly in his bearing, but there was nothing in that respect. All the light we had was from the one candle that I'd lit at dawn prayers and had burnt on for those two hours since. From it I lit six more, put five in sconces around the room and gave the other to him.

'A bit of warmth wouldn't go amiss, either,' he muttered. Then, 'I'm searching everyone's house, you understand I can't make yours an exception.'

'Why should you? You can search with my blessing.'

I waited for the brotherliness I'd seen in him the day before; it soon occurred to me I might be waiting some time. His peevish little light made short journeys here, there, one corner, the other. Up (to find what?). Down (what could I be hiding at knee-level that he hadn't already tripped over?).

'Well, excuse me then,' I said, after a few moments of rigid standing, 'while I go outside to see what's what.'

'It's an upended milk cart, Reve. Did you take the vow of chastity to help villagers clean up milk?'

'I took it to serve my parish.'

'You took it to serve the Lord God, and the Lord God wants to know what happened to Newman. Now, tell me where to start.'

'We know what happened to Newman – he drowned by poor, shoddy fate, like so many men do. Men, women, animals, children.'

144

The dean held up his hand for me to stop. Then he pressed his skirts to his thighs and looked around the room at the business awaiting him, and exhaled.

'I'll start in here then,' he said.

'Start where you like – I have nothing.' I looked again onto the road; a lot of dark motion, four or five bodies scurrying, crouching. 'What happened out there?' I asked the dean. 'Did you see anything?'

'Too dark,' he said. 'The horse slipped on that patch of wet cobble, that's all.'

I sat in the chair. Even your horses are useless, he'd be thinking. Even your milk carts don't stay upright.

He offered his pale light to one corner, another corner, to the room's centre, upwards, then said, 'No wonder you weren't worried about me stealing anything. Looks like somebody's already taken it. Were you robbed in the night?'

'I told you twice, I have nothing.'

'All gone I suppose, when your sister left?'

'You suppose right. The wagon came yesterday.'

The emptiness had surprised even me, when the last thing was loaded and the wagon had creaked away. I'd thrown the words *sanctus sanctus sanctus* into the room, and they'd come back hollow and scolding.

'Well, at least it won't take long,' the dean sighed.

He ran his hands on and under the bed, between the blankets, under the piece of fustian I kept to warm my feet. He looked in the cooking pot, in my cupboard used for food and my chest used for clothes. One by one he nudged the five apples lined up on my table with a fingertip – the apples he had given me. They rocked without rolling, in an apple-ish way that seemed to satisfy and then disappoint him. He passed an unenthusiastic eye over the wash tub. The pile of wood barely interested him. He took the Man of Sorrows from the bedside stool and upended the stool, and gave it a little shake.

I asked, 'What are you looking for?'

'I'll tell you when I've found it.'

'How will you know you've found it, if you don't know what it is?'

'You'd make a sorry sheriff, Reve.'

And you make a sorry dean, I thought; in fact, muttered within my chest. He glanced up, then away. He went into the other room, which had been my sister's room until two days before and was now empty except for two things: a pair of shoes and a bottle of ambergris. Shoes might have been too glorified a term for those unravelling piles of leather, which she'd had as long as I could remember. Stitched and restitched, but now beyond the help of the needle; not shoes to take into a new life.

I suspected the dean would come out of her room with one of these two things, so as to show his trip hadn't been worthless. It was the ambergris he chose. He unstoppered the bottle and inhaled deeply as though it was a full-bloomed rose. His face went stale.

'That was my sister's,' I said.

'No wonder she left it behind. Smells like – '

'Something's arse.' I added, 'So Robert Tunley once said.' Poor quip, ill timing. He didn't smile back.

'It was for her headaches,' I muttered, though unnecessarily. 'She often got headaches.'

'You speak of her as if she's dead.' Said, if not tenderly, then without accusation, and he passed me the bottle.

I rolled it under my thumb, set it on the table, shrugged one shoulder and decided to venture a sentiment I thought he'd understand – he too being alone. 'She's the only person I had left to love. My only family.'

He came a step closer. I thought he might even put a hand on my shoulder, and I prepared to place a hand over his; a clean

146

gesture of alliance. But though he was now companionably close, he didn't put a hand anywhere except stiff by his side, and I was reminded of the only time I'd played chess – I'd watched the other man advancing his piece towards me and marvelled how it could seem that someone was giving you something when in fact they were taking it away.

I retreated one pace, away from the middle of the room, into which he'd stepped. 'Is that all, then?'

'That's all. Nothing found. You'd better get over to your *little dark box* – I've been telling everyone about the pardon on offer if they confess, in the hope it might prompt in them the urgent desire to.' He primly brushed his skirts. 'Oh, and it's a light breakfast for you this morning, I hear. Oakham's little custom of weighing the priest.' At which, inexplicably, he patted his own belly. 'Go steady on those oats, hmm. Now, I ought to get on, sorry if I woke you.'

If anyone ever doubted God's facility for creation, they only needed to stand for a short time and watch a few lowly men and women at work. In the dawn dark they were freeing the fallen horse. They'd unhooked the cart on the upside, the easy side, and were working underneath the horse to free it on the other. They agreed: the mare had slipped, newly shod, on the rain-slimed cobbles. Jane Tunley was passing a soothing, shushing hand down the creature's neck and coaxing it as upright as it could go, while Herry Carter and John Hadlo gave their hands to the straps and buckles of the harness in the cramped blindness under the horse's bulk. 'Breeching dee loosed!' one would call. And the other: 'Backband unbuckled! Trace free!' Their fingers liberated the creature deftly. If God had made men and women in a cruder form, these ones would have either hacked the cart free of the horse with an axe, with breakage to the cart, or forced the horse and cart up by now, with probable breakage to both.

But they were nimble, gentle and full of forethought, and when Hadlo declared that the cart was free, Jane Tunley called for somebody to go further up the road, knowing that when the horse came to its feet and realised its freedom, it would bolt. As it did. And there was Morris Hall and little Tom Hadlo to catch it and bring it to a standstill, and run their hands over its shoulders and flanks, down its legs, checking for injury. The cart meanwhile was brought onto its wheels by several men and women, and that too checked for injury – the axle was off and a wheel snapped, for a start. Its side gates were smashed. Despite that, it was fixable, they said. The spilt churns had already been lined up along the road, Townshend was already on his way down from the manor with a face that bore more concern than anger, and the cart and wheels were carried off to the barns for mending. Only the axle was left.

While I watched – because they wouldn't let me help (and didn't need it, was the greater truth) – the whole scene was efficiently cleared and soon there was nothing left but the cart axle and a few interested dogs. Why they left the axle, I didn't know; if it couldn't be fixed, it'd make good firewood. The darkness was thin and blue by then and the sun soon up. The villagers had come and gone, and the cart carried off like a sick child. There was just the sound of cock crows, and the distantly whickering horse, and the dogs' surprised tongues finding milk, thick, warm and sweet, between the cobbles.

I emptied my bladder in the hazel scrub and went indoors. I ate oats with water and no milk. The dean was right, today was weighing day, that undignified annual ceremony in which I was put in a boat along with another man to see that I weighed less than him, for a priest's substance is, it's claimed, midway between man and angel. I didn't feel altogether angelic, I must say. It occurred to me as I ate that the dean might delight in my failure if I weighed more, and the thought stopped me eating before the bowl was empty.

A brother, I'd thought when he arrived the day before on his lonely little mare with his fearfully creased brow. I'd even felt relief when he dismounted in his vestments – which were a fair bit finer than mine – and squeezed my hands in his. I could see he was hoping to find something in Oakham to like, or something that would like him. I'd been prepared to be both, the liker and the liked. I'd show him the church full of donations – the chalices, the lights, the altar cloths, even the useless little acorn cups; we'd laugh.

But he'd taken one look at the church and got on to other business – the business of Newman's death, for which he'd come – and I hadn't noticed anything about Oakham that had pleased him yet, least of all me. I sat too long in my chair. I unstoppered the bottle of ambergris; if I left it like that, would my sister escape completely and be gone? As a smell disperses and fades? *You talk of her as if she's dead*, the dean said. Well, in a way she was, and also boldly alive. Here and gone. So recently, so long ago. I tried to remember anything from her twenty-three years on earth and nothing came, nothing at all except a memory of her on the eve of her wedding, which was only three days gone. Everything else preceding it – missing.

She'd been in this room, frying bread basted in eggs in a skillet over the fire. It was good bread made with wheat. The room smelt of warm butter and ambergris. The table was set with a plate, knife and cup for each of us; I filled the cups with beer and we sat and ate. Annie ate hers like a wolf. As children we had egg-bread, though it was rye then and never tasted as good as this bread made with Oakham wheat. She sipped at her beer and made shapes with string wound around her fingers, and I noticed her fingernails were dirty, and said she should remember to clean them before she reached the altar.

After breakfast I'd taken the last week's ashes outside and added them to the heap, and cleaned the smoke off the window.

Then I'd taken my razor and soap and shaved first my face, then the tonsure. I wore the tonsure small; England was no place for a bare head. 'Soon you'll be bald anyway,' Annie said, 'then you'll be trying to stick it back on.' She tied her own hair in a scarf; her hair, unlike mine, was the colour of late, ripe grain, and unlike mine it fell lazily down, where mine curled more urgently up. Mine was a wild ruff on my head, hers was a cloak more luxurious than she could afford to buy. I could never understand how it all went inside that scarf, nor how we two could have sprung from the same womb.

'Thank the Lord for giving us another day of dog-hork,' she said, meaning the rain and grey. We each bowed to and kissed the Man of Sorrows before we left; 'Cheer up,' she whispered to him, as she did every day, and she put on her coat and helped me fasten the topmost buttons of my cassock.

There it was: a morning like any other, nothing special in it at all. Yet it eclipsed every morning, afternoon or evening that had gone before. A memory as trivial to the world as a stone to a shore – and yet was everything I had left of her before the great mill of time heaved itself up and over and spilt her out. Annie and I had watched two parents die, and long before that a brother, another brother and a sister before they could even walk. I'd bid farewell to my own flesh and blood, then farewell again and farewell again, until all that was left was Annie. When she had her twentieth birthday I'd begun to wonder if I'd be spared her loss, since a woman not married by then might have seemed (to callow men) to be jetsam washed up. But then John Endall appeared, tepid and pleasant as a lettuce, and there it was: time had dealt its curse – since all things are a matter of time.

When I saw her next she wouldn't be Annie, but a woman in the image of our mother. Fate sealed, fortunes set, belly swollen. Besieged. And our dank, carefree February morning of three days before would give way to the course of life, which shackles us.

And me? Shackled too, by the heart, to God, my last presiding kin and remaining accomplice. Before Annie was pledged to be married, the warmth of her sisterly love had made me less craving for God's. But there it was, he didn't like to be uncraved, and so he'd designed from the very beginning my utmost dependence, and from that my utmost devotion. All things are a matter of time.

Singing that day, my irrepressible Oakhamers. The village road busy with brooms while everyone swept their houses and yards for Lent. There was a rare ceasing of rain, and the brooms flew gusty. They made dust clouds that hung long in the damp air. The hens scattered circularly, the goats sneezed, the dogs ran ever hopeful at swinging broomsticks. *Bring us in no capon's flesh, for that is often dear; bring us in no duck's flesh, for they wallow in the mere.* A drinking song; they liked that one, whether they were drinking or not. They sang it in choruses up and down the road. That morning, the morning after it had been decided Thomas Newman was dead, they sang with defiant good spirits. Everybody was in trouble if Thomas Newman was dead; only in the wake of his death did the village realise fully that Oakham belonged to him, and that he was what protected them. So they sang, and the road plumed with dust like a stampede sent up at battle.

> *Bring no bread,*
> *bring no pig,*
> *bring no cheese,*
> *bring no tripe,*
> *bring no eggs,*
> *bring no meat,*
> *bring us in good ale!*
> *For our blessed Lady's sake,*
> *bring us in good ale!*

* * *

151

'Benedicite.'

'Dominus.'

'Confiteor.'

A sob. Poor Carter. I might have known he'd be the very first to confess. A moment before, he'd been outside the Lewyses' house sweeping their yard, and I'd seen him drop his broom and run to the church after me. I was only half on my stool when his 'Benedicite' burbled like water from a spout and his body dropped to the cushion.

'He was as good as a father to you,' I said.

'He was.' A strangled kind of sound.

'You'll see him in heaven.'

We were whispering; it hadn't been decided that way, but now that we were, it seemed we were committed to it. So we whispered on like thieves, and I bent forward to hear him.

'Whatever's to be done in the village, I'll do,' Carter said through tears. 'I've swept Mary Grant's house, and Fisker's with his bad leg, and the Lewyses' because of Joanna being so bloated with child, and Hikson's. I said I'd help Hikson with his brewing, and there's some slates on the church porch need replacing, and the dean said he'll need help down at – down at – Tom Newman's house, with the animals and that. Now that Tom's – now that.'

Carter went into a pain-racked silence. I couldn't see why Hikson needed any help, able-bodied man that he was. Lazy as a cowpat, was Hikson. If a child offered to carry him to church on a Sunday, he'd let them.

'Why do you have to help everyone?'

'I have grief all through my body, Father, like I'm stung.'

'And so you're running in sore circles.'

Carter said nothing.

'Sometimes we have to sit with our sorrow, not run from it. Helping Hikson mash his grain won't ease the sting.'

'It might help atone for it.'

152

This time I said nothing. The day before, Janet Grant had rung the death bell, and all of Oakham had come to the church as was our custom, and I'd invited them to pray, and told them the death was Newman's, but there was no body to bless or bury. I'd seen Herry Carter's face among the many, blank as a stone, and I hadn't known until then that, far from the absence of feeling, blankness could be the overwhelment of feeling. I thought he too had died, standing there.

Carter was sitting further back on the cushion than most did, and I was making no effort to turn myself from the grille. So I could see him, though the light was never good. He was so young in the face, and innocent, his nose button-ish and mildly upturned. His grey eyes were calm and fetching. His face was slack and melting with sorrow, the cheek I could see held the sheen of tears, his hair a nest, his fingers continually going up to it to scratch or ruffle.

'Do you remember when Newman first came to the village?' he said. 'And we thought he was a criminal, or a merchant, or diseased, and we kept away from him.'

I nodded into my lap, though Carter wasn't to know.

'He came wearing those gores over his shoes and we ribbed him,' he said.

'Yes,' on a breath of laughter, because I did remember those gores, now he said it.

'And then we heard he'd lost his wife and child. And come to make a new life. Why did he come to Oakham? Who would come to Oakham to make a new life?'

This was less a question, more a matter of common perplexity that had passed around our village in the twelve years since Newman came, and it never expected an answer. Then as Newman made his fortune here – fortune relative to the rest of us, anyhow – the perplexity turned to marvel and the marvel to fact and the fact soon went as unremarked as any other.

'One day I was helping one of his sows with her birthing,' Carter said, then realised he wasn't whispering any more, paused to decide what to do, and committed to speaking in passionate tones. 'And when those little things were born, five of them laid along their mother blind and hungry, Tom was looking at them close to tears. Then rushed off all of a sudden and left me there. I sat in the stall at a loss. Then he came back and he was holding a small wool blanket. 'This was my daughter's,' he said, and he said it all quiet and heavy like a sky full of rain. He held it out to me so I took it, but he didn't say anything else. Nothing. Eventually I offered it back to him and he took it, and he held it and looked at the sow, and there was nothing to go by in his face, and then he started walking away. That was when I said in an urgent way, 'I'm here, Tom, here I am,' meaning, I'll try and make up for what's lost. He understood I meant that, I know he did. He looked me straight in the eye and nodded. Then he went and I was left with that sow and I felt – I don't know. I don't reckon he'd ever shown that blanket to another person, only to me. I felt – like a great sail full of the ocean's wind.'

Carter hadn't known much of his parents; everyone in the village had had a hand in bringing him to adulthood, me too. Then Newman came, a wary, childless man, and there was Carter, a wary, parentless child of eight years, and Carter went in to live with him at the old wooden manse when it wasn't much more than a leaky outhouse. Newman used the last of his money to rebuild it, and to feed Herry Carter and get him strong. Gave him love. *A great sail full of the ocean's wind.*

'But I didn't, did I?' Carter said, and now passion had turned to stridency. 'I didn't make up for anything in the end. He paid for my wedding, he hoped we'd repay him, I expect, by bringing a son or daughter into the world, though he never said it. But me and Cat don't seem able to bring a son nor daughter into this world.'

'It's as God wills, and that tragedy is yours, not Newman's,' I said, no longer whispering, either, but quiet. 'Any child you had could never have replaced his own.'

'Not replace, make up for. *Make up for*. That's what I as good as promised that day in the pig stall, and he gave me all a person could and I didn't make up for anything. Now he's in the river, dead and drowned.'

'And is that your fault?'

'It's nobody else's.'

I'd been leaning forward, pressing my own thumb against the hump of the etched-in camel, thinking how strange a creature it was; did the camel gestate her young in that hump? I leant back again, dissatisfied. How little we know.

'When my mother died,' I said, 'I was filled with grief, and then with guilt. What did I do? Did I drive her away, to the other world? Guilt often follows sadness. Who can say why? Perhaps if we imagine we were part of the cause of the death, we can do something to reverse it.'

Carter's hand went to his head again, ruffling that thick, fair hair. He sniffed in the way people do when they've come to the end of a bout of tears.

'The gossip going round is that Mr Townshend did it,' he said.

'Don't listen to gossip, Herry.'

'I heard it's the dean's suspicion.'

'The dean's just trying out notions, is all, to see how they fit.'

'But Mr Townshend would be the last person in England to do it.'

'As the dean will find out,' I said. 'Give him time.'

There was worry in Carter's voice now that the grief had abated, and a thread of it was in me too, though I didn't give it away. I didn't know what to make of the dean, how well he meant, how dogged he was. He'd been with us less than twenty-four hours; it seemed soon to be choosing suspects. And besides, he wasn't supposed to be choosing suspects; he was supposed to be on our side.

'Herry, pray the Paternoster and the Confiteor as many times a day as you can. Try hard with your wife to conceive. Be pure and strong through Lent, and by Easter you'll be ready for the host, for new beginnings. The Lord will wash you clean.'

'And I should fix the church porch where it's leaking.'

'It's not for you to – '

'It troubled, Tom, that leak. I'll fix it today.'

I looked up and sighed. Then I spoke to him in a whisper that was sharper than before, and with my mouth nearer the grille. 'One last thing, Herry – take care what you say. You know that our dean's around, and he's intent on finding a story to go with this death. You mustn't go around saying that it was your fault. You'll find yourself – '

I was going to say *without a head*; I spared Carter the notion, and myself the trouble. In any case it wasn't true, they wouldn't show him the mercy of a beheading.

'Tell me it's going to be alright, Father.'

'If you do as I say, it's going to be alright.'

He raised his voice. '*Mea culpa, mea culpa, mea maxima culpa.* I beseech blessed Mary ever-virgin, blessed Michael the Archangel, blessed John the Baptist, blessed Apostles Peter and Paul, and all the saints to pray for me to the Lord our God, *Dominum Deum nostrum.* Amen.'

'Amen, Herry Carter.'

'I'll go and fix the porch right now.'

'Go then.'

Another sniff, defiant this time, and his young, restless body was already released to the light and cold.

Others look at the fields sloping off up towards the east boundary and think: this is my field, that's yours. Newman

156

looked at them and thought: they could all be mine. Others eye the skies that they know go eventually to Europe, and think: what's that got to do with me? Only this bit of sky matters, the bit that's raining or sunning on me. Newman thought: if the sky makes it so easily to Europe, why not me? If this bit's raining on me, why not go to that bit?

But he battled, did Newman, with the instinct to be his own man and the will to be God's servant. The battle was everywhere in his body – in long legs well capable of striding, but rarely did; in a slight carriage ballasted with a pair of muscly fighter's shoulders; in a cool eye betrayed by a twitch. He'd a staglike way of standing (difficult to explain why, but if you've seen a stag, you'll see how the trees or clearing or mountain stand back from it and grant it space); yet a stag past its rutting days. A stag that's equally hind. An uncolourful, bloodless face with striking, scooping cheekbones, and on those cheekbones a lacing of very fine and broken redness: proof that the blood did try to urge, and then dissipated. A face gone prematurely rugged with the effort of wanting what it feared – since Newman wanted to find his own ways to God, and feared his own ways to God, in case they didn't lead there. And feared, above all things, being separated from God, who keeps company with his dead wife and child.

Twelfth Night, this January just passed, Newman, not long back from his pilgrimage to Rome, installed on the other side of the little dark box – because he confessed whenever and as often as he could. What had he seen on his travels? The whole world on wagons and carracks, he said. Sarplars of wool on mules' backs, the stench of lanolin from wool sacks – ewe and mud and milk and muck in the throat. Sacks going this way, tin going that, traders here, pilgrims there. Tallow, goat-skins, salt, hops, silver, cotton, wax, silk, pewter, wood, pitch, potash, soap, spices, cows, paper, grain, stone, glass, armour, fustian, wine, sugar, latten, coal. Iron as plentiful as the stones on the ground and brass abounding from the hills. Spanish olive oil, as golden-green as those young grain fields; silk from Sicily; Indian pepper, ginger, cardamom, nutmeg; dried rhubarb and galingale from eastern China; aloes from the lands around the Red Sea; cloves that are violent on the tongue; brocades and great noble tapestries; Syrian ash in Venetian glass and scented soap; Asian elephant tusks and unicorn horns that change hands in Alexandria and go to Paris for carving; Indian emeralds, rubies, sapphires, diamonds, lapis lazuli from the Oxus, Persian pearls and turquoise.

A land of wheat, and barley, and vines, and fig trees, and pomegranates; a land of oil olive, and honey, I said, which was from the scriptures, and pounced upon by Newman. To only know the world from the scriptures! Wasn't it an insult to the Lord to ignore the lands he'd made, the colours he'd pained himself to imagine and mix, in preference for some words in vulgate? Only somebody with a mind like a rock could go on with the idea that we on our little island are separate from those other places – that great world is rainbow threads woven into our greys and greens. Where did this leather belt come from? he asked me, of a belt I couldn't see. Not English goats, but Norwegian ones. And the flour for making bread that feeds our great cities? From Baltic grain, high up in the north. And the ironwork on our new weathervane? Spanish iron. Our little land is flecked with foreignness, the Lord wants our colourful mingling.

(Myself wondering how it was that Newman knew so much about what the Lord wanted, and having the peculiar sensation that his words coming through the grille were moths disintegrating.)

Not only that, he said. It's not only *things* that you find when you venture out of Oakham, down to the ports, out to the sea, cutting out across the tides to Europe – not only *things*, which are after all fatuous, but matters of the intellect too, the soul. Did I know that music, being of the air, has a perfect resonance with the air in the ear and the air of the human spirit – that music might therefore bring us direct to the Lord and heal us? So they said in Florence and Rome. (I did not know, I said, and smothered a yawn, which wasn't boredom or tiredness, but defence, since nowhere in this dealing with the Lord is the priest, and yet there Newman was nevertheless, confiding in his priest.) And that, he said, man has been able to take the sprawling and nebulous mystery of time and harness it on a clock face, minute by minute, hour by hour.

And that, abroad, a vision had been seized of us men and women as beautiful. Not tormented sacks of sinful flesh, but fine creatures – that Pietà he'd hung at his altar, for instance, where the Christ, though crucified, was otherwise like any man in his prime, his thighs muscled and his chest firm, and Mary's milky eyes screaming with a mother's love, a real mother, a mother like his or mine.

And that – so he said – some were claiming there were other ways of writing the Bible, since if you looked at the Greek, as they were doing abroad now, it yielded new ways of seeing things. For instance: no longer *In the beginning was the word*, but *In the beginning was the conversation*. I spluttered, I think. *And the conversation was with God*. I spluttered more. As if God is your cousin next door, I said. Yes, said Newman, as if God is your neighbour and friend. He reached the short distance to the grille, asked for my hand, which I pressed there, and which he pressed his against, briefly. John Reve, my redoubtable friend, he said. Crossed himself, and asked me to bless him.

Nobody wants to speak badly of the dead, but I need to admit that there've been points along the way when I've lost patience with Newman for this. Let's say you want a church built, and you say to your friend the church stonemason, I can build my own church, I don't need you. Then in the next breath you ask the stonemason to build it for you. Doesn't the mason have cause to be confused and to not know what's being asked

159

of him? If Newman had entered *conversation* with our great and silent master, why did he turn to me in the next breath and ask me to bless him? Couldn't he have just asked God?

But I did bless him, every time, like that stonemason going back day after day with his chisels and ladders and mortar. Because he was a friend? Because I loved him? Because it seemed impossible for me not to?

(And now I have the strangeness of speaking of him in a past tongue, because he's a day dead. Is it too soon? What is the point, Lord, of official departure?)

'Father, you'll think I've come just for that pardon you pinned up yesterday, but it's a real thing I'm here for, and I don't even want the pardon, I don't care for it at all.'

Our churchwarden, Janet Grant, who cared not for anything except the zealous and faithful doing of the Lord's little works: the lighting of the church, the cleaning of the chalice, the sweeping of the chancel, the straightening of the Psalters.

'On Friday late morning, Father, before your sister's wedding, I was walking across the churchyard as I do, daily, several times a day, as you do too – and I was passing the rowan near the path, you know, where the path narrows and there's that little clump of crocuses that have come up these last few days, and some thrushes come to – in the rowan just there, they come to perch, they eat the berries – '

She paused; her speech was ever thus. Spirals of deepening particulars, then pauses when she saw she'd strayed from the point.

'And I saw an owl. An owl. In good daylight. It flew right above me, and I thought it might have wanted the thrushes, but I don't know if owls have a taste for thrushes, I thought it was mice they liked.'

'An owl,' I said.

'In daylight, Father.'

Which was commonly taken as an omen of death. This was her as-yet-arrived-at point.

'It scared me to see an owl fly by daylight, and when I came to check the church on Friday night, to see if all the lights were out and everything safe, I found that I locked it as I left, the church. Which I never do.'

'Locked it?'

'Yes.'

'We agreed the church should never be locked, except in dire times.'

'I thought it was dire times – there was evil about, death somewhere, and I wanted the church to be safe from it.'

'You tried to guard the church from evil – '

'I know, Father.'

'The church is a refuge from evil – '

'I know, Father. I did wrong.'

I imagined she bowed her head, her head that was big for her small body. A curious sight was Janet Grant, a woman of forty with the shoulder-span and hand size of a child, and a large, pale moonish face that was young and sincere and had an eyelid that drooped, only slightly, but once noticed couldn't be unnoticed. Her entire top gum showed, if ever she grinned.

Her voice seemed to move a little closer to the grille; perhaps she'd looked up again, and turned towards me. 'In the morning first thing I unlocked it, before my rounds – before you'd know. But we all know what happened then.' Whispering now. 'Then we learnt that Thomas Newman had died.' A pause, and the whisper sharpened. 'And it was such horror – because I'd seen death coming, Father, and what did I do? I locked the church; I stopped the Lord finding it. I left death to the devil.'

'But – the Lord isn't deterred by a lock.'

She made hesitant sounds of thinking with her dry tongue before she ventured agreement. 'The Lord can pick a lock.'

'He's the greatest locksmith there is.'

'But Newman wasn't.'

Her next point came rapidly, with rare directness. 'Newman wasn't a locksmith, and if he'd tried to come to the church before he took his own life, he wouldn't have been able to get in and pray for his soul.'

She fell quiet at the foot of her words. Is that what everybody thought – that Newman took his own life? Or what only she thought?

'Newman wouldn't have known to come and pray for his soul before his death,' I said, 'because his death was an accident he didn't see coming.'

'Forgive me, Father, but you can't know it was an accident.'

'Neither of us can know one way or the other.'

'But if he drowned himself and tried to come to the church before that to pray, it was me who stood between him and God.' She gave an incredulous laugh touched with bleak thrill: her! Her with shoulders the width of a child's, her who stood in the way of God!

I might have assailed her with questions: wasn't Newman a rich man? Wasn't he loved? Wasn't he in good health? Rich, loved, healthy men don't hurl themselves in a river, do they? But I remembered where I was – in the little dark box, which was for the interrogation of the other's soul and faith, not for the interrogation of a dead man's motives.

'Your sin was to lock the church door,' I said, 'not to stand between a man and God. Sins are measured – you know – by intention, not effects, and your intention was to make the church safe. A pointless intention. That was your sin: to have a pointless intention. A trivial sin, which is now forgiven if you say your Creed before you sleep tonight.'

'I always say my Creed before I sleep.'

'It'll be no effort then.'

She sat in unsatisfied silence. My hands were cold; I tucked each into the opposite sleeve.

'But did you think he was *happy*, Father?' she said. 'Thomas Newman, was he happy?'

Her question seemed to me painfully innocent, my answer not worthy of it. 'If you could tell me what happiness is, I could tell you if I thought Newman possessed it.'

She swallowed dry. 'I think happiness is being without any of the things that make you unhappy.'

'Really? Then no one is happy.' I thought I'd disappointed her, or taken from her optimism in some way, so I added, 'Most, perhaps. Happiness is being without *most* of the things that make you unhappy.'

'What sort of most? How many most? Everything minus one thing? Two things?'

'More than one or two things.'

'A quarter unhappy things and three-quarters happy?'

'A fifth perhaps.'

'A fifth.'

'Or thereabouts.'

'Did you think Newman was a fifth unhappy and four-fifths happy?'

'Yes,' I said, though not because I had any idea.

'But didn't you see him at Annie's wedding?' she asked. 'He started out well enough, but by the end I saw him sitting on his own, or not on his own as such because people came to sit with him, but he might as well have been on his own, and he didn't dance and he looked very remote. I wouldn't have said he looked like four-fifths of him were happy.'

'Being alone isn't the same as being unhappy.'

'I saw him when Annie danced – with her new husband. Their joy!' She emitted the last word thinly, on a breath, as if it were a wren taking flight. 'Sometimes when we're joyless ourselves, seeing the joy of others can be the last straw, can't it? Seeing others in love, when you've lost your own love.'

'Newman lost his own love twelve years ago,' I said, impatient. I wasn't impatient with Janet Grant but, suddenly, with that wilted groom Endall, whose last few acts of liveliness would be to inject Annie with his weak progeny, then be too spent up to help her raise them. 'Newman's wife and child died twelve years ago,' I said. 'Show me a man, woman, boy or girl who hasn't buried someone within the last twelve years; and if you find that lucky person, show me them again in a year or two. They'll have buried someone by then.'

Maybe she winced; she certainly loosed a small squeak. Her own husband was only three years in the ground, and her two children went there as infants. There were rustling sounds of her gathering herself up as if the squeak had embarrassed her. She went very quiet, I wondered if she was weeping.

Her voice, from the quietness, came like a leaf on a branch that was only that morning bare. 'Are you hiding something, Father?'

Her question startled me. The least-expected words from an ever-bitten tongue.

'Just that you say with such certainty Newman didn't kill himself, but maybe you have to say and think that. If he did, all his worldly things would have to be given over to the Crown: his house, his animals, his money, everything, Father. His land too. Most of Oakham would be given away – and then what?'

I looked down at my handless arms, which were one continuous arm, and I had the feeling that I wouldn't be able to separate them if I tried.

'You have to say it because you want to protect us, Father. That's what you do, protect us – very well, we all think. Better to say it was an accident.'

'Newman was a rich man,' I said, though I sounded a little forlorn even to my own ears. 'He was a healthy man, he was loved. He wouldn't have hurled himself in a river.'

164

'But if he did, and I stood in the way of his last hope of salvation, what will I do? Am I damned?'

'Do rich and healthy men hurl themselves in a river?'

'If I stood in the way of his salvation, will I be punished?

'Do you know how blessed his life was? Do you know anybody who wouldn't have traded places with him?'

'But will I – '

She interrupted herself with a fretful swallow and I, realising that it had been too long since either of us had spoken anything but a question, strode out of the dispute at last with, 'He was rich, he was healthy, he was loved.' As if latching a gate. And my hands, which had worked their way out of the sleeves, gave a strange little clap.

Night Air

Benedicite, Dominus, Confiteor. Pater, Creed, Ave. Have you wronged your mother and father? Have you given in to excessive appetite? Have you harmed an animal? Have you had despairing thoughts? Denied help, travelled to dangerous places in your mind, been unfaithful, let your hair go dirty, your nails grow long, have you stolen, coveted, sworn, doubted?

Father, I spat in the ditch; I let wind while praying; I didn't say Grace; I overslept; I put my left shoe on the right foot and the right on the left; I left the bellows on the table; last Christmas I broke a promise; I overslept; I thought the devil was in my ale, I drank it all up to be sure he wasn't, I thought the devil was in my second and third ale, I drank them up too, forgive me for doubting; I overslept; I overslept; I shaved my husband's face and left stubble in the shape of a heart, he doesn't yet know it; I overslept; I ate a raw snail, snarfed it up out of its shell in one hearty suck; I scratched my name in the chancel pillar in Mass last summer; I fancied a cloud was the shape of a buttock.

To the oversleepers of Oakham, and the wind-letters and ditch-spitters and cloud-fanciers and snail-snarfers and whimsical shavers and doubtful drinkers and confused of feet, I gave forgiveness; they left victorious with a forty-day pardon under their belts. Any other time you'd have to do something strenuous

166

for a whole forty days of pardon, now you just had to embroider a confession – and not much thread had to go into that, just say you overslept; you probably had.

Not far off twenty confessions thus far in a single day – the dean would be pleased. What a day of mixed fortunes it had been for the people of Oakham; they'd lost a friend, and the man who provided land and work and food and worldliness to this soggy little dell, and yet there was a pardon going as a result of his loss, a pardon that forgave them forty days of sinning. *Forty days.* The tears rolled confusingly – grief and gratitude.

Thank you, Lord, some said under their breaths. Thank you, Thomas Newman, said others. For several years the distinction between the two had been growing hazier.

Midday prayers. *God come to my assistance, Lord make haste to help me.* Muttering, hungry, into the rosary. *As it was in the beginning, is now and ever shall be.* Psalms, a hymn, something from Peter. *At this midday hour renew your grace in us: make good our defects.* Out.

At home I took an apple from the five on the table, a corner of bread and a bit of cheese. Then I returned the bread and cheese to the table, in growing dread at soon being weighed. I ate the apple as I went. I walked out past the abandoned axle, southwards past Old Cross, past the birch maypole, the pigs snuffling filthily along the track leading to Newman's woods, and westwards down towards the river in a soup of murk and rain.

In summer the path west would be lined with tall daisies and grasses, and Our Lady's Gloves would put out flowers that were deep harbours for bees. The thick clover at West Fields turned the ground velvet and the cows drowsy. Reflections of trees and clouds would collect in the river's clearness. The birch copse would shiver with light; the million little leaves rustling in a soulful breeze, wild strawberries on the ground. Even the horse tails tied there would flutter like ribbons rather than hang as nooses. I didn't look to my left as I walked past them then. I didn't look at the bare, unstrawberried winter ground nor at the trees, which were brazenly bonelike. I thought only of summer, and finished my apple.

At the river bank I threw the core into the water with a spirited overarm lob. Here was where Newman must have gone in and drowned; his feet on the muddy edge where the bank met what was left of the bridge – half an arch, where there'd been two before the collapse. He'd have been able to see, as I could, that the second bridge was better built than our previous attempt. The stones were hacked to regular shapes and packed tightly, with a little mortar (just enough to add strength to well-fitted stones, not so much as to compensate for badly fitted ones); there'd been none of the lazy daubing or cobbing of our previous try. The keystone – now at the bottom of the river – had been hefty, a strong, pleasing fan, well chiselled. We'd taken costly advice from the stonemasons at Bruton, whose guild dispensed counsel, one pained grain of wisdom at a time, each grain pinching another half-crown from our purses.

The abutments were sturdy, the arches shapely. It had been a respectable bridge, not elegant but noble. It had a cutwater. It had stood proud and anticipatory for three months – finished late in November after a summer of building, and collapsed a week ago after a winter of floods. River's too quick and narrow, Newman had said, and I admitted too late that he was right. Where the river funnelled and surged, it plundered the banks, you could see how it had scooped out the earth. A keen violence at work. That had weakened the abutments, which probably, I could even see now, had been built too close to vulnerable banks and were entrenched (good and deep, said the stonemasons, or the abutments will splay), but maybe not deeply enough (the abutments had splayed). And the bank itself had become more prone than upright, and with mud as slippery as ice. If Newman had stood there in contemplation of the damage – wistful? righteous? melancholic? despairing? annoyed? amused? – and lost his footing, he'd have been whisked in and away, away and under, under and along, arrowed into downed trees and cow carcasses, dragged through silt, lastly shunted by current around a seaward bend, and gone.

I stared at the water. For something going one way so rapidly, it managed a dozen distractions; eddying, folding, spluttering, backtracking, lurching, kicking, bolting, bucking: a bitten mule. Ten shades of brown, one shade of black, and an almighty wet sound roaring from it, a sound so common to us lately that I'd only just noticed it.

In my thirteen Oakham winters I'd never known such rain, nor seen this place so churned and soaked and listless in its mood and colour. I put my hand out and a dewy vapour settled on the back of it. My own chest and lungs had begun to labour from taking in too much damp and windless fug. For years on end nothing happened in Oakham out of the ordinary cycle of birth, strength, illness, death – there were no particular comings or goings, nor things to surprise us. Then in September, Newman went on a pilgrimage to Rome. In November, we finished the bridge. In December, Newman came back from Rome. In January, Sarah Spenser went on a pilgrimage to see a rotten tooth. At the end of January she came back, feverish, and while away I'd been feverish too. In early February the bridge fell down. A week later Newman drowned. What curse was this? Now here we were, besieged by a rural dean who, I'd come slowly to realise, was too intent on saving us wholly to care for the fate of any one of us singly.

I crouched, rolled my sleeves to the elbow and scooped up a wet clod of mud and threw, or tried to throw, it into the river. It landed close by. You must do something, John Reve, you must do something. I picked up a second clod and a third, but wet mud doesn't hurl. I don't know if I thought I might see dry green grass beneath, if I scooped mud long enough. Maybe I thought I'd find summer beneath, and the Lord's mercy, the proof of which would be a fresh, mild western wind picking up from the ground, rising, speeding across the fields.

'John,' she said.

And I said, 'Cecily,' because she'd chided me too many times for saying Lady Townshend, or even Mrs Townshend.

'Let me in,' she said. 'Let me kneel at your feet like we all used to, before this damned box appeared.'

She rapped her knuckles against the screen. I didn't object, not least because she'd already started pushing the screen aside, and her white bony hand fell on it, heavily ringed. Cecily Townshend wasn't a woman you disputed with. She filled that tiny triangle of space I perched in, and pulled the screen shut, and crouched at my feet in a harsh rustle of woebegone silk. Her dress was the one of dusky peony-pink; I remembered the days when it was red. She'd been wearing it most of the winter, with warmth from a fur mantle which she wore now, and which smelt confusingly of lavender and dung.

I pulled the amice up to hide my eyes from her, partly at least, and I turned my head. Though washed, my hands and nails weren't entirely clean of mud, and I tried to put them behind my back. She helped my discretion not a bit by clasping the left hand before it got away, and looking up at me. Not a beauty, but her eyes always impressed me. So lovely, faded blue, lively and curious.

'Thomas Newman is really dead?' she whispered – though even 'whisper' might have been too loud a word for the near-soundless movement of her lips. I heard only the hiss of an s, and the dull blunt fall of the last word, like a foot thudding a campball.

'Yes,' I said.

'He went unshriven,' she said.

'Yes.'

Her knees were on my toes; I worried that her dress had dipped in my cup of beer. There was a smell of cloves and roses among the lavender and dung, I think from her headdress, or some hair pomade. Their medley made me slightly nauseous. I was used to any number of smells, mostly bad, but at least coming one at a time.

'Look at me,' she said. 'Listen to me.'

I turned my face to her but left the amice pulled up. She was cautious about the queue of jittering, fidgeting villagers in the nave; I knew this. It was never easy for the Townshends to come to confession; every ear was turned to hear what they were getting up to, the people-on-high. Oakham wasn't a salacious village, not especially occupied with scandal-hunting, but it never hurt to know what your Lord and Lady were doing that needed forgiveness.

'I can't bear that he's dead,' she murmured.

Her face wasn't anguished, it was pinched and unhappy, but also calm. It was turned upwards towards mine.

'And to not even have his body to bury.'

'If it appears – '

'It will not appear, John. Do you think the river will flow backwards and lay him out on our banks? It will not appear, not until it gets to the sea.'

'Then we'll have to pray he's found the Lord's arms.'

'We'll do more than pray.'

She fumbled with the purse around her neck and pulled out a piece of linen full of coins, which she pressed into my hand. 'This is my prayer. Ten pounds. Let God know I've donated it and ask him to give Thomas Newman a place in heaven, and to get him there soon.'

I stared down at that pouch of coins. A tremendous amount; a year's wages for a priest. What was I to do with it? I could

171

hardly commit it to the tin box we kept for donations, or ask Janet Grant to list it in our church accounts. Every eyebrow would arch at that. It wasn't the kind of money donated for the well-being of a dead friend; it was the desperate sum given for a lover, from the wail of a strangled heart. It felt, in my palm, like the weight of her heart itself.

'Keep it privately and donate it crown by crown,' she said, because she knew the predicament. 'If it takes six months for it all to appear in the accounts, or a year, or two, it doesn't matter. Just let God know *now* that it's there, so that he can act.'

What strange complicity she'd drawn me into, because we'd never before spoken about her relationship with Newman, yet she confided as if we understood one another. And, oddly, I had to admit we did. The love affair between them was there to be suspected, I'd just never allowed myself the suspicion. Now when I looked at her I felt warmth and disdain. Disappointment. Had she loved him? Ten pounds said she must have. I suddenly thought of a hare, the way it looks up frozen and affixed, all eyes and cheekbones, all tapering nose and alert quiver.

I knew I should have questioned her: the nature of the affair, how long, how often. I should have prescribed penance, based on her answers and how sorry she was. I didn't believe she was sorry at all, and I asked none of those questions.

'I can't take it,' I said, and held the pouch of money towards her. Of course she knew I could take it, and would. I wondered if my very thoughts appeared through the light of my eyes and were fully visible to her: with this money we could rebuild the bridge. Otherwise, with this money we'd be a quarter of the way to a new west window, though not one brilliantly coloured. She closed her hands around mine, pressed my fingers against the coins, their curves, their coolness. Those lustful hands, I thought. A heavy ring on every finger can't keep a woman to her husband.

'Take it.' So she said, unnecessarily. And also unnecessarily: 'Say nothing to anyone about it.'

I shook my head. A hare and a stag; they were a fitting pair, she and Newman. As we sat in silence I considered their affair, and felt the lack of surprise settle in me, as when you're told something you always knew. It must have been a passionate affair, both drawing their swords, neither knowing a moment's hesitation or apology. A business of tall, slender bodies and sharp appetite and few words.

'Thank you, John,' she said, and lowered her head to kiss my clutching hand. 'It was Thomas Newman's money anyway – he gave it to me some time ago, to protect me. Oliver squanders money. Thomas wanted me to have something of my own, in case there was nothing left. For clothing, for food, for repairs to the house, for animals. Well, I don't want it for those things. I want to buy him his place in heaven.'

I wondered, what depth of affair was this to warrant from Newman a gift so large, and what length was the affair, and how often, and how equal, and started by whom? Instead of speaking this curiosity aloud, I nodded.

'Listen,' she said. 'Tomorrow morning check behind your house, I'll leave a goose there. A good, young one – for you, only, not for sharing. It should keep you going nicely into Lent.'

I almost laughed, for I was hungry and it was a good thought that tomorrow I could eat well again, that the priest's weighing would be done. She hadn't brightened, but she'd become brisk and curt. Her bargain with me was made. The goose wasn't offered as a bribe, to buy my discretion, but as a gift to buy my loyalty. It was a marker of friendship, of complicity, and I was won over – not by the goose, but by the gesture.

'A goose is more fish than fowl anyway,' she whispered. 'If you look under its wings you'll find gills.'

She stood, unfurling herself to an uncommon tallness. My view was filled with tired rustling silk. I sat low on my stool, knees drawn up, and she touched my head with her fingertips, then nudged the screen aside.

Newman, six or seven months before, had stood in the chancel where the laity weren't to go, and played idly at his lute. I was folding the altar cloth and replacing the host after Mass.

'Hear this,' he said, and he closed his eyes while he played. 'Don't you hear God in it?'

'I hear something, I think it's not God.'

'Then listen more.'

I didn't listen more. He played well, better than anybody else Oakham had known, and better than I'd heard anywhere in my training, and his plucking was cool and deep as a lake, sweeter than birdsong – yes, all the things people said of it. It was that. But it was a sound made by a man's fingers picking at sheep gut. I said this to him. 'God doesn't advise and comfort us through sheep gut, he has better means.'

'You, in other words,' said Newman. 'You're the better means.'

'The host,' I said, because I was holding it at the time. The host was a better means; itself the very body of Christ, here at our little altar. God's own son in his truest flesh. I said this too.

'But only you can give the host,' Newman said. 'A man or woman can't stride up here and take the host for themselves. But they can hear music for themselves, it pours direct into their ears.'

'Such is my point, Tom. It pours direct into an ear and might mean nothing. Or worse than nothing. It might be the devil himself pouring in.'

'Do you think we haven't lived on this earth long enough to know the difference ourselves? Are we infants? Do you always have to be our nursemaid?'

'Nursemaid?' I went and sat on the altar step, slouched forward with my elbows on my knees. I was always tired after

174

Mass. It was a warm afternoon. The church was mellow and dusty, it had its summer smell of ponds and peaches.

Newman had put the lute down next to me on the step and was pacing, loose and vivacious, excited. I thought he looked then like one of those travelling players, the rangy foolish jongleurs who pranced after balls.

'The *divino fuorore*, it's called,' he said. 'The divine frenzy. The musician plays, and in playing transforms himself into a medium for the divine. Music enraptures him, John – he and his music act as priest, as holy man, in channelling the powers of God.'

'Yet without priest or holy man,' I said, sitting up, outstretching my arms in an anger I was trying to tame, 'how can you know these are really God's powers? *There are so many kinds of voices in the world*, says Corinthians. *How shall it be known what is spoken? How shall it be known what is piped or harped?*'

I raised the lute, a dead wooden thing, soundless, replaced it on the altar step. I was aware of his Pietà over there on the altar, lavish with colour; he presumably thought that had something godly in it too. God in the paintbrush, a hog's-hair God. By now he'd stopped pacing; he stood with his arms crossed.

'I respect you, John, your holy authority. Of course I do. But maybe you take your authority too far and imagine we can't have any holiness for ourselves.'

'That's unjust. I help only with the things you can't do.'

He looked down at me. 'And what can't I do? If I sleep with the lady of the manor, do I need you to undress her for me?'

At which I looked abruptly away. 'No, but you need me to forgive you.'

'That's just where you're wrong, John, because I can put my case to God and he can forgive me or not, and he can punish me or not. I'm not sure he needs you to arbitrate.'

Newman now spread his arms just as I had.

'And do you?' I said. 'Sleep with the lady of the manor?'

175

He smiled at me, 'Well, if I do, it's not your business.'

'You play your lute afterwards and God forgives you?'

He grinned. To think God would trouble himself with sheep-gut strings. To think a sheep's innards could do what a priest has trained for years to do, has sworn his body and soul to, has surrendered his man's body for, and has denied himself in service of doing. As if God's ear were cocked evermore in the direction of Newman's lute – no, as if God leapt into the lute itself.

'Have it your way,' I said to Newman, and I took the lute from the step, jumped to my feet, went into the confession box and placed it on my back-breaking little faldstool. I came out to find Newman leaning against the east pillar. 'There,' I said, I suppose childishly. 'If the lute's such a reliable minister of God, let *it* take confession.'

Newman had smiled and said, 'I wonder how long it would take anyone to notice.' Not unkindly; he was never unkind.

As I sat there now, with the smell of Cecily Townshend lingering – lavendery cow muck and fusty midden – I thought it wouldn't do to be angry with a dead man, especially when your hands were full of the dead man's money.

Newman could be provocative; we were like that together – he provoking, me half-enjoying the challenge of it. But it wasn't only provocation that time, I could see that now. I now knew that when he brought up Cecily Townshend that day he was half-confessing to a sin for which he asked no forgiveness. He'd undressed her many times, and then played his lute to God by way of making right; and maybe he believed God had obliged him.

I pressed the side of my head against the wall of the booth a little harder than was comfortable, and saw myself then as I was when ordained, prostrate in front of the altar. The bishop's hands on me; my bones had shivered. You are *in persona Christi*, he said. You speak through him to the Lord. It was as if I'd been called to the edge of a precipice and gone over. Not a leap of faith, because you don't leap but fall, and the fall is terrible, but God gives us no other way. Not pictures, not music. No shortcuts. I'd tried to explain this to Newman: you don't go upwards through air to find the Lord, trilling like a bluebird; you go down, through the pit of yourself. But he'd never taken heed of what he didn't want to hear.

It was then that I heard something crash, or more rightly thud and smash. A thick whump of man contacting ground. I ran out of the booth to the porch where Herry Carter had slipped from a ladder and ended splayed below, with a neat gash in front of his ear, and the slate responsible scattered into some fifty different varieties of triangle around his bleeding head.

On the Devil's Meddling with the Fickle Element of Music

'Once there was a fisherman who sat on a boat that bobbed on a sea, a shimmering sea filled with fish of equally shimmering scales that glinted green, purple, blue and pink at the end of the sharpest hook. Each day the fisherman threw his hook down at the end of the line, secured the line to the boat, and played his harp; that was his way of fishing – to play the harp so sweetly that fish came willingly to his hook.

'At the end of the day he took home nets that were bulging to a family that was well fed and fully expectant of never going hungry. He sold his fish cheaply to the villages all around, and they never went hungry, either. All was well. Of course, when all is well, all is soon not to be well and, indeed, so it was.

'One winter day the devil rowed in on his own boat and anchored it out of sight around an outcropping of rock, and he made a hissing sound that was as airy and sweet as the strumming of the harp – at least to fish, who have (through no fault of their own) limited discernment in these things. Knowing no better, the fish swam to the devil's hook instead. Perplexed by his unattended hook, the fisherman tried different music on his harp, but none made a difference. For days and weeks the devil took up his place by the rocks, unseen by the fisherman whose nets were carried home half-full, a quarter-full, near-empty, empty, until the fisherman and his family and the villagers around were rake-thin and ravenous.

'All might have been lost for the fisherman, whose weakness would soon stop him staying a boat day-long in winter waters and taking the burden of the cold. His heart had been lost too; why would the fish stop coming to his bait unless they'd died (they hadn't, he could see them beneath) or unless the Lord was punishing him, and if the Lord was punishing him, why? All might have been lost, were it not for a bright day on the boat, and the sun catching something glinting in its bow – a hook. A gold hook, to put at the end of his line. And behold, when he fished with that hook, the fish left the devil and came back.

'Which of you know what this story is about? Philip? (About the devil being a gluttonous bastard, Father.) But think it through – Morris Hall, who is the fisherman? (Is he old Clere, down at Bourne, who used to sell fish here and died of an ulcerous leg? Or is he one of the disciples?) No, no, the fisherman is you, each of you. You see how the music of the devil can creep in? But with the gold hook – which is the worker of God, which is your priest, which in this case is me – the distinction is plain and the devil's left hissing to himself.

'Why am I telling you this in a sermon when there's so much else to tell? Well, I know that Thomas Newman, rest his soul, has been advising some of you about the airiness of music and how, being airy, it resonates with the air inside the ear and also with the airy human spirit and, in being so nimble as to do both, can reach between our small puny bodies and the greater heavens. I know he's told you music can channel cosmic influences, to use his phrase (which none of us, in our hearts, understand). And he's played to you several times on his lute so as to demonstrate how you might be plucked up to heaven

179

in the rapture of its sound. I know that, now Newman's been taken from us suddenly, you might feel the impulse to honour his memory and become bound to those notions.

'But I have here a treatise that pours caution on this optimism: *On the Devil's Meddling with the Fickle Element of Music*. Though music can be fair and free and like the breath of God, it's also the most double-dealing of mediums: fickle, close to spirit vapour, capable of being intervened on mid-flight by the devil and used for his means. Between the sweet sequence of notes from your pipe is a pause roomy enough for devil antics, roomy enough even if hardly a pause at all, since he's a foe who can shift to the smallest shape.

'I want to explain to you, my parish, that in spite of music's loveliness, it's susceptible to hell; its very loveliness is its susceptibility. In this, I am your golden hook; I am the one who can attract God's truth, so that those truths can nourish you. The devil can come to you through music, but it can never come to you through me. Enjoy your music, but don't be misled into believing it is a channel to the Lord, since nothing and nobody but the workers of God are a channel to him.

'Some of you believe that you'll hear from Newman in the other world by way of his lute, that it will somehow break through the air and come to you as a sign of his passing through purgatory. Give up listening. If you hear his lute, how will you know it came from him, and not from the devil? I, on the other hand will know, since if the music falls on my ears it must come from God – this is where my ears are more useful than yours. If that happens, I'll tell you, and we can rejoice in knowing the soul is on its way to heaven and leaves a delicate trail of sound, like the effervescence of a shooting star.'

Up to which point the dean, standing at the back of the church, had looked pleased. He'd have liked the chastening tone of the sermon, he'd be rejoicing that I'd for once lectured them on the merits of knowing their own ignorance. The part about the shooting star he'd have liked less, and found it a bad way to end a sermon – too whimsical and glad. You can't lecture them about the perils of airiness and then end with a notion of the stars, he'd be thinking.

But with the rest he seemed pleased, which I could tell by the fact that he stood at the back of the church while I lifted the host, and cast his eyes contentedly down while everybody else raised theirs up to see. Janet Grant stood behind me holding aloft a square of black cloth, so that the host shone ever more whitely against it. Eyes downcast, the dean would have been able to see two hundred strained arches bringing a hundred pairs of feet onto a thousand toes, so as to catch a glimpse of that host. Then he'd have been able to see the devoted kissing of the pax bread that Janet Grant passed around, and been able to hear the quiet while I called for prayers for the Pope, the bishops, the clergy – our dean especially! – the kings, lords and commons, those everywhere in the country in need, and those in need in our own good parish, the Tunley household who'd supplied this Sunday's holy bread, the pregnant, the sick and the dead, in particular Joanna Lewys, Sarah Spenser and – we say it with grief and disbelief – Thomas Newman.

The dean, chin pertly raised, must have been satisfied with the devotion he saw, because at the end he left with the Townshends and not a word to me, and the sated look a man or woman gets after a meal that was cheap and imperfect, but filled a hole. Herry Carter left with his wife and a piece of bloodied linen pressed to his cheek. He looked flushed and excited and slightly wavering on his feet, and he met Jane Tunley's concern with such a buoyant light in his eye and such a blush to his cheeks that she looked at him in admiration, as if she wondered whether a falling slate to the head might do her a world of good too.

The church emptied noisily. The bread-giving Tunleys, Morris and Joan Hall, James Russe the butcher with his wife and child, Bodger Philip and his crew, John and Tom Hadlo with little Mippy, Sarah Spenser, all five of the Otleys, all six of the Brackleys, all nine of the Smiths, the reeve Robert Guy, the lonely miller Piers Kemp. I stood at the pulpit watching, rubbing my thumbs against the downy pages of the priest's manual.

I wished for them not to go. Hither-thither they went anyway like a flock of geese, I thought, then wished it hadn't been a goose that came to mind, since then I had to bear awkward thoughts of Mrs Townshend. A flock of any other creature would have done.

Resurrection

They all went, but a few would turn and come back. Circle the churchyard, utter a quick prayer at a grave, wait for me to be seated in the booth, then return with their rosaries and a 'Confiteor' at the end of their tongues.

One was Gil Otley, whose unmistakable jaw at the grille boasted a patch of hair in the poorly formed shape of a heart. It was so advanced upon by new stubble that I might not have known it was a heart, if his wife hadn't confessed to it earlier.

'There's been a miracle,' he said, once he'd given his Creed. He was a short, brawny, rough man, the kind who looks worrisome in dark shadows. He had a way with bulls and oxen (which must have wagered he was one of them) and he was Oakham's best and sturdiest ploughman, a hard worker, and misunderstood as miserable because he was never wasteful with his words.

'A miracle?'

'My dead son's teeth, in the earth.'

'What earth?'

'I was ploughing up by East Woods and up came a pouch of teeth belonging to my dead boy.'

'East Woods,' I said, 'by the Bruton boundary?' and he made a sound along the lines of 'Euhh', which seemed to me to mean: *what other East Woods are there*?

'You're certain they were your boy's?' I asked.

'My wife has a habit of keeping those first fallen teeth from our small ones' mouths, and putting them bloody in a wool pouch for luck. When the boy died I carried his pouch around with me all places, til I didn't. Til I lost it.'

'Then you ploughed it up by chance.'

'Three years on – brute chance.'

'They're intact?'

'A pearl, each.'

'A miracle,' I said.

'Ep,' he said. Then: 'I don't come to confess, just to ask you to pass on my thanks to the Lord Almighty for giving me a bit of my boy back.'

'That'll be a great mercy for you and your wife, to have that back.'

'Yeddup,' is what he replied. I didn't know what it meant, but it sounded like he was chivvying a sheep. I wondered whether anyone would tell him about his wife's shaving prank. She was always a prankster, Ann Otley, ribald and ruddy and given to jibes about her husband's lack of romance – not that anyone could have begrudged her husband the same complaint. That heart, so close to his eye and never seen by it, seemed a tender, innocent thing. Besides which, his beard would be back in a day or two and the heart would be taken into the forest of it and disappear, and he'd never need to know any better.

'A right miracle,' he said.

'A miracle,' I said again, though I suspected it was more fluke than miracle; a fluke was for improbable happenings, a miracle for impossible ones. But how flashingly bright that miracle would sit in the midst of this day – the teeth of a dead child brought back to the mournful hands of the father.

'It might be that you didn't as such find those teeth,' I ventured, 'but that the Lord made it so that they were never lost.'

'They were good and lost for three years.'

184

'Yet the Lord can reverse time if he wants to, and in your case he could have reeled it back to the time before they were lost.'

'Can he?'

'In the scriptures, Hezekiah was sick, about to die. God promised to give him fifteen more years of life as a reward for a lifetime of perfect worship. To show Hezekiah he was sincere, God moved the sun backwards ten degrees on the sundial. To say: Hezekiah, I'm here, your God, don't doubt me. I can turn the very sun back on its course.'

'Is that what he did with my boy's teeth? Un-lost them?'

'He could have.'

'Can't see why he'd bother.'

'To show you: though you've lost a child and have reason to doubt me, I'm here, your God, and your son is well in heaven and whole-hearted.'

When an ox is deciding whether it's prepared to pull the plough, its thought takes over the whole field and steers the clouds. Its thought has such simple magnitude. Gil Otley's deliberation filled the church in a similar way.

He said at last, 'Might have brought the whole boy back, not just the teeth.'

'But we all have to go sometime,' I replied, 'and God can't bring us all back. It was your boy's time, his calling to heaven was strong and urgent.'

A deep, rough breath in and out. 'Well, if the Lord turned back time, how am I not three years younger?'

'When he moved the sun backwards on Hezekiah's sundial, the sun didn't move back everywhere, only there. When Balaam's donkey spoke, not all donkeys learnt to speak. Miracles are precise. The Lord can reverse one portion of time and leave the rest of time as it is. *I am the Lord of all mankind; is anything too hard for me?*'

'Not so much hard as pointless, getting a donkey to speak.'

But Otley conceded a sigh; even a pointless miracle was a miracle.

The afternoon light on the stone was flat and grey. Sometimes I could look at it so long the grain of the stone separated out into pebbles and rocks on a beach seen from extraordinarily high above. Itself a miracle; the miracle of distance. A small thing is a big thing seen from afar, a big thing is a small thing seen up close. The miracle of the changing size of fixed and rigid things.

Otley had been coming to his feet. Once he was standing he added, in a thick voice that fell heavy from a height, 'Please pass on my extra thanks to the Lord then, for the strangeness of the miracle. I don't always approve of his ways and reasons, but at least he has ways and reasons, which is more than can be said for most.'

Oh, we all have reasons, I thought. Only that they're not always good ones. I reached down to Cecily Townshend's money, which was pressed against my foot, took out the coin that felt smallest – a shilling – and passed it to him through the grille.

'For you and your family – buy some meat before Lent.'

Some scrubbed, scarred, weather-beaten fingers took the coin. 'Glory be,' he muttered.

Sarah's face came to the grille. 'I wasn't sure if you were in there, Father.'

I turned so as not to meet her eye.

'You were so silent, I thought you'd gone.'

Gone where? I wondered. Seeped like a draught out of the window?

'I need to ask forgiveness for disturbing you and Thomas Newman in the church on Friday night. I came in feeling very unwell.'

186

'If you couldn't come here for help, where could you – '

'I interrupted the last conversation you had with him.'

'You interrupted *a* conversation I was having with him, it was any old conversation. It only later turned out to be the last.'

'Father, that seems an odd logic.'

To me, odd logic seemed an odd logic, since if it was odd it was hardly logical. Back when her mind was bright, I might have put that idea to her.

'We were talking about nothing,' I said. 'He'd come in to pray at his altar as he always did. Nothing more.'

He'd prayed before the painting of Mary, made a joke about me looking guilty, standing there with the taper. I'd said, You make a handsome couple, you and Mary. Then he made his reply about how she settled for the browbeaten cuckold Joseph instead, and that was the size of it. To think that was the last time I saw him, the last discussion I had with him, about so little, nearing nothing.

'Are you any better?' I asked.

'Today I feel different,' she said. 'I'd say cured.'

So then I broke a rule the priest's manual clearly gave: *Don't look at the penitent, turn your gaze. Their hearts will open in the place your gaze vacated.* When I looked at the grille, where her face was turned three-quarters my way, I saw she was far from cured. Her eyes were dark and large and sunken, and her expression was plucky and tinged with lunacy. Still, if she felt distress she hid it, and her voice was the even and soft voice of her old self.

'I slept most of the day yesterday. On Friday night, when Tom took me home, he made me a broth, disgusting enough but it made me sleep all night and most of Saturday, until that little man woke me up.'

The dean. Sarah must have been the last person Newman was with, given that he was drowned by Saturday morning; the dean would've taken great interest in that. Hers had been the first door the dean had knocked on, only to learn nothing except that he needed to knock on several more doors before he could properly think of himself as a sheriff.

'Was the dean kind with you?' I asked.

'He was very kind, he gave me some of the leftover broth in a cup, he sat in the far corner, he explained that it was alright, he knew I didn't murder Thomas Newman. I had no idea that I might have. I didn't even know he was dead.'

I'd looked away from her again by now. I was emphatic in dodging her gaze. Instead I studied the besmirched black of my own lap. She was curiously calm about that death, but she was curiously calm about all things in that moment, as if her illness had bewitched or drugged her. On my looking away, she too moved away and sank to a low kneel on the cushion where I could no longer see her.

'You need to pray hard for your health, Sarah,' I said. 'With me, now. Virgin most faithful.'

'*Virgo fidelis.*'

'Mirror of justice.'

'*Speculum iustitiae.*'

'Seat of wisdom.'

'*Sedes sapientiae.*'

'Cause of our joy.'

'*Causa nostrae laetitiae.*'

'Mystical rose.'

'You've missed some, Father.'

'All the same, mystical rose.'

'*Rosa mystica.*'

'Morning star.'

'*Stella matutina.*'

'Health of the sick.'

'*Salus infirmorum.*'

'Refuge of sinners.'

'*Refugium peccatorum.*'

'Comfort of the afflicted.'

'*Consolatrix afflictorum.*'

'Grant, I beseech thee, O Lord God,' I said, and she knew to join with me, so that we said in chorus, 'unto us Thy servants, that we may rejoice in continual health of mind and body.'

And she, the last part alone: '*Perpetua mentis et corporis sanitate gaudere.*'

Her Latin was sure, her memory perfect, even in the distress of inexplicable sickness. Prayers were carved into her very bone; she was faithful to the marrow. There – she and Annie by the bulrushes in summer, unhooking a fyke net from the rushes where the river ran rich, slow and muddy; they were bold thieves. In the morning sun the eels they took from the net were bolts of light flashing in their hands. Arms aloft, some smaller eels thrown back into the river. They were calling and toiling like men, as busy as foxes at a chicken coop, as bright and fast as morning, as avid as soldiers at war.

'*Perpetua mentis et corporis sanitate gaudere,*' she chanted. 'May we rejoice in continual health of mind and body. *Per Christum Dominum Nostrum.*'

A day or two or so after Newman and I had talked on the river bank about time, when he'd thrown the yew into the water – the day we'd first spoken of building a bridge – I'd found myself rambling at my sister. Why can't time go backwards as well as forward? If time's not a river but a circle, and if you can travel round a circle one way or another and end up where you started, why can't it go this way and that?

I asked her, not because she'd know an answer, but because she was supple enough of heart and thought to not throw the question out of the window. It was a question that'd troubled me those few days, because I didn't have an answer. If time could go backwards, why didn't it? If God could undo what was done, why didn't he?

We were eating stew; she didn't stop. God moved the sun backwards ten degrees on the sundial of Ahaz, I told her, as a sign to Hezekiah that he, God, had absolute command of time. Like you have command of that spoon in your hand – you can flip it this way, that way. So why couldn't he have brought our mother back from that fire?

Annie stopped with the spoon near her mouth, its contents just dispatched within, a smidge of meat juice cleared neatly from her lower lip. She said nothing, so I ate to fill the silence.

If you want to stop dead people being dead, she said at last (laying the spoon on the table and then sitting on her hands), you might as well just bring them to life in your heart. You might as well not wait for God to make a miracle.

I told her our mother was alive in my heart.

Listen, she said, here's how you make her alive. There was a woman, Agnes Reve, who died in a fire; eight years before that she had a daughter; seven years before that she had a son, who became a priest. A year before that she married a labourer with narrow shoulders and no humour; for seventeen years before that she lived peacefully with her own mama and father and sisters, right back to one special June morning, or was it afternoon, when all the heavens aligned and all ill fates were defied, and she was born.

There, Annie had said, she's once more alive.

I scraped my chair back somewhat huffily, swilled my empty bowl and had nothing to say in response except, forlorn: No, Annie.

Yet as I was hearing Gil Otley, this conversation of four years earlier had come back to me. Why, suddenly? Because Newman was dead? Because Sarah was sick and dying? Because Annie was gone? Because there was nothing in the world I could do to make it otherwise. Because, in the futility of Gil Otley losing his son, why not have hope of some kind of resurrection? Because Annie was right. She was right, that there in the curved chamber of our hearts was all the circularity of time, and all the tools for its both-ways navigation. For while it happens one way, our imaginations have in them all the dexterity of turning it the other, a facility God has given us that I don't suspect he gave a cow, nor a bat, nor an eagle. A facility he gave us that we might grasp this audaciously flexile and amenable element of time that he made, that he can turn and bend.

As I sat in the booth, I fancied I could feel that plump roundness of my heart, and time milling inside it. The moonish cycle of seasons and days. There was a tingling in my fingers and feet and up my wrists and forearms, as if my blood was dragging contrarily up channels that were meant to go downwards. Annie was right; our imaginations do restore the dead to life. The last dialogue she and I had about our mother had begun in lament of our mother's death, and ended with the words that stayed with me since: *she was born*. You could bring the dead back to life without waiting for God to provide a miracle; you could defy the reaper in your plump old heart; you could change things. You could say of any ill fate: it is no longer so.

A body entered the booth, slow and breathless, and knelt with a few cracks to the joints, and chewed at dry gums, and breathed out long, and shifted without ease, and blew out another breath without appearing to have taken one in between, and then settled into a quiet but not silent repose.

I waited for him to speak (because no doubt those cracking joints and blowing breaths were a man's) and when he didn't, I sat back with my head against the wall and scratched my knee and felt the tingling recede in my hands. Time stopped clean. A robin chirruped in the churchyard. Rain tink-tinked at the window. The other's breathing lengthened. Horse hooves were distant on the cobbles. A faint waft of wintersweet. The candle at my foot threw a lame shadow as the light failed.

Eventually I looked through the grille to find the man fast asleep. It was old Maurice Fry, in from the fields. Ancient and exhausted. Sometimes the drape of the curtain and the quiet of the church and the give of the cushion are all it takes for the already-weary. I didn't wake him. No need, there was no one waiting. I took Cecily Townshend's money, slipped past him and out, and went home.

Cheesechurn

I put Cecily Townshend's money in both of Annie's forsaken shoes. The worst hiding place in the world, I then thought – a pair of shoes in an otherwise empty room. Albeit a room the dean had already that morning searched, but you could never put it past him to search it again, for the sheer pleasure of it. So, I buried those shoes in the small chest where I kept my few clothes, which was lockable. I kept with me the key, in a burse. Not a moment too soon, because before I'd finished crossing the room the dean was at the open door saying, 'Reve, let's walk.'

I excused myself for a moment behind the hazel scrub while he stood in the doorway. He must have been able to hear the heavy stream of my relief; *an overfull bladder is the curse of confession*, I was going to say cheerily when I came out. In fact I kept quiet.

We walked in seeping rain a short way towards Old Cross, and I thought we were aiming for Newman's or the river. Perhaps the dean had something private he wanted to say, or wanted to amble while I betrayed what had been confessed to me. At which I'd launch forth: Paul Brackley overslept, Gil Otley dug up his dead boy's teeth, Janet Grant saw an owl by day, Emma Prye put her left shoe on her right foot and her right shoe on her left – until his inevitable impatience urged me to be quiet.

Instead he stopped where the broken axle lay in the road, and he assessed it with disappointment.

'Why is this left here?' he said.

I told him I didn't know.

'I know. They think it's bad luck to move an axle on a Sunday. Because it looks like a strut from the cross.'

His raised brow told of lost hope. It asked: how do you reason with people who have the intellect of children? Then, without a word, he turned on his heel and wandered back tiptoe-ish the way we'd come, up through the village northwards. I followed.

The milkmaids' singing drifted across and down from the manor, and on that dull and damp day it was more sombre and needful than sweet, and lingered in the rain. 'Not much of a day for singing,' I remarked, and he made no acknowledgement that I'd spoken. 'Even the cows aren't lowing,' I added. Nothing. We walked on. From Bodger Philip's croft, a merciless thwacking at wood and grunts of effort. The road stank more than usually of ale. Hikson was brewing some fifty yards up from us and there was no wind to weaken the smell. It collected and mushroomed in the dampness to a sour musk that prodded the tonsils. The dean coughed, though I thought over-pointedly. When we walked past Sarah Spenser's we saw Herry Carter go in. 'Good old Carter,' I said. 'Our Samaritan.' But I suspected that the dean would be thinking otherwise: *Ah, an afternoon assignation, the village do-gooder has a quick roll with the village witch! Eve calls another man to the apple!*

Morris Hall passed with the mare that had fallen that morning with the cart, only now she was cartless and had a slight but unarguable limp in her right foreleg. She had one stack of wood strapped to her back and Morris had another stack strapped to his, to save the mare trouble. It was a tenth of what a cart might have carried, and both of them looked fed up, and Morris Hall's attempt at a smile landed more as a snarl. Still the dean said nothing, only proceeded with his hands behind his back and eyes wandering without his face moving much, and his expression the bland indifference of someone idling through a market with no intention of buying.

It was reaching that time to down tools and there weren't many stoopers up in the fields, but those that remained on Townshend's land were as filthy as if they'd been wallowing in the furrows, and looked abject even from a distance and in the coming dusk. Without turning his head, I knew he'd seen them and was thinking that Oakham's mud was muddier than most, and Oakham's rain wetter. Oakham's beer mustier, Oakham's milkmaids more melancholy. I almost believed it myself for a moment. A vision arose of a swaying sea of French barley, all honey and gold – no sludge of soil there, no spines snapping in toil, no collapsing furrows. Just a vision of effortless French golden barley at a soothing sway, the clearness of which was made up because I'd never set foot in France. Well, so much for France, I told myself, and pronounced, in the way of someone who didn't know when to give up, 'You might not know it now, but Oakham is golden in summer. All those fields there – golden as anything.' I brandished an arm in their direction. Silence.

Passing the Lewyses' house, we caught what must surely have been the final cries of sex – such are the perils of these earth-walled houses, they let any sound in and any sound out. By now we were at the brew-house and the smell of fermenting wort was enough to wallop the throat. I looked in there, so as to turn away from the sounds of Adam Lewys's carnal triumph across the road. Hikson was still and silent over a yeasty vat, somehow seedy-looking even when doing nothing. At our other side the lovers were gaining, not losing, stride. The milkmaids' song was growing thready. We persisted onwards at the dean's slow pace. I went to say something else jaunty and anodyne, but tripped on a stone or pothole that wasn't there. He lifted his head up a touch and his chin probed the air.

At New Cross he stopped once again, and I, beside him, privately cringed. The crucified Christ had been given his usual Shrovetide shawl to keep him warm during the hard times of Lent, and if that bout of sentiment alone wasn't too much for the dean, then the frilled skirt fastened round Christ's waist must have persuaded him: Oakhamers really do have the wits of children. Our good Christ looked like a clown or marionette in a street show. A harmless village joke, I wanted to say, but even I couldn't see the point this time. I thought the dean would tear that fancy dress from Christ's body and have harsh words for me, but again he said nothing, did nothing, even when I took the skirt off myself. I crumpled it in my palm.

Shortly past New Cross the road bends to the right, and before the bend we heard retching coming from the thicket that lines the road, then a girl's sobbing, then retching. She was there when we rounded the bend, it was little Jane Smith, the middle of the Smiths' seven children. She lifted her head to look at us – her wet hair was splayed against her chin and her pale face was streaked with sweat and sick. She motioned for us to go away. Pregnant, then. Any young girl throwing her insides up into a bush is with child and unhappy about it. The dean tilted his head towards me and raised a subtle brow. *Just what you need – another unwanted Oakhamer* is what his travelling brow said. Though he indeed said nothing.

The barns were the last buildings this side of the village, except for Mary Grant's and Robert Tunley's houses all the way out by the brook. I hoped the dean's strange tour might end at the barns, and sure enough it did. It came to a halt near the last of the four barns, where our grain and rushes were stored and, for now, the cart that had broken that morning.

Down the far side of the last barn was Deep Ditch, where boys like Ralf Drake shovelled waste – animal, vegetable and human. Shovelled and buried, shovelled and buried. The stench was a knee to the groin. Because the day of stinking slog was ending, the boys were – playful. That was the word I wanted to offer the dean. Better playful than defeated, surely. And though their sound was raucous and had driven the dean on with new and quickened interest, their game was harmless enough. It seemed to involve them lifting one of the boys above the ditch and lowering him towards it until his nose, twitching like a rabbit's, rested on the sewage and swill. We were only yards away but they didn't see us. The dean probably took this as proof that they weren't only debauched, but oblivious: Oakham's boys are lazier, deafer and blinder than most. Not to mention Oakham's shit, which is shittier. He cleared his throat as if a whole ear of wheat were stuck in it; they swung round. The poor suspended boy dropped into the ditch with a haw like that of a donkey. The dean turned away.

He didn't make any motion to walk further. Then he spoke the only other words he was going to speak on this walk, spoke them loud and not to anybody in particular.

'Do you know that out at Bruton and beyond you're known as Cheesechurn, Cowudder, Milkpasture. I try to set them straight. I say, It's Oakham. They say, Where? They think you're all dwarves and sleep with your own mothers and sisters. I try to put them straight.'

He shrugged sadly. Then he swivelled on his heel and walked back as we'd come, faster now and not at his ruminating stroll. The mist of rain had given me a quiet soaking. I followed. There was one thing at least that the dean didn't know: that those copulating in the Lewyses' house weren't husband and wife, since Joanna Lewys would be milking at that time, and anyway far too pregnant to be that energetic under the covers. I prayed that his spiteful logic wouldn't work that out.

Oakham is golden in the summer, I wanted to shout as we passed the first of the barns – the barns filled with Townshend's willing cows, cows that would be plump on clover and would slosh with milk: the creamiest of milk. Oakham is golden and plump and God-loving always, no matter what it might seem! But as we passed that barn, the dean ahead of me, a furore kicked up – one cow avidly and violently mounting another. The afflicted one's eyes languid with sufferance. A dreadful hollow moan of protest like the sound of slaughter. Cow-at-cow; *quite unnatural*, said the dean's bland contempt. He stood to behold it for the shortest of moments before walking away home.

Golden hook

I knocked at Sarah's door, only to get no answer. I went in and found her sleeping. I crept out and closed the door as tight as it would go.

'John Reve?' I heard. It was Carter, approaching from the land behind Sarah's house.

'Herry?'

He was carrying a spade. He prodded the handle towards the wall. 'I went in to check on her.'

'How was she?'

'Disturbed, I gave her milk and tried to ease her.'

'And you did, now she's sleeping.'

'The sleep of the dead.'

'Don't talk that way.' I bent to pick up a bucket that was side-on to the ground and put it against the wall, then realised I still had the little skirt-of-Christ in my hand. 'Earlier she was fighting fit,' I said. 'Clear and calm as a bell.'

'Huh,' said Carter – a laugh, a chide, a refutation, a grunt. I added nothing about the strange nature of her calmness and how it had seemed to come from something fraught. He looked as exhausted as a dog mid-fight. The cut on his face was blood-crusted and the piece of bandage gone. Poor soft young face of his, it had lost hope to worry and flashed a hint of the old man he might become. 'She hasn't got her ground ready for sowing,' he said, and he walked back towards her plot. I went after him. 'Look at it, the most unlikely bit of ground you ever saw. What'll grow here?'

Not much, I had to admit. Two robins were making much of the unearthed worms; that was something. That pleased the old bewintered heart.

'Will Sarah die?' Carter asked. He'd started digging and didn't look up from the task.

'I don't know.'

'She's decided she wants to.'

'Earlier she said she was better.'

'Earlier's nothing – earlier's gone.'

'Well, isn't that true,' I said, and squinted at him through the mist of rain. 'What is it, Herry?'

He struck the spade into the ground and straightened. 'She's going to confess to killing Newman, that's what. She said so.'

I laughed. 'Well.'

'Don't just stand there and *well*, John Reve.'

'What then?' I asked. 'What then, Herry Carter? Stand here and do what else?'

We watched one another. Chickens squawked around us hungrily. The air had collected a drizzly mist; everything felt moist and spongy. I understood what he was saying – Sarah's suffering had come from only God knew where, a rotten and tortured suffering, and in Newman's mysterious death she'd seen an opportunity to end it. Her own sorry life must have seemed a small sacrifice, burning at the stake no dreadful fear for a body that burnt night and day already. People confessed to all kinds of things when they were desperate, just in case. Better to own up to too many sins than not enough: the greater the punishment on earth, the less time needed in purgatory. That was her calm of earlier – not a calm of peace or ease, but one of scheming. Carter knew that as well as I did. He was staring at me with his hand whitening around the spade handle.

Chickens stabbed their beaks at unseen things. I received a brutal peck to the toe.

'Nobody will believe her confession,' I said.

'They will, if they really want to.'

'Nobody will want to.'

'No?' He flicked his gaze outwards towards the road. 'Anybody who's looking for a murderer might want to.'

'The dean isn't here for a lynching, Herry. He's a fair man – he knows as well as any of us that Newman's drowning was nothing to do with Sarah.'

'I don't trust him.'

'But you can trust me. Do you think I'd let any harm come to her from the dean?'

I heard my own voice hang in the air between us, heavy with confidence. I thought: when he next speaks, he won't call me John or Reve or John Reve, he'll call me Father – he has that look of needing somebody to believe. The look of somebody climbing a cliff and dangling his unseen foot, in the hope it finds a hold.

'Father – are you sure?' he said.

'I wouldn't say it otherwise.'

He stood, looking towards the house.

'Maybe she'll recover,' I said, trying for optimism. 'The truly sick don't have the wherewithal for designing their own death. She's young, besides. Earlier she recited the Litany of the Blessed Virgin without a pause.'

He tugged the spade from the ground and poised himself to dig.

'That can wait,' I said, and he looked at me. 'Go home.' He nodded and let the spade slide through his palms. No resistance; the boy was finished.

Father, I'm sorry I let the cart tip this morning; Father, I took the Virgin's name in vain; I just finished sleeping with a woman

201

not my wife, it isn't the first time; I spoke with my mouth full; I overslept; I helped chuck Fin Brackley into a ditch of shit; I lobbed a stone at a bird; I'm ashamed you saw me throw up in a bush; I found an egg with two yolks and ate it all for myself; I lost my lucky bent coin; I've been unhappy; just today I slept with a man not my husband, it's the last of many times; I landed a rock on a spider that looked like the devil, did I cause Thomas Newman's death?; I burped Ave Maria to amuse my boy, did I cause Thomas Newman's death?; we ate with thirteen at the table, did we cause Thomas Newman's death?; I dug without sharpening my spade, was I asking for trouble?; I stepped over my child, did I bring bad luck?; I overslept; I underslept; I overslept; did I cause Thomas Newman's death?; the dean says God'll suppose we've all caused Thomas Newman's death, unless one person admits to it. Was it me, Father? Did I?

Fires were lit and Oakham took to supper. The air was one-third water, one-third spirits and one-third smoke, and the smoke was flavoured with chicken and pork. It was a proper stew that evening, what with the cooking meat and the brewing wort and the windless rain. Lungs were steeping. And it was after supper – which I didn't have – that we all went down to the millpond, as was routine on Shrove Sunday each year, and we toed a rowing boat onto the pond, tethered with a rope.

Oakham's men were assessed for size: John Hadlo was half a head too short, Oliver Townshend less short but too stocky, Morris 'small' Hall too small in every way and not worth trying, Robert 'Rotundley' Tunley too big in every way and not worth trying, John Fisker too hunched at the shoulders to sustain comparison, David Hikson so wiry that his height was irrelevant, and Adam Lewys too drunk to stand upright on solid ground, let alone on the quivering floor of a boat. Robert Guy seemed the best bet, he was subtly fatter than me everywhere on his body, but when I was set back-to-back with him, it was proven that he was also subtly shorter. The notion was born that the match was perfect: he, being our reeve, was surely the equivalent of me, John Reve. And he, needing to equal my weight, was our accountant and used to equalling any two things that came his way.

He was chosen to a round of cheers, which were muted, since nobody had forgotten that for the last twelve years the man who'd taken this role, the man most like me in build, was Newman. But everybody seemed to do a decent job of pretending that Newman wasn't dead, only away for the day on business, and so we got on. The boat was pulled parallel to the bank, its prow held firm by Tunley and its stern by Hadlo. Robert Guy removed his shoes and stepped in. I removed mine and stepped in after him, so that we were both standing entirely unsteady in the middle of the boat, all but hugging.

'Take your places,' growled Tunley, and with no skill we each wobbled to opposite ends of the boat. Robert Guy lurched and grabbed the side and almost capsized us. 'Sweet shite, what are you, a blind cow?' Tunley asked. 'It's a mill-pond, not the Atlantic.' Guy scowled and righted himself. I was more adept, maybe because I did it every year – adept enough, anyway, to stay on my feet and shuffle without dignity to the stern.

The crowd, which was a good two-thirds of the village, jittered. Usually they heckled and prattled as if at a dog-fight; even though the spiritual dignity of their priest was being tested, it was never really in doubt. This year, they weren't sure. Was it a spectacle or a reckoning? They looked on, concerned, while Robert Guy tried to come to his feet and stay on them. If my end of the boat sank less than that of the other man, it meant I weighed less; and if I weighed less than him – whose build was similar – it confirmed my ongoing priestliness, in weighing more than an angel but less than a man. More fleshly courage than an angel, less fleshly burden than a man. It confirmed my right to take my parish into Lent. And if my end of the boat sank as much as the other man's, or God forbid more, then I didn't know what would follow because it had never happened. In twelve years, with Newman at the other end, it'd never happened.

Robert Guy teetered to his feet; we couldn't have picked a less water-going man than this rigid accountant. He stood scarecrow-like with his arms spread. It didn't seem to me that there'd be much between us; I was glad I'd gone without dinner and wished I'd gone without breakfast. The boat rocked and steadied, and Tunley gave another grunt: 'Hands off!' At which he and John Hadlo let loose their grip of stern and prow and left us to our fates. Oakham's eyes were on the stern. Did it rise? Did Robert Guy at the prow sink? I turned my eyes up to the line of great oaks, which were each a universe of life, jackdaws swinging on the branches, woodpeckers in and out of the boles, finches pecking at the bark. Nests. So many nests.

I didn't feel the boat tip at my end; I didn't feel that small, unweighted moment. I tried to know the lightness of the heavens in my limbs instead of bone and flesh, and I had that feeling again, that beyond the ridge was the sea, an intrepid vastness; that if I stood on tiptoes I could see the topmost masts of ships tacking their paths. I didn't look at Robert Guy, and couldn't – for the sake of balance – look at the crowd. My knees didn't feel strong, my stance didn't seem steady, and the boat bobbed evenly, or so I thought. I drew in breath. Did that help? Or maybe I should give breath out? Did breath lighten or make heavy? Somebody in the crowd began to clap, and then the rest broke into a guarded and staggered cheer and Tunley cried, 'Prow down! Stern up! Amen!'

The boat was pulled to the bank; Robert Guy tripped from it longingly onto dry ground and I stepped without pride or honour, for if the boat had tipped, I'd never felt it. Still, Tunley's cry of success remained the last clear sound on the air. There was relieved murmuring but no celebration, and the crowd dispersed – it wasn't a cause for celebration that your priest was proven at least a little holier than your accountant, any more than it was a cause for celebration that you woke up each day with both feet still on the ends of your legs. It was as it should be. It was only if a foot was missing that the day became memorable.

I walked back to the church on my own, my heart shuffling itself like a pack of cards. When Newman had been at the other end of the boat, he'd look me in the eye, and I him, and after the weighing he'd grin and pat me on the shoulders, and we'd walk back to the church together. That's when he'd come to confess this, that or the other. On the third or fourth year he confessed that he always took time to load some fist-sized rocks into the wide, rough hem of his surcoat when he was at the prow. No need to, he'd said, it just adds to the spectacle. I knew there was no need to. So I forgave him his little theatre and let him do it the next year and the next.

The best part of half an hour elapsed while the light went from the dull of day to the dull of dusk, and the grain of the wall came apart and dissolved into shadow. Nobody came to confess. There was a pardon on offer and they didn't come. They'd flurried in before, Father Father Father – but now? Were they tired? Perhaps my end of the boat hadn't tipped up at all and they knew it, and no longer put their faith in me. I sat on my hands to keep them warm, though my face was hot. What would it be to lose their faith and trust? What would I be? Anything at all? If not their Holy Father, their *golden hook*, then what? Nothing, or even less. Then I realised that it was raining hard, and that the rain was sluicing from the sky, effortless and relentless, and that this was surely the cause of everyone's absence, this rain. Not my performance on the boat. Then a deep muffled thunder unfurled, and I looked up to wait for lightning. I don't know if it was boredom, or the strangeness of the day, or the hammering of the rain, or the low, long companionship of the thunder that rolled around the sky like a horse's whicker, but I was filled with a sudden longing. I sat forward with my elbows on my spread knees and the pads of my fingers drumming together without sound. My heartbeat accompanied. I clasped my hands together.

When I wasn't much more than a boy I met a woman. I've told nobody else about her. She was a married woman and was older than me; it wasn't only a husband she had, but children too – I never asked how many. Some of them might have been almost as old as me. I was already in training for God's work when I met her, and when I fell into the deepest, most sudden infatuation, as if into a hole, I looked up at God with the blood coursing through my loins and challenged him: how much, Lord, do you deserve me? How much do you want me? Is it worth your while to rescue me from her?

The infatuation lasted a summer, and it ended with the first frost. She ended it; I'd have gone on all winter and into the next spring. I lived then a few miles from Southampton where I was born, and our parish was big, about three hundred, and the woman and I didn't know each other. She lived in a coastal village, not like mine. Mine was four miles inland, all we had of the sea was a salty mouthful of it when the wind blew up and north-west.

She travelled, though, on a mule, selling seaweed – nets full of dulse, which was good fried with butter, or else rinsed and mixed with hay for animals. Eelgrass for fertilising fields, or for drying and stuffing pillows, mattresses, roofs. Bladderwrack for curing goitres and headaches. I went to her for that reason, to get bladderwrack for my sister's headaches, and she sold me some and told me when she'd be back. When I went again, she gave me the seaweed without charge, and told me when she'd be back. When I went again, she led me to the birch wood near the village.

She came to our village twice a week, and she always made sure that she reached us at the very start of the day or the very end, and she'd take me to the wood where nobody went outside of daylight because birch was considered thick with spirits. The first time she took me I had no idea what she wanted, I was a boy who'd not long since lost his mother, and to strangers' eyes she might have been my mother. 'This way,' she said, just as my mother might have, and I walked by the side of her mule, watching the movement of the holy black cross that ran over its shoulders and down its back.

Over the weeks we became intrepid with each other; if it was she who led at first, it was me by the end. She taught me how to please her. They'd said that women were ravenous and empty and tempted men into oblivion. I found her hungry, yes, and her eyes were beautifully wicked at times, and she treated me like her mule, as her mule looked on. But she wasn't empty, she was full inside and soft beyond any softness otherwise on earth, and I made it my task to find the emptiness if it was really there, and to be taken close to oblivion to see if God would save me from it, to see if he wanted me more than I wanted her.

I began to imagine her as Eve, naked as she was under trees and lying in soil and leaf at first shrill and green and later gold and mottled and dying, and the ground damp and mushroomy. I let her tempt me all she could and I would succumb, and ask for more, and succumb again, and do as she asked. I was waiting for God to tell me to stop and come to him. I began to think that he was encouraging me to search every space in her, either to show that I'd find nothing true or everlasting there, or else to let me have my pleasure while I could. I thought that the mule was his servant, come to watch and send a sign. The clusters of primroses that broke out on the spot we used were his approval, his will that we should know beauty. Then the forget-me-nots and Virgin's Tears and wild strawberries, our thrilling, ever-changing bed.

She did what she pleased with me, the game was her own and the rules of her making and breaking – the traps, the taunts, the temptations, and the grateful ecstasy of fulfilment. Her stench was of salt and fish and tar, and her hands were long and slim and coarse. She gave me bruises where her fingers had gripped, and she might leave me lying on the ground, dazed, without a word of affection, not even a goodbye. But in moments she was less Satan's bait and more the gentlest of mothers, she would give strawberries to my mouth and sing to me and cup my cheek in her palm, and I'd imagine her with her children and be more inflamed than ever, and force her shoulders back to the ground and open her legs. Now come for me, I would say to God – now, at my very lowest, pluck me out, punish me, show me you want me. I would glance up at the mule, and the mule would hang its head heavily on the end of its neck and gaze liquidly, and do nothing.

There was one time only when I went to her, instead of her coming to me. She couldn't do her round of villages because one of her children was unwell. So I walked the four miles to her village to meet her before daybreak and we took a path down to the shore, in a cove where the fishermen weren't, shielded by a rock. We might only have been there half an hour, but in that time ships passed to and from the port, ships so large that I could see them from the corner of my eye even as her body absorbed me; I could feel them passing, these great wooden cities. Life. Extraordinary life – the flesh, the world, the wind, the flags, the unending glory of the woman sent to test me, how she opened all around me, how the world appeared to me at her edges.

That was the end of August. When she came to me during September she was milder and less voracious, without explanation. She laid herself down more obligingly and lifted her skirts, as if it was for my pleasure and not hers. She took less from me, no longer buried her hand in my curls and pulled my head back to run her tongue up my neck, and no longer left me bruised. I took what she offered, and then took what she didn't, and I was made frenzied by her sudden inertness and drove myself at her; sometimes I was anxious that I'd finished her, and had to kiss her and ask a hundred times, Are you alright? Are you well? She was kind, docile and remote. For the first time I believed that she could be a wife.

So one morning in mid-September I borrowed a horse and went to Southampton where there were markets selling jewellery, and I bought her a good silver bracelet from Germany with all the money I had and some I'd stolen from my father. I rode back and waited for her. Why not my wife? I wasn't realistic: there was every reason why not, not least that she had a husband. Well then, my wife in nature if not in name, our bodies wedded. I could share her, if there was no other choice. I could share her two ways – with her husband and with her children, and she could share me with God, since God was offering no objection. So I waited that night and she didn't come, then I waited the next daybreak and she didn't come, and I waited night-day-night-day with the bracelet in a burse around my neck and she didn't come.

On the last day of September she came, finally, but not to me, only to the village – not at dawn or night, but in the middle of the afternoon, and when I saw her (because my ears were sharp as knives to her call of *Dulse! Eelgrass!* that chimed like Vespers bells from a voice unexpectedly sweet), she saw me too and looked away. She came to our village once or twice a week as usual after that, but never deigned to know me.

I went back to the piece of ground in the woods where we'd encountered each other, to see if God, even yet, had something to say to me. I expected punishment and none came. I wanted encouragement and none came. I asked him: Is her change of heart a sign from you? Nothing came to say it was or wasn't. I forgot about the woman, in case that was his will, which it surely was. I asked: Shall I give myself to you? He didn't seem to hear. I went back to the market and sold the bracelet for half what I'd paid, and with the money I bought the carving of the Man of Sorrows, and a chalky painting of the Pietà. Later, when I was offered my first stole and chasuble and my hands were anointed, I wondered if he'd strike me down. He didn't. He let me become a priest. I asked for a church newly enlarged and improved, its roof vaulted and its buttressed walls pierced daringly high with windows. He gave me a parish between river and ridge, and a church that was like any other. Though I knew he wouldn't reply, I said, Let me serve you well.

We hang between the devil and the deep blue sea. Priests are the light of the world, they say when they anoint us. The light of this world, of this heavy earth. The Ghostly Fathers, the golden hook. And I feel burn in me at times a cool unearthly fire, and my skin unpicks and is halfway to light and air. Yet we're also men, men among others and like others, men of the parish with muscles that ache and eyes that blur with sleep, and stomachs that nag and needs that nag too, then beg.

We have faces that flush with heat, ears that burn with desire, teeth that get infected and drop out, skin that rips; we sweat, we itch, we squat like a dog to evacuate what's inside. We're so like men, they have to weigh us against another man in a boat to make sure there's no mistake. They weigh me like a pig at market! We're not men, but so like men it's hard to tell. So like men that suddenly the Ghostly Father is on his knees at his

210

own confession stool, his face pressed anguished into his hands – imagining the hard floor he kneels on is a copse and his knees are in loam and he's as much an animal as any man could ever be, as if time had given way and he was with that woman still, with her salt-and-sea-stench on his stomach. With her, and looking up from her legs towards the mule, and trying to argue his holiness to a God that he doubts, for a moment, is interested, or listening, or even there.

Goose, cooked

'Well, Father, I'm neatly shafted.'

I folded my hands and turned my face up to give it some air. At the sound of someone scuffling the curtain I'd sat properly on the stool again, straightened myself, put my hand to my neck to cool it.

'Perfectly shafted,' he said, 'as if God arranged the shafting himself.' A lively pause. 'Felicitations, by the way; your end of the boat stood up nice and proud.'

Was he joking? With Townshend it was hard to tell. He might look like someone's kind uncle at first glance – stout and small-handed and with well-spaced eyes – but he was as dry as a twig and sometimes sharp. He'd stood watching the scene at the millpond without much humour, his tabard a bit tight around his middle and his face purplish-grey. Now we sat on either side of the screen with the thunder rolling like rocks loose on a mountain.

'You know it as well as I do, Reve – with Newman dead, we're fish on a hook.'

I didn't say anything; it was always better to let Townshend speak in his own way.

'Not even fish on a hook, minnows in a net. We've been in that net for a while, and now it's about to be dragged up.'

Minnows can swim out of most nets, was my thought, and I didn't know if it was pedantic or significant.

'You're talking about the monks coming?' I'd only heard about the monks the day before, from the dean, but I wagered that Townshend already knew. He was the one with messengers, fingers in pies.

'Yes, the monks,' he said. 'And everything else that's coming for us, but mostly the monks.'

'What else is coming for us?'

'The world, Reve. Taking little bites out of our flanks like a horsefly.'

'Minnows, horseflies. The Lord wants to hear things plain and straight.'

'He wants it straight? Here's a straight tale then – they wrote to me, the Bruton monks, back in January. They asked if my land was available. They didn't ask if it was for sale, they just asked if it was available – *procurable*, they said. *Would it be that your hectares of wheat-growing land are procurable?* No, I said, it wouldn't be. Was that plain and straight enough?'

Oliver Townshend had a voice of velvet, skin of satin, eyes of summer dusk. It didn't matter how hard times were for him, or how grey his face went with worry, or how well or badly he ate, or how much milk his cows produced; money and good breeding were deep in him. I envied that. He was a nobler man than most, with more weaknesses. I could imagine him penning that short and righteous sentence to the Bruton monks: *No, it wouldn't be procurable. Yours in faith, OT.* With a vehement full stop. Then standing and pushing his shoulders back and pulling his tabard in.

'I had a pact with Newman – neither of us would cede any land to anyone outside this parish. We'd keep a tight grip on it, we'd keep Oakham's land to Oakham, we'd rely on no one and give nothing away for free. If we sold land, it was to each other.'

213

Your land to him, I thought. Never the reverse.

'Well, now he's dead and his land is nobody's and I have only two hands, how do I keep a grip on it all? It's as ripe for the plucking as – '

He stopped as if reeling back from another metaphor, lest the Lord take umbrage. He swallowed loudly. God only knew what he'd do or say if he knew of the money his wife had given me that very day, now stuffed in Annie's shoes, or if he knew of the deeds Newman had drawn up that left everything to him and his housemaid.

'And if we all bought Newman's land, between us?' I said. 'That would be a hundred pairs of gripping hands.'

He gave a short laugh. 'Little hands, worth nothing. As good as a gaggle of children clutching at straw dolls.'

Which I knew to be right. It wasn't about the land being owned, it was about who owned it, whether those who owned it would be able to put up much of a fight to keep it. In one man's hands – Newman's – that land was safer; one man with a lot of land had power, because he had money, had proven himself either by right of birth or by wit and cunning sense. In many poor, weak hands it was for the taking, as if offered. It needed to pass to Townshend, but that would be to reveal the deeds, which would be to rouse the dean's suspicions and have him fling about predictions of murder. Which would be to the peril of us all. So silence, for now, was my only refuge.

'I think my wife was in love with Thomas Newman,' Townshend said, and the swerve of the conversation set off a tic in my neck; I half-expected the thunder to rip through its constraints and split the night. 'Not that it matters, because nothing can be done.'

'Is that your confession?' I said, I hoped not too hurriedly.

'Is what my confession?'

'Your suspicion of your wife.'

'If you like.'

'Then ask the Lord forgiveness for it, because it's no good a man having no trust of his wife, especially when there are other worries. It isn't what marriage asks of him.'

'And if he's right not to trust her?'

'Then her deceit is her own sin, to be forgiven separately.'

Though I let that sin go, I thought. I let Cecily Townshend go without settling her score.

'Well, he's dead, so even if my wife goes on loving him, he can't love her back. She'll tire of that, my wife. She tires when there's no attention.'

I thought of Cecily Townshend's skirt in my beer and her silks near my cheek; perhaps her husband could smell the traces of her lavender and hair pomade here in the booth. I thought of her sharp, stricken face; I doubted she'd tire of a dead Newman. What happens to unreturned love? It becomes powerful, rampant – I'd already seen that in her darting eyes.

'It doesn't make me glad he's dead,' Townshend said. 'Before you ask me to confess to envy and gratitude at another's misfortune. I wish with a passion he weren't dead.'

His voice had become a mutter, a thought aloud.

'Reve, listen, I want to give money for rebuilding the bridge. I've done the calculations – '

'You mean to build it in the same place,' I said, 'just so it can fall down again?'

'Further downstream or further up would do, where it's slower and wider. Come on, Reve.'

'Where it would need five arches. Who in Oakham has the skill for that?'

We'd tried to find bridge masons before, they wanted too much money. We sent four Oakham men away to Exeter to learn the skills for themselves, and three never came back. The last, labourer James Monk, spent his time away suffering the French pox and returned with the strength of an old man and no bridge-building knowledge whatsoever.

'Listen to me, Reve,' Townshend said, and I sank back on my stool, for it hadn't been so long ago that Newman had put to me the very arguments I was now putting to Townshend, and I'd been the one saying *Listen to me*, knowing that what I had to say wasn't entirely worth listening to, and wanted to be said all the more doggedly for that.

'Listen,' Townshend was saying. 'With the herd I have, I can produce around six hundred gallons of milk a week, that's six pence a gallon, which is fifteen pounds, but if I increase the herds three- or fourfold – let's say fourfold, which is modest – that's two thousand four hundred gallons and sixty pounds per week. Granted, only in the summer when the grass is good and there's lots of grain. If we have a bridge we can get the milk to the nearest towns within a day, which means we can trade it fresh. The rest we can use to make cheese, which can become our speciality, Oakham cheese, like Venice glass, like Portugal malmsey, like Dutch flax. Within half a year we could be doing ten times that much, think of it. I'll borrow the money to buy back some of Newman's land, I have cousins – I'll write to them. We'll be a place to be reckoned with. Oakham cheese. Sounds wholesome, doesn't it? Sound and homely. Think of it.'

I did think of it, there and then. A bridge handsomely built further downstream where Newman had said, five miraculously vaulting arches, conveying cart after cart of milk and cheese; the cheese bridge. We could rename ourselves just as the dean had said: Cheesechurn. A proud sign on the far bank.

It was all very well making two thousand gallons of milk a week – the milk would be on the turn before it reached the other side of the bridge. Cheesechurn, also known as Milkturn. And where were the mouths that wanted to swallow it? Anybody could get a cow and anybody could milk it and anybody could churn its milk and make that grainy, pallid mulch Townshend called his finest. You could swab your face with a slab of Townshend's cheese, so wet and giving it was.

'We'll find the skilled men to do it,' he said. 'We have to make a go of ourselves. We have to be a place that can stand up for itself.'

I hesitated; I leant sideways to rest my weight against the wall. Suppose we could find skilled men; suppose Townshend could pay them, as he suggested he could. A bridge is a bridge. If we had a bridge, and if that bridge carried milk and cheese, it could one day carry sugar, and if we could make confections with that sugar and trade it outwards, then we might begin to stand up for ourselves. If the bridge carried in traders and pilgrims on their way elsewhere, if those traders and pilgrims paid tolls, spent money for a bed or some food, spread the word about our parish, our sugar, our wheat, then we might begin to stand up for ourselves.

'If you'd donate money for the bridge, Oakham would gladly accept it,' I said.

'I'll speak to my cousins.'

'Are they rich, your cousins?'

'Richer than us.'

'There are goats richer than us.'

A lord elsewhere in the country had left his worldly goods to his herd of goats, or so it was said. Meanwhile Annie's old shoes were packed with Townshend's wife's money, which was neither fortune nor pittance, but a help, a great help. If only I could tell him of this dubious good fortune, but there wasn't a delicate way of explaining its provenance.

And what of the other dubious good fortune? 'Townshend,' I said. The words were ready in my mouth – *Newman has left you almost everything he owned*. But once those words met his ears, they'd steal his ignorance, and his ignorance went some way to protecting him, since a man who didn't know he'd benefit from another's death is less likely to have brought the other's death about. Once he knew, he knew, and he couldn't prove when and where that knowing started.

'What?' he asked.

One day soon I'd have to tell him; when the dean was gone. When it had all blown over and Oakham was once again forgotten to anybody who mattered. 'It's nothing,' I said.

'You know something about my wife you want to tell me?'

'No, not that.'

'Then what?'

'I'm only sorry. Nothing's as it was.'

He let out air through his nose. Circled, so it seemed, his wrists, which cracked once with each rotation.

'You're not far wrong,' he said. Then, 'Reve, a last thing. If there's any suspicion over Thomas Newman's death, if that dean – God's own snoop – decides it was more than an accident, eyes will turn to me. We weren't friends, I'll admit we didn't like each other much. I was the man who was losing everything at Newman's hands. But we had a shared cause and an under-standing which kept us both safe, and all of us safe. His death could break me. It could break Oakham, as we've discussed. I'm asking you to defend me if ever it came to that.'

Genteel, purring Townshend, a cat among dogs. He gave off a delicate smell of camomile and cloves. His dark outline through the grille was tense and proud – I knew a life of small, cruel selfish worries collected in the furrow between his eyes, while the heavier selfless worries bore his shoulders down to a worn kindness. He was always shuffling them back, adjusting his tunic or coat. Making himself taller. I could hear him do it now.

'I would, of course,' I said. 'If it came to it, of course.'

'I see woods and no easy way out of them.'

'There's always a way out.'

'But not an easy one.'

I wondered if this was the time for my observation about minnows and nets, but I couldn't remember its point. If we, the minnows, swam out of the monks' net, what did that even mean? Swim to where?

'Is anything in this whole world easy?' I asked.

'Parting with your money is easy. And dying, apparently.'

'Dying is the hardest part.'

'Well then, I'd thank you to stop it happening to me any time soon, Father.'

He blew out some air; his belly rumbled. Then he came to his feet with the assistance of the grille. His hand clutched it and he hoisted himself upright.

'Do you know why I came here, Reve?' he said.

'To confess, I suppose.'

'Confess, my arse. Confess to what? I came because you're the last friend I have in this place. I just wanted to come and see a friend.'

When he'd gone, I drank my beer down. His smell of cloves left warmth and comfort, as did the beer, though my tongue was as dry and rough as a board.

It was with worryingly little trouble that I envisaged this pack of monks Townshend forecast – or at least their brief-bearers or door-keepers or carriers or gardeners – coming from over the hill that marked Oakham's boundary with Bruton, through our East Woods and onto the land bought up by Newman. I saw them look with approval at our furlongs parcelled into well-marked strips that were newly ploughed to what would be a good till, once it dried out, a till capable of wheat. I saw them look at the leys where a few wilful horses and goats and sheep grazed. I saw them appraise and project, count and calculate – you could get fifteen, sixteen, seventeen bushels of wheat or barley per acre out here; that's how many? There's some two hundred acres that the eye can see, that's some three thousand two hundred bushels of wheat, more than any abbey of monks can eat – and wheat is like gold, no trouble selling it. That's not to mention the rest of the land as you near the village, and all those meadows by the river. And the mill, and the manor, and the church. All those would be useful.

I envisaged the army of monks and I thought: now Newman's gone, what stops them coming? As soon as they get wind of his death, they'll come. His land is for the taking. Oakham slips down another notch or two in their estimations because the respectable Thomas Newman, man of wit and business, is no longer in it, and died a death that shames us. If a murder, then it shows our savagery; if a suicide, then it shows how we wore him down to despair; and if an accident, then it shows that twelve years with us makes even the most able man clumsy and hapless. When there's nothing left of Oakham for them to respect, they can take our land without even having to ask for forgiveness. They can take it as if granting a favour.

Newman, at Annie's wedding: his face lean, clever and quick. Janet Grant was wrong, he wasn't unhappy, he was serene, and inside that serenity, I believe, elated.

He stood as he often did, left leg rooted, right leg kicked out at rest. He looked at me; he was the slightly shorter of us two, but something about him towered and made me feel half-grown.

'You should give it up, John, this love affair with the bridge.'

'Hardly a love affair.'

'In any case, give it up. If two wives died on you, maybe you'd think twice about marrying a third.'

'Or maybe you'd hope for the third to outlive you.'

He'd drunk nothing all night as far as I could tell, except one cup of beer, which he was still cradling. Amid a barnful of people dancing his body was quiet and still, the toe of that kicked-out right leg resting on the ground, where usually it would've percussed a tap-tap-t-tap, tap-tap-t-tap. A wreath of rosemary was tied around the oak strut against which he leant, and it was just above his head; its smell would plunge intensely between us from time to time. He seemed to have no great investment in the music and dancing close by.

'I know you've given enough money,' I said, 'but – '

'You're right, I've given enough.'

'Who else can Oakham look to, then?'

'For yet one more bridge? It can look to its priest, and its priest can reassure it that another bridge would be unnecessary, and that other things are more essential for its well-being.'

'Is that so?'

'That's so.'

'For instance, its bridge to the Lord,' he said, glancing at me before looking elsewhere, but not at anything; not cross or waspish, but not warm, either. 'A bridge they can navigate alone now and then, without you standing taking tolls, as it were. There are times when your best intervention is to get out of their way. When they need to, let them make up their own prayers, let them know – feel, in their hearts – that he's *their* God as well as yours. That bridge, from their hearts straight to him, is worth any number of bridges you might orchestrate across the river.'

'Make their own prayers?' I said. 'Have you heard the kind of prayers they make?'

Newman looked into his cup of beer, and swilled it, and said nothing.

'Peter Green had a jammed lock – what prayer did he give? He invoked Christ's breaking down of the gates of hell. Do you think it worked?'

'Do *you* have a prayer that would have worked?' he asked.

I turned my shoulder from him. He was mild with me, never raising his voice except above the music, or even showing signs of being vexed. I watched his right foot to see if it tapped or if it made ready to join the other and walk away. It was still as a clam.

He was watching the wedding dances without attention – Annie going from arm to arm in the blue silk dress she'd

221

borrowed from Cecily Townshend, and taken up at the hem. She'd a chaplet of Star of Bethlehems around her head that kept falling loose, and which she repinned as she danced. Cecily Townshend herself was leaning against a table, picking at a boar's head; if Newman was less indifferent to her than he was to anyone else, he didn't show it.

'What is it, then?' I asked. 'What is it they do in Rome, or Florence, or wherever, that's made you so certain about a man or woman's way to God? What – is there some holy water you drank there that gave you all the answers? In which case, bring me some.'

It came out unmistakably bitter; another time I'd have raised a brow to show there was a tease in there, and another time he'd have raised his in return and crossed himself and muttered, *Fornax ardens caritatis*: burning furnace of charity, forgive me for stravaging around Europe and drinking water without you, Reve, *rex et centrum omnium cordium*: king and centre of our hearts. All of it said with some sarcasm. I might once, when we were younger, have nudged him with my elbow. Not now; the wedding wine had doused my *burning furnace of charity*. And neither was he in frivolous spirits.

'Listen to you,' he said. '*Bring me some*. If you think there's some holy water that gives you all the answers, wouldn't it be worth going to find it, not waiting for it to come to you? You could know something of the world, but you'd rather stay here trying to shake money out of the trees for a bridge. I don't know why you're so beset by it.'

'What do you think I want a bridge for, if not to cross it?'

'For other people to cross it, and pay you.'

'To bring wealth to Oakham,' I said, 'to guard us against winters that leave us starving. I've repaid you well for the money you've put in – a plenary pardon, Newman, which is more than anybody else in Oakham's been granted.'

'For which I thank you.'

'I want to rebuild that bridge,' I said. 'I want it, Tom. To stroll each morning on that opposite bank.'

Meaning: Do you remember that friendly morning, when we watched the others on the opposite bank? Do you recall?

'It's your business what you do,' he said. 'I'm not willing to give more money. And business is just what it is – a man of business builds a bridge and waits for people to pay tolls to cross it; a man of the spirit seeks across the bridge himself, pays with his faith and opens his heart. Well, I'm not a man of business, Reve, I'm a man of the spirit, and I've sought, and prayed, and find myself finally in a state of grace.'

That's what he said. *Unlike you* (those first words not actually spoken), *I'm not a man of business, Reve, I'm a man of the spirit*. Those were the words he said.

'Ah,' said the dean when I appeared at his – Newman's – door.

He let me in. We sat by the hearth where a fire was getting up. It was darkish by now, and the last thunder was a distant, soft rumble. He'd lit the room amply and the floor was strewn with the violets and rushes we'd laid the day before, in the hope Newman's body might appear and could be laid out at his hearth. No such fortune – and the place was traitorously cheerful and warm in his absence.

'I just thought I'd let you know what I know,' I said.

'And what do you know?'

'Well,' I said, 'in a single day, about a third of the parish has confessed.'

I expected him to be glad; it was his idea to lure them to confession, and he had. A man is glad when others do his will, so my experience had shown me. But he showed no sign of gladness, so I went on. 'After a day of confession, nothing's surfaced – Herry Carter's stricken with grief and has cut his face. Drew Norys lobbed a stone at a bird, the miserable fool.

223

Maurice Fry came for a sleep. Gil Otley found his boy's teeth. Sarah Spenser is willing to confess to anything in her torment, including murdering Newman with an axe.'

The dean spluttered a laugh.

'Which we know she couldn't have done,' I said.

I sipped the beer he'd poured me and waited for his response. He yawned. A tear of tiredness glistened in the outer corner of one eye. All the light in the room had found it and made it bright as a jewel.

'I wanted to say how I appreciate you being here, in Oakham,' I said.

He turned his face and that bejewelled tear blinked at me.

'Your friendship. Your support of us in our grief. Sarah, for one, said you were kind to her.' I turned the cup in my hands. 'I can be lonely here at times, with nobody to talk to. About the works of the Lord, I mean. About problems.' I smiled. 'And then a brother comes along.'

He nodded slowly. After a while of nodding, and then a while of sitting so still that the tear – which had trickled slightly – rested as a single pearl on his cheekbone, he inhaled and said, 'Yes, it can be lonely being a priest. So much to decide – some of it trivial, some not, but still. All yours to deal with.'

The truth of his words had a weight, and the sympathy in them a warmth, and I was rendered heavy in my chair as I murmured, 'Yes, indeed, yes.'

'When I was a priest,' he said, 'I had an odd thing happen in my parish. Our church wall supported the wall of a house, meaning that the church and the house shared a wall. I suppose it's not that uncommon a thing – '

'Like at Bourne,' I said.

'Precisely like that. Well, a hole appeared in that wall, just about big enough to squeeze a hand through. The man living in the house, John Brews, decided he liked this hole because he could watch the consecration of the host without getting out

224

of his underwear. He was an odd parsnip of a thing, he looked like he'd just been pulled up from the ground.'

The dean reached over with the jug to pour me more beer, which I took.

'I couldn't give Mass and sermons, with the noise that came from Brews's house,' he said. 'He had eight children and a wife who liked to sing more than people liked to hear her, so I had the hole fixed. A while later it was miraculously back. I told Brews that since he'd made it, he ought to fix it, and he refused. I'd be at the chancel and there'd be his little parsnip-face at the hole, all knotty and pale. I had the hole fixed again, and he sued me and had me arrested for trespass.' At which the dean turned to me and said with a little huff, 'Trespass!'

'That's a sad affair.'

I leaned forward to scratch an ankle. Floor rushes always gave me cause to scratch; if they laid me out on rushes for my own death, would some flickering, leftover force of life in my limbs still feel the itch, though my hands were dead clay and unable to scratch? It seemed to me that would be purgatory indeed.

'I've heard of the same,' I told the dean, to show fraternity, and because I had, 'of priests being sued by their own parish, and it's always a sad affair.'

'Oh, it happens,' the dean sighed, and seemed so minute in his chair that a surge of feeling occurred in me, at least some of it affection. The tear rolled down his cheek finally, and he wiped it from his jaw. 'It happens alright. And what do we do about it? Right and wrong aren't like man and woman, they're not so easy to tell apart.'

'I'd say they're just like man and woman, you can usually tell them apart, but not always.'

'Fine, then,' he said, lifting his cup as if in salutation. 'And in that case, was John Brews right or wrong? It was his wall as much as the church's. Besides, he saw Mass a lot more when the hole was there. Well?'

225

'It's hard to say.'

He turned in his chair to look at me. 'Yes, it's hard to say, but you still have to say it.'

I raised a brow at him. 'Do I have to say it?'

His stare was nothing other than cold, though I tried for a moment to see it as something else.

'All I mean is, I'd be interested to know what you did,' I said.

'And I'd be more interested to know what *you'd* do, Reve. Would you concede John Brews had a right to his wall and his hole, and let it be? Or would you concede that the church had a right to its wall without a hole, and block it up?'

'A compromise perhaps,' I said.

'A compromise!' His left leg lifted and fell as if on a string. I'd delighted him somehow. 'Yes, Reve, a compromise!'

'Leave the hole, and ask his wife not to sing.'

'And his children not to speak or cry or babble or squabble. And Brews not to snore and fart, and his wife to bite her tongue in the pleasures of – '

Intercourse. I wanted to speak it, because you should never leave unsaid the awkward-to-say word, else it repeats itself in the silence a hundred times over and swells like a fruit between you, hanging, dangling, ripening by the moment. Begging to be picked. But I delayed too long, and by the time I went to say it, the fruit had fallen and landed, overripe, at our feet. We both looked there, towards our feet.

'Shall I tell you what I did in the end?' the dean said, becoming upright in his chair. 'I convinced the chancellor to drop the charge against me, and we fixed the hole, and told Brews it would be the last time. Or, if there was a next time, it would be him being arrested.'

At some point between the plump, glistening tear of tiredness and the now-upright rod of his back the dean's mood had turned. His lips thinned and his fingers curled with defiance.

'You see, Reve, in the end I had to show guidance and example. Where there's no right or wrong in a situation, you have to supply the answer yourself. This is the meaning of strength and leadership. You have to say: This is what I'm going to do, for want of better ideas. You have to say: There's some unexpected trouble, and I'm going to take charge of it.'

'You aren't talking about the hole in the wall any more,' I said, because his glare didn't leave any doubt that the anecdote was turning its pointed end towards me.

He tapped a rigid finger against his cup. 'I never was.'

'No.'

We gazed, I at the floor, he at me. My cheek hot and hollowed where his scrutiny bore at it. In that scrutiny, the failure of our friendship. The failure of myself to inspire him.

'Is there something you want me to do?' I asked.

'Where there's no clear answer or wrongdoing, but nevertheless a problem, you have to lead by example.'

'As I try.'

'And not let your parish fall to mishap and – degeneracy.'

I could think only of the little skirt that Jesus had been dressed in. Had it troubled him that much? Surely not the grunting, pounding cow in the barn. 'Is it about our walk?' I asked.

Nothing.

'Is it about that skirt that Jesus was wearing at New Cross? You know that's a prank. I always think that a village that can still find the spirit for pranks is in good health, don't you?'

I was tired of his silences, and angry, and distressed at sitting in Newman's house, in Newman's chair, when Newman was dead.

'What, then?' I said. 'Is it about the cows in the barn? Did you expect me to part the two beasts with my hands, mid-thrust, mid-shunt? Did you want me to catch the barn boy mid-flail before he landed in a ditch of shit? Push my palm against Jane Smith's mouth mid-vomit? Do you want me to clean up the seedy weather?'

227

'I saw Cecily Townshend walk around the back of your house this evening with a large bundle in her arms,' he said, 'and I thought it was odd for a woman of her standing to be running errands. Is there anything you want to tell me about that perplexing sight?'

I'd been at my ankle again, but stopped. My hand fell loose and I sat back.

'What does this have to do with our conversation?'

'So there's nothing you want to tell me?'

'She was bringing a goose,' I said. There was no point lying, and anyway I guessed his question was a formality, and that he'd already been to the back of my house to check for himself. 'Just a goose.'

'A goose? Why would you need a goose, when we're about to fast for Lent?'

I rested my hands flat on my splayed knees.

'It was just an act of kindness on Cecily Townshend's part.'

'Will you share that kindness with your parish?'

'It's hardly big enough to share.'

'So while the rest of Oakham does their best with bread and barley and stew and one piece of fish in forty days, if they're lucky, you'll get halfway into Lent before your meat runs out.'

'If I share it, it'll be a mouthful each – '

'What you mean is that you can't share it, because then you'd have to explain that Cecily Townshend gave it to you and that would be – awkward, I assume. Particularly if you tried to explain why.'

'I told you, she gave it in kindness; it's not uncommon to want to thank your priest.'

'Will you be able to eat it all before you fast for Lent?'

'Lent's only two days away.'

'Then share it with your parish, a mouthful each. Or is it that you want it all for yourself?'

The dean stood, went to the fire and showed the palms of his hands to the heat; his fingers were a bloodless white. 'Do you know how much you need your people to pull together, now that Newman's dead? Do you know how close your churchyard is to becoming another vegetable patch for a monk? How can you ask your parish to pull together if you, yourself, are pulling away? One rule for you and another for them. Can they trust you?'

I took a short gulp of beer and let it sit in my mouth for a moment without swallowing. When I did swallow, it was audible and the dean wheeled round to face me.

'You're their guardian, Reve, you're the single greatest force that stands in the way of the Bruton monks taking this village. You might as well be standing up at the boundary with a pitchfork. Maybe one day you will be.'

Woe betide us then, I thought. I wouldn't have the first instinct of what to do with a pitchfork. Wave it, jab it, charge hell-bent and full-pelt with it, like a spear? At a monk?

'It might have been my eyes,' the dean said, 'but I don't believe I saw your end of that boat rise, by the way. If anything, it sank slightly.'

I don't know what my look conveyed to him, because I tried not to show panic, but panic isn't easy to disguise. I was ordained, I wanted to tell him; I gave over my flesh to the spirit, a pound of my own blood for a weightless whisper, a hope. If the boat didn't rise, isn't that a fault of the test, not of the man? Do you really mean to say that, when offered me, the Lord refused? Or only that I'm a fake?

I said, uselessly, 'I'll send the goose back to the Townshends.' Though useless, the urge behind it took formidable shape – to be rid of that goose, which seemed now to mock, deride, belittle me.

'How incriminating *that* would be for Cecily Townshend. Wouldn't her husband wonder why she was giving the priest little Shrovetide gifts? Perhaps he'd wonder if she had something to hide.' The dean went back to his chair and perched on its edge. 'No,' he said. 'No, no. You won't take that goose back – you'll eat every sinew of it, and there'll be no trace of it left by Shrove Tuesday. Think of it as eating your weakness and affection for compromise, and at the end, when the weakness is gone, you're left only with resolve.'

The sniff I gave, snatched up through the nose, was like the ones I often heard on the other side of the oak screen – defiant, but helpless.

'Resolve, Reve. Do you understand? If times get worse here, you are going to have to be the strongest of all men. Not some man hiding at his table eating a goose and hoping for the best. Not some man waiting for a rural dean to help him. I say this for the good of Oakham, not for my own good. Why should I care what kind of man you are? But there are close to a hundred people depending on you. Compromise will get you nowhere. Some difficult decisions have to be made in this world. Can you stand up and make them?'

I got up, not easily, from the chair. I nodded, though I didn't know if it was a nod of consent to his question or simply a gesture of parting.

Bring in the goose, I thought. But when I stood to, I thought instead: leave it outside. Surely the foxes or dogs will get it if it's left outside – and if they don't get it, it's the Lord's way of telling me it's mine to eat. But of course the foxes and dogs will have it. I hoped for that, then felt hungry at the thought of it gone. I ate some milky, humid cheese.

I went outside to see if the church was in darkness; some lights still glowed. I crossed the churchyard unevenly. The night was wet, close and cloudy, bruised by thunder that had rolled around it for most of two hours but had cleared nothing. Inside, Janet Grant was over in the north aisle snuffing out candles.

'Father,' she said.

'Let me help.'

As she worked from north-east towards the door, I worked the opposite way, snuffing the candles one by one. It always surprised me how much light a flame threw, and how bleak and deep the darkness that replaced it. And how a small, steady flame could cast such a prancing shadow.

I went from light to light in silence, while Janet Grant did the same. At the door we met with only the light of the tallow she held, and the one candle that burnt through to morning. This world that advances on us was shrunk to a flame stuttering in the black of her eye. This hurly-burly world, what was it suddenly but the fennel and goaty staleness of her breath, and a waxy umber that stopped and gave way to giddying dark before it even reached the door.

I fumbled and opened the latch and let us into the porch, then fumbled again at the second door. We went into the sodden night. The door shut heavy behind us.

'Sleep sound, Janet,' I said.

And she returned, 'Sleep sound, Father.'

Day 1
The previous day, Shrove (also Egg) Saturday

Burning

'John. *John!*'

A banging at the door; I rolled over in bed, glue-eyed. One eye managed to open, but only one. The other was gummed in groggy sleep. The more willing eye saw that it was either night or the thick, dark night-side of morning.

'Let me in, John.'

It was Thomas Newman; I'd know that voice even five fathoms under sleep, though its usual melody was flat.

'John, please.'

He pushed at the door (which was never locked and would barely close or open in its rain-swollenness). I shut my eyes and burrowed my head down into the covers. Anyway it was cold. My head registered a searing pain and my eyes, my eyeballs – they felt like stones being ground underfoot. Cropsick. Too much of Hikson's brew at the wedding yesterday. Newman was by then in the room with the door closed behind him; he was a voice in the dark an arm's length from my bed.

'John, wake up, get up. I need something.'

I need something. As if we didn't all need something.

'I know you're awake. I need the final sacrament. I need you to get up.'

I need the final sacrament! Only Thomas Newman could be cocksure enough to ask for the final sacrament, as a blacksmith asks to be handed his swage.

In the burrows of my covers, behind those painful orbs that I used to know as my eyes, his face appeared to me from the evening before – fresh, imperturbable, fixed on an unseen hope.

'Look, you can do it here. I can kneel here – you don't even need to get up. You just need to hear my confession. I can go to the church and get the oil, the host. I'll bring them. No need to get up.'

He'll wake Annie, I thought, and then remembered that for the first time in many years my sister wasn't sleeping in the next room, but had gone and was married. My body froze in a cold and impotent fury. Did Newman think the holy oil and the host in its pyx were his for the taking? Was the altar his table? Here was the man who'd claimed his lute was as good a path to God as any priest could be. So go and kneel to your lute for the final sacrament, I thought; ask your lute to anoint your forehead and drive out your demons. Why wake me?

He was standing by my bed, shaking as if a wind were at work on him, and his breathing was caught. He must have had no light to see by, except for the night lantern that burnt by my door; no candlelight of his made a rosy umber through my eyelids. For the first time I noticed the rushing of rain against the house. Then I heard him lower himself, I supposed he'd come to kneel.

'The trouble with feigning sleep is that the oblivion of it is ruined by the effort to seem oblivious. And you are a bad actor.' This last he whispered straight into my ear.

My breath pooled stale in the cocoon of blanket; Newman was right, it was too uneven and shallow for a sleeper. It was scattered by the fast beating of my heart. He must have been able to hear my lungs on the cusp of bursting.

'Please, John. With your permission, might I go and get the things for sacrament and bring them here?' He waited for me to answer. He clapped his hands to his thighs. 'Why, John? Aren't we friends?'

Poisoned and sick is how I was; Hikson must have put something mean-tempered in the wedding brew. When Newman's voice came next, it shot softly in a burst of colour like a well-fletched arrow from the darkness, straight towards me.

'When my daughter died of the sweating sickness,' he was saying, 'I took up all my grief and turned it in my hands over and over until it resembled love, and I gave that love to my wife. We had eight days of this love. I hadn't properly loved her before then, since I wasn't a warm husband, and nor was she a warm wife. We had eight days of discovering we needed one another, and then she too became ill and died. I'm not convinced by this life. This life we're given. I've lived as well, adventurously and kindly as I can and I've found the kindness returned, but all the same I don't find much to hope for. This life, John – I'm suspicious of its logic, if it has any. You tell me it does and I believe you. But I'm willing to gamble this life away, in the trust that the next will be better. You tell me it's better, and I believe you. You tell me there's a place set up for me already in heaven, which you yourself have negotiated for me through pardons on account of my good doings, and I believe you. What harm can it be to take myself there?'

I pinned my body to the bed. Newman added, as if we were in conversation, 'My death will look like an accident, a drowning, there'll be no harm done. You know about the deeds; I want to die without trouble to this village and these people, and I beseech you to guide Townshend to take care of their needs. You'll do it. You're a good man.' A pause, and then: 'Let me die by the word of the church and of God. I want to die.'

The muscle and bone and bloody sinew that stewed in a soup inside my skin quickened itself as if for action, but as I was about to sit up and speak to Newman (tell him not to consider what he was considering, that his life was precious), that tide of blood and will seemed stopped by my skin itself. Then all I could feel was the coldness of my skin and the pain in my head, and the betrayal from the night before, which had provoked a rage I'd never known. I'm not a man of business, John, I'm a man of the spirit, he'd said. *I'm a man of the spirit.* As if to say: You, John, are not.

His hand landed on my arm and grasped it. 'I need the last sacrament. I can't die without being shriven.'

I gave nothing. He waited with his hand there. The bones in my jaw ached for want of speaking, of sitting up and telling him the plain truth: If you're such a man of the spirit and I'm such a man of business, then it should be *me* coming to *you* for the sacrament.

My heartbeat was a bird flinging itself around a closed room. His fingers flexed, then loosened. Still I gave nothing, until the hand relaxed and he lifted it away. He stood and loomed lengthily. The rain was drum and fiddle, beating and skittering. It touched me that he should keep standing there, hoping – but that was the kind of man he was, patient and determined. It took all I had not to sit up and put my hand out to his, and to hear his gentle word: Benedicite, and to offer him mine: Dominus. He stood without moving and I lay without moving, and the battle between us was waged with our eyes – his which refused to leave me, and mine which refused to open.

At last there was a gathering of breath and motion and the darkness was scrambled; he was somewhere in the room but I couldn't tell where, not until the candle by the door was extinguished (by draught or breath?) and the door itself creaked open and was shoved closed.

Some moments came and went. How many? Enough for something leaden to pass down my legs into my feet, and for a sudden heat to inflame my soles, as if, in the absence of a well-apprised head, it was my feet that were doing the thinking. For what priest let one of his parish go to death unshriven? What would he be, to do that? I came nauseous to those feet, those lumps of conscience, wrapped myself in a blanket and discovered, as I unlatched the door, that my whole body was now alive with conscience, and the rage had ebbed out of reach. I ran down towards Old Cross in a drizzle that seeped from lifeless air.

Up ahead, in the dissipating dark, was Newman, going towards his house – not towards the river, but home. I followed enough to watch him cross the threshold of the door, and I stood long enough in the woods to know he hadn't come straight back out but had stayed inside. The smoke plumed so soothingly from his chimney, the air smelt of oak. It had passed, his moment of whim and spleen, he'd changed his mind – of course he had, because no man who still had hold of his senses would die willingly without being shriven.

I was a priest in his nightgown and blanket in the rain, shoes unfastened, and cropsick, and shivering. But I assured myself: you did not let Newman down, John Reve, far from it – you dissuaded him from death by refusing to grant his passage there. Who could say you let him down?

My trusted feet were cold with relief. They took me home.

I must have had sleep of some haphazard sort, and while asleep I must have worried about the loss of the candle flame by the door, and dreamt about lighting the fire, because when I woke I was sure it would be burning steady and that I could reach my hands towards it. It was the sound of the door opening that woke me and brought me upright. No fire, no flames. A cold, dark dawn, and Carter standing before me, with teeth chattering and the reek of the river.

Get up,' he said.

I sat with Carter's cold hands on my arms; he was soaked, and some wet part of him dripped onto my wrist – his sleeve, or hair? Weak daylight fell in, but it was grey and mundane. Newman was here, I thought, and though it occurred to me as if a dream, I knew it wasn't. The moment I caught the smell of the river on Herry Carter I knew what news he had for me, and still I sat in bed, blank-faced, and must have stared through him, because he brought his face up to mine and repeated, 'Get up!'

'I – '

'Thomas Newman has just drowned himself at the bridge. Gone under. I saw him.' Carter prodded at his eyes with two splayed fingers, then he was rendered down into sobbing with his face in the blanket.

I scrambled up and pulled on my alb. I don't know that I understood precisely what he'd said, even though I'd anticipated him saying it – I only got into my alb and found the cold pinching at my skin. These endless winter nights with their dark dawns and morning moons. Enemy of bare flesh. Herry Carter was a shape made clear only by the sound of sobs. 'Me,' he said, 'it was me.'

I stood away from him and didn't expend effort to light any candles. 'What was you?'

'Me who forced him to drown.'

'You're not thinking straight – come on, sit here.'

The table had two chairs. I pulled one out. He scowled and stayed kneeling by the bed.

'He went there to drown himself,' he said, 'of all the depraved things, to *drown* himself. Tom Newman, of all the men. And I tried to stop him, and we tussled and he tried to push me under, so I fought and somehow – ' Carter's face and fist clenched at once. 'He tried to push me under.' Then deformed in tears and disbelief. 'He tried to push me under.'

240

'So you fought back and it was him who ended up under?'

'I didn't mean to do it.'

I sat in the chair Carter had refused, while he knelt in fust and shadow with the whites of his eyes trembling and his hands milky in half-prayer.

'It's before dawn, Herry, why were you even by the river?'

Herry Carter came to his feet, then sat lumpily on the edge of the bed with his elbows dug into his knees. Sorrowful sighing. He ran his hands against one another like he was trying to get a spark, then clasped them and chewed at a thumbnail.

'I don't sleep much these days, my wife's twitchy and restless in bed, except she can sleep through her twitches and I can't. The rain was coming down like someone was throwing buckets. I couldn't sleep, I tried my best.' He bit off a sliver of nail and spat it elsewhere. 'I got up and found myself going down to the river. The floods – I worry about the sheep down on that ham. Had anxieties that they were drowning.'

'And Newman was there?'

'No, but then he came. Dressed up in his coat and boots. He was surprised to see me.'

Carter stood and began pacing, also shivering. I got up, took my blanket from the bed and put it round his sodden shoulders. He was wet as water itself, and skin as cold as granite, and shoulders as blunt as a cudgel. He tugged the blanket tight to him.

'At first he lingered and made light of things and said he'd come for a breath of air, to clear the wedding wine from his head. That's what he said. He kept trying to persuade me to go back to bed. I knew there was something amiss with him, so I didn't. We waded about in the flood looking for animals, and there was a certain amount of bleating from up-ham, but in the light we had, which was as good as no light, we couldn't tell if animals had got themselves mired in the flood. So Newman said he'd stay til first light and check again, and we went back towards the bridge – or, I should say, what was left of the bridge – and talked about the stars, which he said were other worlds like ours, with life involved.'

Carter sat again on the bed, and I told him, 'You should breathe, breathe deep', because he was shaking and his breath was frail as wool snatched on bramble.

'Then Tom Newman stopped talking about the stars and said, Excuse me Herry, and went to the bank and started wading in. Like that.'

The sobbing took up, and a whine of pain. Which in this dark, cold shuffle of bodies and words was real, and which was illusion? Newman at my bed, Carter at my bed, Newman at the river, Newman wading in, Carter standing soaked, Newman's hand on my arm, Carter's hand on my arm. The fletched arrow of Newman's plea, which I now saw as a real fletched arrow, as if Newman had taken aim at me in a dream. None of it was dream, but none of it had the straightness of reality. Hadn't Newman gone home? Not to the river – *home*? I assembled the blanket around Carter's shoulders where it had fallen.

'That's when it started,' Carter said. 'I don't know what happened, how can I say for sure? Just that I realised Tom Newman was walking straight into that demonic wild river and not stopping, so I went after him and he asked me to leave him alone. But we were both up to our waists even though we hadn't properly left the bank, and we were both holding on to what's left of the abutments, so I thought: if he really wanted to die, he wouldn't be holding on. Isn't that right? If he really wanted to die, he'd be in by now.'

I found myself staring out the window while he spoke; the moon was paling and shivery and the day was coming for it. But the day was pale and shivery too, and not convincing, and songless.

'There wasn't much talking,' Herry Carter said. 'Between Newman and me. I knew what he was trying to do and I knew

242

why, no need for words. He'd talked to me before about being reunited in heaven with his wife and child, and that his life was only to do enough good deeds to gain him entry there, the sooner the better. I knew that's what he was up to. Those hems of his coat were filled with rocks, that I also guessed from the way his coat plunged downwards in the water where my own splayed like a skirt. I tried to pull the coat from him. He fought his way out of it as though to tell me I might as well not bother, since he'd drown anyway, it might just take longer. But I took that another way – the fact that he struggled out of his weighted coat and hung on still to the bridge, well, all that meant his heart wasn't committed to dying. I think his coat went off and sank downstream. So then I hung to his waist with my arm that wasn't hanging to the abutments and I yelled to him: "I'm your son, I don't intend to let you go, we'll go home and light a fire. We'll be alright!" And what did he do?'

I turned my head, and looked at Carter over my shoulder. Newman with his hems loaded with rocks, just as they were each Shrove Sunday when we came to be weighed. My heart, too, filled with rocks at the sudden thought of him gone. Out there, the moon pulling its pale breaths, away from us. 'What did he do?' I asked, because Carter needed me to ask.

'He eyed me, did our friend Thomas Newman, amid all the chaos and noise and not knowing where our feet were, he eyed me so steady and calm that I thought he'd understood my love and what it meant, and then he let go of the bridge. I clung to him, I can't tell you how much, until just my fingers were at his shirt and tearing it and pulling it. But you see the problem – I had no arms and he had two, and with one of them he pushed my head under.'

At that, he bowed his head and looked down – maybe at his hands, which were, I imagined, crablike on his knees. But none of this was visible to me in the light we had. 'Do you hear what I said? He pushed my head under.'

His teeth began chattering so violently that they gnashed, and I wondered why the Lord thought up chattering as any kind of help with cold. I asked, 'Where's that blanket, Herry?' I couldn't see if it was still around him. 'Put that blanket tight round your shoulders.'

'He pushed my head under,' Carter said, 'and I saw death coming closer than I've ever seen it, and I was thrashing out of control and mortally cold, and when I came up for a breath, I saw him and I kicked him away, went under, and when I came up again I was still holding on to his shirt, but he wasn't in it.'

There was no sound except for the scratch of the blanket, a fumble; I could see him manoeuvring it around him, a black shadow like a wing, then a tugging of it, wool on hemp. And I imagined Newman's shirt flailing in the current, empty of him.

'I could have just let him go,' Herry said. 'But I kicked him away. Used both my feet. I kicked him away.' Herry Carter raised his head then and pinned me, or so I imagined, with his look. 'Does God see what happens underwater?'

'Listen – '

'Could he have seen me kicking my feet like that into Newman's ribs?'

'The river's fast and murky, Herry, and God isn't always looking.'

Which we knew to be untrue. Carter held steady with his gaze; the oval of his face marked itself out against the dark.

'God saw my legs alright.'

'He saw into your heart,' I said. 'That's where he spends his time looking. And your heart was good.'

'Good? If he saw into my heart he'll know my intention, which was to kill Thomas Newman – not just to let him die, but to kill him.'

'Only so that he might not kill you.'

'*Thou shalt do no murder.*'

'There's murder and then there's murder.'

'Each Sunday at Mass you tell us, *Thou shalt do no murder. Thou shalt not kill.*'

'In spite, in greed, in hate. But your heart has never been anything but full of love for that man. God sees that.'

'I never heard you say, *Thou shalt do no murder except with a heart full of love.*'

'I'm saying it now. *Thou shalt have a heart full of love.* And whatever action is inspired by that love, God will look kindly upon.'

Carter slumped, head towards knees. I went to him, sat beside him, put my arm across his shoulder. He was silent as if he'd died. My forehead was dull with cropsickness and a too-deep sleep, my body top-to-toe queasy, with only one sharp sensation that arrived in the neck, like a board partitioning head and heart: shame. Tell him, I thought: tell him Newman came to you earlier that morning. That he stood there hours ago, still alive, with death preventable – or can you not?

'Do you know that Newman was drowned?' I said finally (choosing, over honesty, a swerving shot at hope). 'For all you know, he might have drifted downstream and got out, right as rain.'

'Right as rain!' Carter managed, his shoulders jerking as if in laughter.

'Well?'

He lifted his head. 'Well, I saw him sucked under and then I never saw him again. I got out and ran downriver along the bank and saw nothing. He certainly did not get out.'

I didn't doubt him. There was no getting out of that river, once it was in spate and you were in the middle of it. We'd seen cows pulled down in its tow. Newman could swim, but he wasn't a particularly good swimmer; and besides, nothing could last long in its icy waters; and besides, he wanted to die. So why would he swim?

'Herry,' I said finally, 'say nothing about what happened this morning.'

No word from Herry Carter, only the back of his abundantly haired head, his wet hair that smelt of weeks of smoke and dirt.

'If anybody asks, you were still in bed. You saw nothing.'

'My wife knows I was not in bed,' he muttered.

'Then you must get her to share your account.'

He swallowed. Cat Carter was as loyal and unquestioning as any wife in Europe, in this entire world; she'd back up any story he gave her.

'You said you still had hold of his shirt. Where is it? Did you let it go after him into the river?'

Nothing.

'Herry?'

'It's over there.' This, muffled.

'Where?' I got up, went towards the door. I found it on the floor – it was easy to identify, a sopping heap. I put my hand to it but didn't pick it up.

'You need to get rid of this,' I said.

He lifted his head.

'How will you explain having his shirt?' I hissed, though I hadn't meant to. 'How will you explain it?'

'Easy, the truth. I'll just say I murdered him.'

'Take it away now, before it gets light, hide it somewhere. Later, we'll burn it or bury it. For now, just hide it where it won't be found.'

So Herry was going to sit agog as if what I asked was madness, when the madness was in doing nothing but sitting agog.

'You'd like to be hanged?' I said.

Debate there in his body, which hovered between the choices of slump and stand. His shoulders said yes, why not be hanged? But his feet, two dark keen shapes on the floor, said no, not hanged. One slid forward to be ready to walk. I picked up the shirt and wrung it over the bucket.

'Bury it,' I said.

He came to his feet, juddery.

'And tell nobody.'

I urged the clump of shirt into his hands and he drew it fully up against his stomach.

'Do you have plenty of wood, will your wife have a fire?'

He nodded, shaking with cold and barely fit to speak.

'Then go and get dry and warm, don't delay. Warm clothes, something to eat – and say nothing. Say nothing, do nothing. Cease knowing what you know.'

I went to the wood pile and hoarded two logs under my arm for my own fire, and took two more. Behind me, Carter left. Dear God, I said to my empty house, and God replied only: *queasy priest*. A bruising rebuke; I busied myself in its wake. Char cloth, flint, fire striker. Get the fire burning strong. There wasn't anything I could think of but the sight of a burning flame and the feel of its warmth. I snicked the fire striker repeatedly against the flint, impatient. I'd light the fire and then, once the fire was lit, breakfast. My hands shook with – was it fear? Regret? Despair? Because, now what? Light fire, breakfast. *And having food, let us be therewith content.*

Eat we must

Boiled beef. Plenty of it left over from the wedding. A bit of rye bread to gnaw on, better for breakfast than for supper, else you go to bed indigested and stone-stomached. Sinner's bread we call it here, because why else would you eat it if you weren't doing penance; God gave us wheat for good reason. But the rye bread was left over from the wedding too, so I ate at the table with the noise of rain abating and fog bearing in.

The rye from today travelled to my stomach, met the rye from yesterday and sat on it. The beef was tender, though, and a solace that went easily down. I drank some watery wine. The puddle by the door, which Newman's shirt had made, was mostly dry by now, just a dark patch in the dirt. I stared at it, and it was only after staring for several long moments that I noticed how the piece of beef in my mouth remained tucked unchewed, forlorn, between tongue and tooth.

I went to Annie's room and dragged out her chest, and a sack of things that clanged – her plate, bowl, spoon and fork, I supposed. Her brass pot, her ewer. When I carried the sack to the door a box fell out, the wooden box our father had made for her ninth or tenth birthday, which she'd covered with shells.

I opened the box and in it were her needles, reels, snips, awl, lucet, scissors and a bundle of dull thread. Once the box was in the sack again, I tied the strings tighter and put the sack on the chest, ready for the cart to come. I put her chair with those things, as she'd asked. Could her husband not provide her with a chair? Had our times really come to that, when a woman was supposed to bring her own chair and table into a marriage? And what next? Would she bring with her a door and window? Her roofing?

I sat on the chair that remained. Here, Shrove Saturday, come round so soon in the flip of a year; and look how the day had started. With my sister gone and Thomas Newman drowned. *Run to the river and find him*, said all areas of my being except for the area that had sense – the heart. *Knock on doors, rouse a search*. The heart drew up its knees and bid wait. *Waiting might make us too late*. The heart claimed to know that it was already too late, and remained stoic. The heart drew lines between love and fear, and in its constant travel between the two it knew all there was to know. It grew stubborn and heavy in my chest until the beef and bread I'd eaten could find no way past. I tidied away the crumbs and wiped my fork and plate with a square of cleaning linen.

In any case it wouldn't be long before Janet Grant did her morning rounds and found Thomas Newman's house empty, and then the cat, as they said, would be out of the bag. So I did as my heart said, and waited.

As it was, Robert Tunley brought the news, not Janet Grant. He came oafing up the road at his own top speed in his fine miniver-collared coat, which he got from nobody knew where and wore for everybody knew what. Hollering, 'Man in the river down at Odd Mill!' Waving his arm through the pelting rain. 'Man in river before the Odd Mill oxbow!'

It was still barely dusk but the birds were now singing, songs so piercing I wondered if it was that which was bursting the clouds. Much of Oakham came out of their doors.

'Tunley!' I called, because he'd run past my house, New Cross-wards. He didn't hear. He was shouting for all men and women to join a search at the river. I can't say there was over-whelming interest in the notion, not with the rain and the meagre light and the lack of care for a drowned stranger. They'd have been more motivated if it had been an Oakham cow that'd gone in.

But then Janet Grant came upwards from Old Cross, looking puzzled and troubled, saying to me that she'd knocked on Newman's door on her rounds and had no answer. I told her she might well speak to Tunley, and I pointed up the road. She hurried over to him, shawl-headed against the rain, and asked what the fuss was for. That was when the two items of news, taken together, raised alarm. Could the person in the river have been Newman? they asked Tunley, and Tunley replied yes. It seemed to be a man. In the brief wild shuck of the body, it seemed not to be a small man; it seemed long of limb – although maybe that was just an illusion of speed and chaos. At the very least it seemed not to be a woman or child. And though it was quite dark at that hour, Tunley's view was close-up as he made it home along the bank (after a night of his own wild shucking amid miniver with a widow from Cooper's Ash who liked to be rid of him before the sun let her see the extent of his gut, and let him see the extent of her age; none of this he divulged to the village, but he'd divulged it to me in the past).

So a search began. The firm half of the village bolted or trotted or walked down towards the river at Odd Mill, and the more infirm stayed back to light fires and start breakfast and wax eggs as Egg Saturday gifts, since the day must go on.

I made my way too. A priest doesn't call, and he doesn't run (cassock-bound, he can't), he just scuttles forward like an old man even when he's young, and he wonders, if he's really in the body of Christ, why he's so unable to do such a simple thing as move his legs at speed. I was alone; the rest of the search was up ahead, scattering into the light of a gloomily breaking day, Herry Carter not among them. For which I was glad – he needed to get warm – and apprehensive. What would people think of his absence? That he had no cause to search? That he knew it was pointless?

Some forty or more villagers went the half-mile down to the Odd Mill oxbow, which is where I caught them. There was no sign of a drowned person. The fog was rolling up the fields towards the village, and the river, impeded by the oxbow, travelled at a slow, muscular surge like the straining hind leg of a beast at the plough. Trees had fallen where a wet winter had worn at the banks; plenty of places for a body to get caught, but nothing was there. We followed it round to the next oxbow at Burn Wood. Here the river coiled back on itself so sharply that the neck of its meander was far narrower than the river itself – a piece of ground no more than four strides wide. The loop of land within its meander was almost an island, which we now stood on, teetering at the bank, shouting into the river, 'Newman! Thomas Newman!', as if he'd emerge from the water from a swim.

But our calls went unanswered. A certain excitement grew. Chatter and a chorus of voices: It might have been an animal Tunley saw, not a man. No, it was a man, did you ever see Tunley flustered over nothing? Newman might be out on his fields, might be out shooting, might be out walking. In this rain? No, that's not like Thomas Newman. Might be asleep in his bed – did Janet Grant check or did she just knock on the door? Ha, if he's asleep in his bed and I'm out wading in rain and shit and mud, I'll kill him myself. Tom Newman drowned! Doesn't seem right. He can't be drowned. He must be. Father? Is he drowned, Father? How would Father Reve know if he's drowned, he was asleep like the rest of us.

I shrugged, solemn. Others had run on past the Burn Wood oxbow, westwards where the river began to straighten on its way to West Fields. If the body had got that far, we'd never find it now. In the commotion I left. I walked back upstream a good quarter-mile to the bridge, alone at this point and wholly drenched. I stood at the bank by the fallen bridge where I knew Newman to have gone in. I whispered to myself: Look at it. The river pushing at its banks, the useless abutments, the deep cow-hoofed sludge, the perfect uncertainty as to where river met land. An accidental drowning here was plausible; no, near-inevitable. It was a wonder nobody had before.

I tried my foot on the mud. Yes, like ice. Anybody standing there would've slipped. There were rain-filled wells in the mud, those of a large-booted person, and there, perhaps, evidence of skidding and slipping, two narrower, longer tracks not deep enough to be made by anything that lingered – just there where the river met the bank. Though it was difficult to tell in the mess of mud and water.

It was only as I was about to leave – and as I was thinking that we needed to call for the rural dean straight away, and show him this scene if he wanted to see it, and let him conclude an accident – that I saw in the mud a length of rope. I braved the deepest sludge to retrieve it, holding the broken abutment myself. The rope was the length and width of a belt – not Newman's because his belt was leather. No, it was Carter's. I'd seen him wear it every day for the last few years. I picked it up and wrapped it round my fist.

Thank you, I said, and squinted into a thickening fog. If anybody else had found Carter's belt, then what? Thank you, Lord, I said again.

Then the cart arrived with two men driving it, men from Bourne, who loaded it with my sister's things. How empty the room, full with emptiness, so brimful with it that it felt there wasn't space enough for me to stand inside its awful fattening hollow;

sanctus, sanctus, sanctus, I said aloud, and the words dropped like a stone on tin, and the room seemed to shove me outside, where the searchers were arriving back from the river.

I washed the piece of rope in the water pail at the side of my house. I tucked the rope out of sight behind the pail, rinsed my hands, came to the front of the house. John Hadlo was striding head-bowed up the road, shoulders locked down against the rain. 'Search has failed,' he said when he came past. The failure seemed to have removed his heart from its warm cavity.

I asked him to find a boy who could take one of Newman's horses and ride to Bruton, to persuade someone at Bruton to send a message to Wells, telling the rural dean there'd been a death in Oakham and asking him to come that day if he could. Hadlo received the word 'death' with a wince. But he was dutiful, and he nodded.

I watched the men take Annie's things away. They covered the cart with pig-skins to keep off the rain, and while they did, a boy from the barns harnessed Newman's liveliest horse. The boy and men set off in tandem, one heading for Bruton, the other for Bourne.

Little dark box

When Annie told me she was going to be married, I took the news in two ways at once: with shock, which was utter, and expectation, also utter. It's possible to be both surprised and unsurprised in the same moment, and to know something could never happen and is also inevitable.

That was how it was when Carter spoke those words to me in the dark of my house: Thomas Newman has drowned himself, gone under. It occurred to me that of course he had, because he'd been recently in my room telling me passionately he was going to do as much – and it also occurred to me that it couldn't be true, because he'd been recently in my room talking passionately. I claimed I didn't understand precisely what Carter had said, but of course I did. What I didn't understand was how I could know and not know, and be shocked and unshocked, and be struck by grief while also feeling something innermost harden in an instant, something that perceived the dreadful inconvenience of his loss, but not the woe of it. Like walking two opposite paths at once, as those riders to Bruton and Bourne – one taking, one bringing. Both at once.

I didn't expect the dean to come with any rush, what with so much on his hands. It didn't matter to me if he came. If he finally arrived halfway through Lent looking distracted and duty-bound, and stayed for half an hour, it would have been enough. What importance was Oakham to him? What magnitude a little death there? I'd heard about his overworked, under-compensated, overlooked, under-recognised deanship. His no-nonsense holiness. A death is but another piece of paper to be signed in a life beset by pieces of paper. Why would this one trouble him?

I'd him told about the death only so that nobody could say I'd kept it secret. He could dismiss the news if he chose. Just another drowning by accident, he could say; what would you like me to do, Reve, put the river on trial? But if we let nobody know, and word got out – which it would – that the richest man in Oakham was dead, then our silence would look covert and shady. Better to bore the dean with our news than to titillate him with our lack of it. I'd sent for him in the bout of doing that comes with rush and alarm. A whim, you could say. Otherwise a brief clear-sightedness.

I was so unprepared for the dean to ride into Oakham the same day that I watched a man and horse come sploshing down the rutted river of our main road and had no idea who it could be. They emanated from the fog just as the sun, at its low winter pinnacle, broke and scattered through the air, made the fog glow and gave the impression of Oakham existing under the sea. It was around midday, only four hours after he'd been sent for. I'd stepped out of the church when I heard the splosh-clop-splosh of the mare's hooves. The bell for midday rang in the midst of the clopping, and the man and horse stepped through the sun-seeped fog so that I could see he wore priest's robes. And, as the sun vanished and the fog closed back in, I ran to him.

It was the sight of a church brother that made me run forward – this small, unsure man in vestments that conferred on him a borrowed greatness. His feet were so miniature they might have been a child's. His smile was imprisoned in a narrow, burdened face. The neat tie of the amice around his neck, the embroidered apparel on the cuffs of his alb. A brother in the flesh! Relief ran through me so hotly I could feel the skin on my shoulders and the back of my neck – the relief Gil Otley must feel when another pair of hands comes to the plough and the acre shrinks under their combined moil. I clasped his gloved wrists. 'Welcome,' I said.

He dismounted lightly. 'John Reve. Our first time to meet for over a year.'

'I wish under happier circumstances.'

'I rarely meet people except under sad ones.'

'Glad's the man who never meets his sheriff, and has little cause to know his dean's name.'

'So they say.'

In fact they didn't; *his bishop's name* is what they said, but since ours was in prison, it was no harm to lightly manipulate the adage. He smiled and took in what he could of our church, though it was mere grey shapes in a shapeless grey. He looked about uneasily.

'I didn't expect you to come so soon,' I said.

'I was already in Bruton when I got your summons.'

'More a request than a summons – '

'And in fact I'd already been thinking of coming your way.'

To which I answered, surprised, 'I can't think why.'

I must have shown the surprise because he put gloved fingers on my arm, like laying snowdrops on a grave, and said, 'To discuss something with you. For now, John, let's not worry about that. Show me inside.'

Nothing like being told *not to worry for now* to cause worrying. Still, his gentleness eased me, and his familiar use of my given name. He led his mare through the churchyard and untied one end of her rein, and looped it around the rowan. She was scraggy with her winter coat, no thoroughbred her, only middle-aged and pot-bellied with a downward cast to her mouth. I ran my hand down her cheek. Her murky eye kept watch. Had the dean come prancing in on a skittering, fire-eyed colt all up-heated and horny, all flank and loin, well, then I might have put up my guard. But this wrecked mare made me soften to both him and her.

The church porch was leaking badly. A quick drip from the roof truptruptrupping *as rapid as a felon's feet*, as Tunley said. The dean stepped around it, eyeing the roof. I let us in.

'Please,' I said. 'See the church for yourself.'

His hesitation was fair; there was nothing to see. He'd encountered a church or two in his care of our Hundred, and was a man fairly well acquainted with that cathedral at Wells which they said existed in God's estimations somewhere between glorious and vainglorious, and left every other church wanting. He'd wandered towards the mural on the wall opposite.

He stared. He needed to stare; the mural didn't exactly launch itself at your senses. It had never been vibrant in its colour, and the light was at its usual poor, dim watery pitch, though Janet Grant had lit the wall sconces all around.

'St Christopher,' I said. 'Carrying the child Jesus across the water.' Which I didn't need to say, since St Christopher never did anything but.

'I'll take your word for it, I can't see much myself.' The dean was frowning as though he could barely believe the insufficiency of colour.

'The kingfisher manages a blue that man can't,' I said, in defence of an attack he hadn't made. 'The May leaves are far better than us at green.'

Those shining, unbelievable greens. The scarlet of a damselfly. The yellow of a goldcrest. Things airborne and suggestive to the heavens, where rainbows form. I saw him close his eyes for a spell and wondered if he, too, had pictured the rainbows and

257

the goldcrests. Perhaps we could be friends, the dean and I, even if we'd been indifferent before. Wasn't the face that I'd used to find stern really just – doughty? Brave (if sour)? And didn't he nod when I spoke, in the way friends do? Even if he did also stare inscrutably at the giantly stooping, washed-out figure of St Christopher, and Jesus cupped in his hands.

He squinted and scratched at the pigment of the child Christ's skin with his nail, then half-said, half-sang, 'The beech leaf can put on a yellow – '

'*Unrivalled by the coat of any fellow,*' we finished in unison. We smiled. It might have been twenty-five years since I'd thought of that rhyme.

'The man who drowned,' the dean said suddenly. 'What was his name?'

'Thomas Newman.'

'A wealthy man?'

'By Oakham's standards. He'd bought a good two-thirds of Oliver Townshend's land from him.'

'He died shriven?'

I lowered my head. 'He didn't.'

'Did he take many sins with him?'

'He was a decent man, fair-minded. He had no enemies. But nobody is entirely without – '

'No enemies? Not even Oliver Townshend? If somebody took all my wealth – if I had any wealth to take – I might begrudge them.'

'If the transaction of your land for their money was what had saved you from ruin and kept food in your mouth, maybe you wouldn't?'

'They were friends, Newman and Townshend?'

'They understood each other.'

The dean stood back from the mural, pursed his lips and extended his hand towards it.

'Might he have seen St Christopher just before he died?'

258

'Newman?' I joined him in watching the mural, as if it might move or relinquish a detail to chew on.

'He'd have needed to see it within a day of his death for it to work its – charm. We could say from sunrise to sunrise. So, since Friday morning.'

'I don't know. He was in the church the night before he died, he has an altar which he prays to. He brings his primer and he sings his Hymn of Adoration. But did he see it? I don't know. How long would he have to look on it, before the miracle was worked?'

'*The eyes must have their fill*, is all the manual says.'

'But what's their fill?'

The dean made an odd jerking movement of his head, a very pedantic little motion that seemed to wish my question away. He moved towards the chancel, looked up at the witch hazel, dogwood and wintersweet splayed in yellows and reds, all fine frills and waxy petals, and waves of perfume that defied the dullness of the season.

'A wedding?' he asked.

'My sister's, yesterday.'

'Felicitations.'

The word trailed off with him towards Newman's altar, where the bright scrolled Pietà hung by two nails.

'This is from where?' He pinched the burnt corner of canvas between thumb and finger.

'Rome – Newman took a pilgrimage there last year, he came back in December after three months away. He brought this.' And some odd ideas, but I said nothing of those to the dean.

'Colourful,' he said. 'Un-English.'

By which I guessed he meant no compliment; our rural dean was known for his view of Italians, French, Spanish. Degenerates, mavericks, showmen, mask-wearers and puppet-makers. Masters of the fake and the flimsy. I thought then of Newman telling me how the Italians could produce blues to rival any dragonfly, reds bloodier than blood, purples worthy of Our Lady's Gloves. The dean looked long at the painting; his lips moved in minuscule, half-formed silent words as if he were trying to commune with this woman and the slain man on her lap – not any Mary or Jesus we'd ever seen in the Pietà. There was flesh, bare skin that had the pale lustre of real skin, the faces that were as human as the man or woman next door, eyes that knew things, saw things. Mary's little bony clutching hand.

'It turns the Virgin into a whore,' he said softly.

He relinquished his hold of the painting and went towards the chancel and altar. I saw the meagreness of the church through his eyes, and the clutter and cheap trinkets on the altar that had been left the day before as wedding wishes for my sister. Those two painted bride-and-groom stones would surely, to the dean, look like a child had doodled them; and the other stone, with the glint of tin through it, must have seemed a poor approximation of festive razzle. The wooden doll *un-English*-looking. The dean picked it out and ran his thumb along the silken wood.

'Do you know where Thomas Newman entered the river?' he asked.

'I have my suspicions, by the bridge – the river's high on the banks. I could show you if you like?'

He wafted his hand, no need.

'And he was seen, drowned, further downstream?'

'By Robert Tunley.'

'Are Robert Tunley's eyes good?'

'They find women.'

He gave a quiet, good-humoured *Hmn*, and then, in time, 'If he's really dead, as you say, then this is a sad day for your parish.'

This he said with a compassion that was missing from all reports of him; yes, he was small; yes, he was furtive; yes, his forehead was cramped and dishonest-looking, but a man couldn't help how his body was. How could a given face be the sum of a man, when he was given it while in the womb?

He knelt at the altar. 'Your man's unshriven soul will need all the encouragement it can get if it's to pass through purgatory,' he said. 'Shall we pray for it now? I advise you, pray for it now.'

I knelt next to him. I was touched by his neck that bent so quickly and deeply that I'd barely had time to arrange my knees. We went through midday prayers, though it was past that. And as we prayed I became overwhelmed by the fact of our praying there together, when every day I prayed alone. I was overwhelmed by the knowledge that Newman was dead and had brought about his own death because life had failed to satisfy him. I was overwhelmed and crushed by the notion of his shirt in the river, empty of him. A shirt empty of its owner. Close to tears at my own regret that I'd done too little when Newman came to me. *Too little?* a voice said. *You did nothing!* Lent was not even four days off, and I'd failed to do my duty by a member of my parish, and now I was lying about it. Two sins that would come with me, if not purged.

The dean murmured about the flame of love. Again I saw Newman's shirt dragging against the current, held only by Carter's hand and then released. The dean was tucked small in prayer to my left and I reached across to him, put my warm hand on his cold one, fully anticipating a jolt away. He laid his second hand on top of mine.

I knew that if there were ever to be a chance to confess to the dean what had happened that morning, such a chance lived in this moment and would disappear with the next. I gathered the words in my heart: Newman came to me in the small hours for the final sacrament and I didn't give it, I pretended to be asleep. Eventually he went away. How could I have given him the last sacrament? How could I have shriven him? I thought that if I didn't shrive him, he wouldn't go through with his suicide. Even he would see the dangers of it. I thought that if I didn't help, I'd be saving his life. When he went I followed him back to his house, and assumed he'd gone to sleep it off – I thought I was saving him.

The dean slipped his hand from mine and sat up out of prayer. When I opened my mouth to expel the confession from my heart, I found that the moment (so ripe and abounding and warm) had already passed. Tell him later, I thought, knowing that every increment of time that elapsed between now and a confession would make the confession harder and less likely.

'John,' he said suddenly, and his use of my name was like his hand once again around mine. 'I've been in Bruton, as you know, and the monks are excessively keen on your wheat-growing land, which they'll pay well for.'

He seemed grave; was he really? His brows, the most expressive thing on an otherwise bland face, were drawn down in concern.

'Shouldn't we be flattered they think so highly of us?' I said, and there vanished entirely, almost without trace, the opportunity to confess. 'But then and again,' I added, 'Oakham's not for sale.'

'If their offer is declined, I've heard of them persuading by fire and force. Within five years this village could be cleared, the church will become their private chapel, and you'll be gone.'

To my ears these words were ludicrous, but in the dean they provoked what I had to admit looked like the sincerest of anxiety.

'That's why I was planning a visit here, to warn you,' he said, 'and why, when I heard about this death, I came without waiting.'

He was looking at me as if for a response, or a solution; I sat back on my heels and dusted from my cassock what might have been crumbed remains of rye bread, though I couldn't fathom how they'd withstood the motions of a whole morning.

'Considering this interest from the Bruton monks, it doesn't bode well to have your richest man dead and so much of your land newly unowned.' He put one hand over the other in his lap. 'Indeed, is it unowned? Are there any deeds?'

'I don't know if there are deeds,' I said, since nothing was gained by telling your secrets to a near-stranger so early in dialogue, before knowing if they were a friend.

He put the palm of his hand flat against my back. 'On my ride over here I was thinking about what I might report to the archdeacon. You see, had anyone else here drowned – you excluded, of course – I could have signed a death certificate saying it was an accident, and been done with it. But on account of Newman being so wealthy a man, and known indirectly to the archdeacon, I don't think his death can be signed away so easily.'

'And yet a winter with floods like these must cause a thousand accidental drownings.'

'I've been thinking about it,' he said again. His hand left my back and rejoined its counterpart in that hollow of his lap, as if, though they tried, the two hands couldn't bear to be apart. 'As chance would have it, it's the season of confession. If we grant a good pardon, a forty-day pardon, for anybody who comes to confession in the remaining three days, before Lent, I can go back to the archdeacon, wave the pardon about, tell him it produced a good turnout but no surprises, and tell him that, having investigated, you see no reason but to confirm it was an accident.'

Here; I was delivered of another moment in which to confess, to say, *And yet it wasn't an accident.* My hand, animated by the intention to speak, lifted towards him.

'That's only the half of it, though,' he chimed, filled with a sudden purpose that made my hand drop. 'Not only will it show we've been scrupulous and serious about the death, it'll show that you have a parish full of people who are lively, willing and faithful penitents. Others are still wary of your *little dark box*, in truth. If we get at least half the parish to confess in these coming three days, that might alleviate their doubts. It would make Oakham look favourable, that's certain. Most parishes get a handful of confessions, perhaps none before Lent, and then they all come at the last hour, a day before Good Friday – a game of nerves, as you know. Who can hold out the longest. Confess last and least, when everyone else has shown their hand. No wonder, if everyone can hear your confession. But with your contraption there in the corner, well, no longer a game of nerves because you can't be easily heard. So half the parish confesses nice and early, and confesses well. Then, you see, Oakham would look favourable indeed. And you a good priest.'

Even if I cast my thoughts back years I couldn't remember anyone in Oakham – and certainly nobody outside it – give so much thought to saving it. His purity of motive startled me, and even while I knew there was self-interest at its heart, I convinced myself it didn't matter, not if those interests were the same as mine. Besides, I liked him. His modesty, his petite hands.

'With a good pardon, we could get at least half the parish to confession,' I said.

'I agree.'

'And he'd be satisfied by that, the archdeacon? If I said confession uncovered nothing fishy, nothing untoward, he'd take my word for it?'

'You're the parish priest – your word weighs a hundred times a normal man's, two hundred times a woman's, three hundred times a child's. Your word is a silver weight in the palm. Your word is worth trading money for. It would cut like a stone through water.'

I dropped my head. He stood, an ankle bone easing with a crack. He walked to Newman's altar in the north aisle and stood in front of the Pietà. With his back to me, I dared take him in. I'd remembered him small, and he was, and narrow-shouldered, which he was, and spiceless, as he was – a man made of the very fog from which he'd that day appeared. I hadn't remembered that the small, narrow monotony of him was in some way sturdy, like a pillar, a table leg, something reliable, something honest. A thing seen in the fog can appear foglike at first, but then shows itself to be solid and constant.

He gathered his skirts a fraction and pivoted to face me. 'I'll need somewhere to stay for these few days. I suppose Thomas Newman's house is free? You arrange it ready for me, I'll arrange the pardon, we'll have it up within the hour. You'll need to announce the death.' He pursed his lips, looked down his nose, which was halved longways by shadow and was rendered girlish and slender. 'We'll make things right, John Reve,' he said.

Desire

Near Old Cross, through fog, the death bell chimed three flat, watery clangs. Janet Grant, ever faithful, would ring it through the village, up to New Cross, and out all the way to the parish bounds and back.

I went past Old Cross towards the outwoods. Newman's was the only house that far down and was bigger than most of the rest, easily as big as mine. It had once been the manse when the old wooden church was there, long before our days. Newman had been rebuilding; he'd slept where the last priest had slept and lost his wits, through loneliness they said. Behind his house, on the wood's edge, stretched an enclosure of pigpens and horse stalls and runs for his geese and hens, with a paddock behind for horses – and it was here that the dean's mare was led by Agnes Prye. By the pigpen, fiddler John Green was praying to Newman's sow. Little Jane Smith clutching a hen and muttering, *Show mercy on the soul of Mr Newman, place him in the region of peace and light.* Outside the horse stalls, Fisker was hanging stones with holes driven through, so the devil could be lured in and disappear (though I feared the devil wasn't so easily tricked).

Hanging a cross outside Newman's door, the wife of Bodger Philip. Inside, the Tunley girls and Cat Carter laying clean, dry straw and rushes on the floor, into which they scattered some tired pressed violets left over from summer. Adam Lewys's wife, back-achingly incumbent with child, arranging Newman's primer and prayer books along the shelf by his bed, while her husband restocked the fire as you'd do for the newly dead if you had a corpse to lie before it. Robert Guy, the reeve, humourless and diligent as ever while he collected up fresh food into a cloth bag – milk, cheese, apples, a bowl of fish rissoles (still cookable), a leek (not firm), a pile of stubby parsnips (not washed) – and humourlessly, diligently, emptied them out again when I told him the rural dean would be staying and might like to have them. I asked Cat Carter to make the bed anew, Adam Lewys to bring some of the wedding beef and boar, his wife to bring some stew.

In the short interval alone, while Cat Carter had gone for bedding, Lewys and his wife for food, and Guy and the Tunleys back home, I lit the fuming pot stuffed with bay leaves and thyme, and brought the same taper to the wall lights all around. I was disbelieving that it was the house of someone dead. And what if he wasn't – how could we know? It could be a trick Newman was playing, not that he had an ounce of trickery in him, but life is strange, death stranger. In this house of his I encountered a voice which might have been his, but might have been the devil's, and I hoped wasn't the Lord's: Newman came to you for help and you didn't even open your eyes. This man is dead for want of you opening your eyes.

To which I felt I must object. When there was so much in this life to regret, lament, blame and fear, did it make sense to expend righteousness by reproaching a priest – tired to the core – for keeping his eyes closed? Was there such evil in keeping closed those very instruments the Lord made lids for? *For the Lord hath poured out upon you the spirit of deep sleep, and hath closed your eyes.*

But then what about the bands of muscle that could and did, a thousand times a day, lift my eyelids without effort, a movement

that the Lord had no stake in, one that, in his infinite busy-
ness, he left to each man to make for himself. Maybe I chose
not to open my eyes out of convenience to myself, or out of
spite for Newman, or out of hatred of a kind. *For this people's
heart is waxed gross, and their ears are dull of hearing, and
their eyes they have closed, lest at any time they should see
with their eyes, and hear with their ears, and understand with
their heart.*

I went to Newman's bed, which he'd got out of only hours
before. His pillow was barely dented. I lay my knuckles in that
dent and pushed it down, because I couldn't abide that a whole
life should make such a faint impact. There, a bowl, nice and
deep. And yet – how weak a man must I appear to God, to be
bending reverent and sentimental over the pillow of someone
who'd shown no reverence to me; preserving his existence in
the world when his words had all but annulled mine. *You are
not a man of the spirit*, he'd said. Grief in that, a notion of loss
so great it had left me speechless that morning. So I flattened
the dent away, cool and sober, and busied myself. Only to find
grief in that too, as if my hands had just destroyed the last
remnant of him.

When the dean came, I was fetching in a bucket of water to
pour into the pot above the fire, ready for warming when he wanted
his nightly wash (for I heard deans washed nightly, even rural
ones). He inspected the house with approval, tried the give of
the bed with his hand, looked gratefully at the hearth, assessed the
parsnips and was glad to know that stew was on its way. As for
the apples, there were five of them and he didn't want any, said they
griped his stomach; so he wrapped them in the cloth and gave
them to me with such generosity you might have thought they
were his to give. He thanked me for everything, patted my arm.

By the time I left, the house was warmish and smelt of
meadows.

* * *

'Man is a foul thing, little and poor, a stinking slime, and after that a sackful of dung and, at the last, meat to the worms. In his final hour he lies with a shooting head and rattling lungs and gaping mouth and veins beating, his fingers cooling, his back aching, his breath thinning and death coming. His teeth grin grimly in a bony head, maggots make breakfast of his eyes. Man is weak and fruitless, a clothed cadaver clutching at his worldly things, a skeleton that will one day clack for want of blood and flesh; a festering mound of skin and nail, and after that an unlubricated heap of bone. Is man the master of his life? Does he own the moments that make it up? No, those moments are God's, to add to or subtract as he wills. Man is a sinner whose life speeds him day by day towards a tomb, not a master of his body but a slave to it; his red lips will turn black and his eyes will fog over and his feet will stiffen and his tongue will slacken and his ears hiss with death.'

Amen, they said, as they trailed up the nave with gifts for the dead. I saw Carter's face blank with sorrow and lips shaping the same repeated words, *Mea culpa*, while all others persisted, Amen.

The ledge of Newman's altar filled with lucky pennies and small velvet socks and gloves to adorn the statue of Mary at Easter, and scraps of silk to cover her grieving eyes on Good Friday, and a key to help Christ unlock the gates of heaven; and things of nature, like acorn halves that resembled the chalice, and stones shaped (if you worked the imagination) like the dove or the mother and child, and berries splashed red by the blood of Christ, and twigs that were the branch of the Tree of Knowledge, and almond-shaped leaves that were Mary's womb, and sheaves of wheat that were her son's earthly form, and ivy cuttings and flattened violets and the furry backs of dead bees, and a cup of milk, a cup of ale, a piece of bread, four painted eggs, a packet of seeds, a bolt of velvet, a tin ring, a pair of dice, a lock of hair, a back tooth, a toenail, to help Newman on.

* * *

'First we believe, and only then do we seek to understand.'

Sarah nodded. She'd knocked on my door only moments after I myself arrived through it, and she stood by the fire pit, though the fire wasn't going strong. I was trying to revive it; better to throw attention on the fire than on the sight of her, grey and partway to skeleton. It was the subtle twist at the left side of her mouth that haunted the edges of my vision. The more I tried to dismiss it, the more grotesque it became. Was it pain? Her fingers, when she passed me kindling, were twisted likewise.

'How long do we have to believe for,' she said, 'before we can understand?'

The dry kindling managed a new, small, thrusting flame. I shook my head minutely.

'I was well,' she said, 'do you remember how I was? So full of health I might have vaulted over a cow, I might have lifted Robert Tunley over my shoulder and carried him to Fox Hole. And now I'm dying.'

'Not dying,' I said.

'Rotting.'

'No.'

'I want to understand why.'

'I don't know.'

I didn't know; whatever she'd done, the punishment surely was too much. A divine balance, I'd already told her. The Lord is asking you to make amends for something. She said there was nothing she'd done to make amends for. Our sins can be invisible even to us, I'd said. Then help me understand, was her reply. My reply was silence; I didn't know. I didn't know.

I cut her some beef and gave her one of the spiced buns from Annie's wedding cake. I took one myself. Now that there was only one chair, I offered it to her and I sat on the edge of the bed. We ate, I fast and hungrily, she hardly at all – but still, she tried. It was the willingness to thrive that mattered, even if the body itself was beyond thriving.

'Silence from the birds,' I said, nodding towards the window where fog and an early dusk pressed in. 'Though it's supposedly their day to find a mate.' Meaning the day of St Valentine. Coy and private they were in this business, then, for there was no song and no heckling call and no beating of wings that I could hear. 'So much for that,' I said, unable to bear the quiet.

Sarah had put down the remains of her spiced bun and was staring, hands folded, into her lap. I was glad to have her face in shadow so that I didn't see the warped mouth and sharp cheekbones and sunken eyes. Her eyes were too dark, too large, all pupil. They brought to me the devilry of a full black moon on a white sky, which is, they said, what the end of the world would hold. There was only her forehead and the strong line of her nose, the nose of a queen. It had always looked misplaced on her roundish young face, and now disease had misled her face into a brutal kind of womanhood, which was queenly all over, and had a troubling beauty. Or had before the warping, the twisting.

'Sarah,' I said, and went to take her hands. I touched the warped mouth. Love comes in ways not known or understood. First we believe, and only then do we seek to understand. Two years I'd been in love with her, two years, and those bruising and thankless, which no doubt they were supposed to be. The Lord doesn't set us easy tests and temptations. He won't ask, Are you ready to be in love? He won't give warning that this girl, your sister's friend who's also to you a kind of sister, will suddenly develop an ankle you can't take your eye from, and make you see that ankle every time you try to invoke Mary or the saints.

He'll just put her in front of you one evening, with your sister there as normal, and change her in front of your eyes. Her tucked-in babyish chin will transform into the chin of a woman concentrating. Her childish wrists will become articulated and strong as they flex. Her little kicking girlish toe will be lost to you and abruptly replaced by a foot made of splendid bones, and her pressed-together knees by muscular legs made for hours of pacing and rocking to calm a child.

When the Lord tests us he doesn't give warning – no, he throws the ball to see how you catch. So when he chose to transform Sarah's chin and wrists and ankles into instruments of seduction, and to both sweeten and ennoble her face at once, and lace her words with invitation, I promised him: I won't touch her. As I didn't. Instead I thought all those things a man is built to think, and for almost two years acted on none. But one day, this last November, on the day of celebration of the bridge being finished, she came to my house when she knew Annie was at the barn carousing with the others, and she sat me on one chair and herself on the other (in the blessed days when my chairs numbered two), opened her shawl and let it drop behind, released her hair from its coif, lifted the tunic up over her head and laid it on her lap, tugged her worn blue dress down to the waist where it bundled around the girdle, and showed me her upper self in full nudity.

You'll think I gaped or stuttered like a choirboy. I didn't; I quietly stopped breathing and then I nodded. I've seen you looking at me, she said. Poor John Reve – I wanted to give you what it was you wanted to see.

I was surprised by lack of surprise. I felt I'd known all along the secret shape of her. I remembered Tunley comparing a bosom to young pears, dropping sweetly yet weightless; shoulders that were downy peaches. I knew it was nonsense – a man refers to fruit when he's trying to clean up the images of his desire, which have no resemblance to fruit. When I saw Sarah there was only a grit of wanting and remorse and need in my throat that I could have choked on. I could have swiped the ewer aside just to smash something.

I only nodded and looked, knowing that this was the next stage of God's testing of me. First he put a woman in front of me and filled me with a love for her that had no grounds, no past and no escape. When I resisted indulging that love, he had her take her clothes down and show all that was stark, sickening and beautiful about a woman. Curves that he'd made and that I could barely comprehend, even when seeing them. Curves moving downwards and inwards and outwards like nothing else in nature.

No man should go his whole life without seeing a woman, she said. Even a priest. Here; look all you will.

Little did she know that she wasn't the first I'd seen, nor that she was the long-delayed answer to the pleas I made many years ago. When my affair with the married woman ended, I'd asked for punishment for what I'd done, and for encouragement to be a priest, and I should have known that these might not come immediately, but would come. At last, they'd come. The punishment of his temptation and baiting, and the encouragement of his love. I'd heard of tests like it, when God subjected a priest to that which he could never have; they said that the sharper and more prolonged the temptation, the more jealous God's love. The more jealous his love, the more demanding. The more demanding, the more he expected of that priest, because he knew the priest was capable.

In three months of that, which was five times of visiting, I didn't once touch her. I didn't even know for certain that I was in love – love being a state of voyage and adventure, and me voyaging nowhere except deeper, I hoped, into God's approval. She'd come by, sit and face me bare-fronted as if it were a game, while my breath rucked at the back of my mouth and my hands splayed on my thighs. If I were standing while she sat, I'd be able to see the ivory white seam of her skull in the parting of her hair. It was this nakedness of head that completed the temptation – that she always took the time to remove her coif and flaunt the pinned clump of her dark hair.

When she went on her pilgrimage she was gone for a fortnight, and in that fortnight I'd sit in front of the fire with my elbows

273

on spread knees and my head low, and think what a particular and severe test this was. Within a week of her being gone I got taken down with a fever, became thin, imagined my fingers were the legs of mayflies, I had garlic and wormwood and scrubbed myself with myrrh; the doors of my house were open and candles lit to drive the devils out, though there weren't any devils. Only God, raging and spiteful.

Two or three days after I recovered she returned to Oakham, herself burning with a fever that made her mewl and strain high-pitched, and which we thought would go, as fevers do. We gave her garlic and wormwood and scrubbed her with myrrh, and a great use all that was, because the fever bit back harder.

She fumbled now with her hooked fingers to untie the coif (from which fell hair that was lank, unbunned and had been listlessly stuffed), take down her tunic, then her dress, then her undertunic. I was still kneeling in front of her. Her poor shoulders. No pear nor peach. Nothing plumpish any more in the journey from neck to breast, but more a rack of pulled skin. She'd taken on a haphazard mottled hue, as if stained. The bosom, though, still kept for itself the spirit of life and miraculous roundness. Whatever was left in me to burn burnt most urgently then, in the sight of her ripeness mid-fall. Whatever devil was at work in her was howling through flesh that still remembered vigour and health.

But her twisted mouth; it was there that I looked with a stumbling heart. This hopeless flame of desire had taken up a vigorous dance. I realised then, doesn't a flame flicker at its fastest because it gasps at air before going out? With each flicker it spends itself. Hasn't the Lord decided, at last, to bring this temptation to an end?

'It must be this then,' she said into a cold silence. 'This has been my only sin, to come here and make you glad. It's for this I'm dying.'

'Sarah,' I said again, as if I couldn't recall another word, and I was due to make a request that she dress herself, and an apology for what suffering was coming to her, in case it was coming on my behalf. Not as she thought – not that she'd disappointed God by coming here, but that her coming here was part of his plan to test me. That she was a stake in his game. He'd given me a fever so as to burn out the longing. Was his intention to transfer my burning onto her, so that she suffered in order for me not to?

She sat opposite me without movement, bony as the devil, crooked-backed, breasts bare, stomach caved, eyes deep, hair loose and fingers bent into eternal beckoning, and when there was a curt clipping knock on the door from someone who didn't plan to wait to be invited in, she still didn't move. So it was that the dean walked into my house and found her half-naked; found us, I should say, since I of course was kneeling there before her nudity. Friendship fell from his face. Something patient departed.

Superstition

Sarah left with her shawl wrapped tight around and her coif hastily tied, incanting to herself a prayer I couldn't hear. A half-hour passed and dusk accrued at the end of a day that had never quite managed to be light. No sign of the dean; I'd been certain he'd come back. I put on a mantle and mud-crusted pattens and went out.

Fog, thicker still. There were voices through it that were chattering, some debating and arguing, nothing unusual except I couldn't hear where they were coming from, whether in the street or from inside the houses. The fog disunited sound from sound, so that a shout seemed to come from just there and a laugh from over there, and then the same laugh from far along the road. Now the strum of an instrument, now a shout, now a voice gruff and terse, now more laughing, now a woman's coo.

In the church, candles burnt at Newman's altar and on the floor all around. I took off the pattens and let myself into the little dark box; I sat. I blew into my hands to keep them warm, and rested my head against the oak screen. After a while I must have fallen asleep, given the fact that I woke up – not a deep sleep, or restful. I cupped my hands in front of my face and blew into them to warm my nose.

I came out of the booth as six bells chimed, and saw that the dean was kneeling at the altar giving evening prayers.

'John,' he said, without looking up. Which meant he wasn't surprised by my appearance, which meant he'd known I was in the box – presumably from the pattens outside. Still *John*, though; that surely bode well. 'Not much in the way of confession? Where's your queue of penitents?'

'I expect many don't know the pardon's there yet.'

'You're right, I'm sure.'

'And they're shocked, and mourning, distracted.'

He stood but didn't turn. Then he walked to Newman's altar and he still hadn't shown me his face.

'What are all these?' he asked, picking up and putting down the trinkets, the charms, the cuts of cloth, the acorn, the dice, the twigs, the bees.

'They're offerings for the dead,' I said, though he must have known, because there was nothing uncommon about them.

'Would you say Thomas Newman was quite an influence on your village?' he asked.

'He owned most of the land – '

'I mean on the villagers themselves.'

'He had many friends – '

'I mean, in matters of the spirit.'

Now he turned round, and his face was as it had ever been – merciful enough, no sign of a smirk or reprimand.

'I just spent an enlightening half-hour up at the house of Morris Hall,' he said, 'and I admit to being confused. A group of them there – they had Newman's lute and were trying to play it, to hear, they said, God in it. To hear news of Newman's death and how long he'd been assigned in purgatory. Then, extraordinarily, they began shaking the thing, when none of them could get any meaningful music from it. Shaking it, in the hope the Lord was inside.' His frown was deep and genuine. 'Why would the Lord be in Thomas Newman's lute?'

'They seek,' I said, evenly and without giving air to the wave of anger the dean's news brought – not at the lute-shakers but at Newman, who'd filled their heads and hearts with false hope and then died, and left me to the consequences. 'It seems strange to you,' I said, 'dealing with parishes that are more worldly, that have more to give to the dead than acorns and leaves. But they seek the Lord everywhere, in everything. It seems crude to you, but it's all they have.'

'I've seen parishes as poor – poorer, even. That's not my concern. My concern is that you, their priest, are here, with God at your side, waiting to take their confession, while they are there, shaking the lute of a dead man in the hope God drops out. Have you let them go astray? Find holy authority outside of you? In Thomas Newman, in his music, in their gifts to him of twigs? Why aren't they asking *you* about his stay in purgatory?' He paused, exhaled. 'Have you a candle?'

I got him one from the vestry and he lit it and placed it at Newman's altar, in the holder of one guttering and due to go out.

'Two things,' he said. 'I've decided, while I'm here, to search the houses of all in Oakham, not so much to find something that disputes his accidental death, but to prove there's nothing to be found. At least I hope – although we both know it can be surprising what you discover, when you wander into somebody's house.'

There it was, though only an edge of it and nicely dressed and given with the slightest of smiles, but there it was – the reproof, the acknowledgement: *I saw you with that woman.* There it was, the sourness of spirit I'd remembered in him from the last time we met, something in his temperament that didn't mean well and couldn't help itself, though it wouldn't speak out plainly. I crossed my arms, I nodded. If he wanted to search the houses, he could. He'd find nothing.

'The second thing – no small thing. Wouldn't it be consoling to have a sign from above? Rather than shaking a lute to find out if Newman's in or out of purgatory, wouldn't it be helpful to have word from God himself? Something that isn't hysteria or superstition, trinkets or charms.' At which he picked up the acorn half, appeared to squint inside it. 'A positive sign, from God. That's what would be good. If a man, woman or child moves promptly through purgatory, what better way of knowing they neither carried heavy sin themselves, nor died bearing the sins of others? What better proof of Oakham's wholesomeness if all its people die well and hotfoot it to heaven? What firmer proof to take back with me to the archdeacon? What better proof that Oakham is worth my efforts to save it?'

Down went the much-scrutinised acorn, carelessly replaced on the altar's edge, left to roll off and land with a sweet tap at his feet.

I asked, 'Proof of what kind?'

'I don't know, Reve, that isn't for us to decide. But aren't the scriptures full of signs from God? How am I to know what sign he'll deign to send.'

Reve, now, not John any more. What a face he had, which barely moved yet held, in its creases around the mouth and along the brow, irritation, anger.

At the sound of voices calling in the road, he jerked his head up like a newt detecting threat, then made to hurry from the church. I hurried after. When we came out onto the road, it was to the tail end of a group of running bodies whose cries were vanishing into the dusk and fog.

'Go after them,' the dean said. I gaped, I fear. If he wanted a chase, why didn't he go after them? But there was nothing in his two-footed hands-on-hips stance that conveyed a man about to get swift on his legs. I turned in the direction of the runners, which was down towards Old Cross, and broke into a kind of trot.

'You'll catch them up by Monday at this rate,' he called. 'Go!'

The trot extended into a lope, skirts hitched. I wasn't wearing my pattens, so any mud and wet would go straight through my shoes. Much to resent in that prospect; if the dean so wanted to know where the villagers were going, it should be his feet that got mired. Besides, I'd lost them by then and could only follow the voices, which came impossibly from everywhere. At Old Cross I went down the track that led to West Fields, since the voices seemed stronger that way. My feet were already finished, no point trying to skip around ruts and potholes and newly sprung streams. It was only when I came near the birch copse that I began to see movement again, and hear voices more distinctly. That of Ann Otley, goading and feisty, saying something about the copse.

'Ann,' I called and then, seeing others, 'Morris Hall, John Mersh – ' Also Joan Hall, Piers Kemp, Paul and Simon Brackley, John Green, Jane Tunley, Richard Prye, Adam Lewys, all gathering near the opening of the copse. 'What on – ?'

'We thought we saw the form of Thomas Newman, Father,' said Ann Otley, 'and we chased it down here. We think it went in the copse.'

Her look was bright and salacious; she was panting.

Much as I wanted to, I didn't indulge this theory by looking in there myself. I said nothing.

'It was emitting a curious sound, Father, an unearthly moaning.'

Nodding all round, except Jane Tunley, who looked less sure. It was only my head that managed to shake.

'Newman trapped between worlds,' said Morris Hall.

'Unshriven, unblessed,' said Morris's wife, Joan.

'No corpse to put into the ground, so it's bolting free,' said Adam Lewys.

'Might only be half-dead, and headless,' was Piers Kemp's offering.

I did now look in at the copse, which was a den of low fog and ghostly birches slender and damp. No man, no soul, no headless devil, nor sound of one.

'Who saw it?' I asked.

'Jane Tunley,' said John Green.

'Adam,' said Simon Brackley.

'Mrs Otley,' said Jane Tunley, while Ann Otley pointed to Richard Prye.

They eyed me, the ground, the copse. Their bodies were vague accumulations of greys and browns against a veil of white that was thrown in all directions; Jane Tunley's red woven brooch seemed the only definite thing in the world, every other shape and hue could be bartered with – something reckoned down to nothing, nothing reckoned upwards to something. It was a day that made ghosts of everyone.

'All of you, go home,' I said.

'Father.'

'Go home.'

I turned from them, towards West Fields, as if to set off in search of the spectre myself. I heard their murmuring and bemoaning, and their reluctant retreat. They were spooked and skittish, and no surprise. In my time in Oakham we'd never once had a death that didn't yield a corpse; without a body to bury away, safe, in the ground, it was as if the dead were too much in limbo and prone to be plucked by the devil, or as if they were hiding and might jump out.

I went into the copse. How could it be that these trunks were so fine and papery and silver in summer, when in winter's wet they ran dark as tough leather? Each spiked dead branch housed in it a soft soul. To think summer lived somewhere in its memory; that it could summon a leaf of green from a miserable sepia knub. The horse tails tied to the branches were soddenly clumped and the yellow velvet, so joyous when it went up in summer, hung heavy and burnet. Fog, the dripping of damp from branches, the mulch of winter undergrowth – but no man.

But I stooped, because there was something on the ground that wasn't earth or mulch, but a lump of cloth poorly scattered with leaves as if for cover, and I knew what it was. I hurried to it, picked it up. Newman's shirt. So this was Carter's notion of *hiding* – stashing under a sprinkling of five leaves. Unless of course he'd hidden it well and it had been dug up; the ground around it did look disturbed – but of course it would, since to bury was to disturb the earth. I dug a more concealing hole with my hands and buried the shirt properly, then piled leaves on top of it, then smoothed the pile to look like something naturally occurring.

I stood, washed my hands off in a puddle and made my way towards the river, though unsure why. (Thoughts raced, in that restive, dipping and swooping way of wrens: perhaps it had been Newman trapped between lives after all, come to claim his shirt. But no, because he hadn't claimed it; and besides, nobody had actually seen Newman, they'd only taken each other's word. If it had been a real un-Newman thing they were chasing, I might see it – it could only have gone this way. If they hadn't been following anything real, what scent, instinct or fate had led them to the birch copse? And what fortune had led me to follow them, and find Newman's shirt before they did.)

At the river, nothing, at least as far as could be seen through the fog. I walked along the edge of the flood through swampish ground until I reached the crowding of bulrushes that were so tall in the summer, and now stood only half an arm's length out of the water. That's what they seemed to be: arms reaching. In the dusk and dank of the riverside they were hopeful; I'd never seen them that way before, or thought twice of their existence.

A sound, an ungodly cracking, which I thought at first was thunder, but was coming from low levels and not high, and was anyway too harsh, raw and near, the sound of splitting. I'd have crossed myself if I'd been able to move. As it was, only those parts of my body that went without my consent continued to work – breathing, heart beating, ears hearing. It was the crack of breaking bones, and an otherworldly creak that made even my breathing struggle to keep on. Then, in the wake of that sound, an almighty splash.

I ran back upstream a few paces to where it was. Indistinct but distinct enough, through the fog, a tree lying felled in the river.

Bulrushes

Night stole in, but so stealthy and inchwise who would notice? Then it was installed on us heavy, and listless, and black. There was some coming and going in the road and a scrimmage of sorts between Gil Otley and his brother Rob, over how they'd divide up the bit of land adjoining theirs – some thirty selions of fertile till belonging to Newman. Soon enough they stopped and went indoors; drinking began. There was leftover wedding brew that had been shared out among households, and they'd eat well enough for one more night on slices of beef, boar, chicken and goose; cabbage tossed with bacon; pears stewed with honey.

I ate, and cursed the pallid John Endall for thieving my sister and her furniture. There was nothing more solitary than having no kin and only one chair. I placed on the table in front of me the cross I kept by my bed, rough and Jesus-less – you could ask for more from God when Jesus wasn't there, reminding you of what he'd already sacrificed for you and what you hadn't sacrificed in return. You could venture a small request:

Tell me what to do.

Newman is dead, I petitioned. Herry Carter is frothing with the desire to confess to killing him, I myself have lied, the dean has asked for a sign from you and expects nothing less, Oakham is a low-hanging cherry waiting to be picked. This day has been long, blundering and not good. Tell me what to do.

I imagined myself some days hence at a roadside partway to Bruton, or further still, whispering into the musty hood of a travelling friar, because who else could I confess to now, and what would befall me if I didn't? *I was asked to shrive one of my parish before death, and I didn't, I pretended to be asleep.* I practised saying it, and it sounded tawdry and bare to my own ears. Some elaboration: *He was an important man, who died a bad death. If I'd shriven him, he might have died a better one, or not died at all, and then the rural dean would have little or nothing to sniff at, would have stayed for a half-hour, a nibble of Oakham cheese, and gone.*

But no; that small word *if* was tawdrier still, a gateway to all manner of heavens and hells. It would be better to start not with what might happen, but what did happen – to begin with the end and journey backwards, like kicking against a current, away from the rock against which you've washed up and out to the open waters, the waves the intentions that carried you in. Not the sin, but the intention behind the sin – this is God's interest. Not where you washed up, but the waves that washed you there.

Your priestly duties will strain you, I was told in my training. You'll feel like a bow whose string is pulled back and back until your flex is used up and you feel you can't flex more. Then you'll be held, taut and tested, and you'll wish for the string to go slack. But if you wait, you'll learn that this flexing is in order for the arrow to fly, which is the part of you that belongs with the Lord and is directed towards him, finely fletched and shooting fair. How can the arrow fly without the strain of the bow?

I opened the Bible; full of signs from him and not short of miracles. There was really only one I wanted to ask for, and I searched for it to find the vulgate words, those being his preference. Please Lord, I said aloud, if you send a sign, I'll know you're with me – how else to know this straining isn't in vain? There: the Lord, through Moses, blows away the plague of locusts with a wind; *ventum ab occidente*, a wind from the west. *Vehementissimum*, strong, strongest. The strongest west wind, to blow away the locusts. I looked up at the white, sheepish fog through the window. The air was so thickly flocked and spirituous. A thin-capped mushroom had found life in the sawn crevice across my table. Amazing audacity; I picked it out.

If the journey from my house to the privy outside was short enough to be done before finishing a rapid Paternoster, it was long enough for me to feel elated (a strong west wind to blow away the spirits) and then defeated (he'd never do it, it was too big a sign, bound to fail; ask for something smaller, have the humility of a man), then doubting (if I was the strained bow, how could I also be the fletched arrow?), then elated again (was it possible, a strong west wind?).

The fog was clearing at last. When I was finished at the privy I let my skirts fall back around my feet and walked out of my croft, across the road, through the churchyard, to the back of the church where the fields rolled away upwards towards the boundary Oakham shared with the Bruton parish. I imagined a pair of monks coming over the brow there, and then the pair became a pack, the pack an army, and I wondered if the dean could be wrong. Weren't the monks our brothers?

Yet I'd never felt as small as I did then, nor as faintly made, like the first marks of an etching – nor had Oakham ever filled my heart more, nor made it more heavy with worry. There was no way now of telling the dean about my part in Newman's death, and nobody else for me to confess it to, except one of those friars on the loose. The shame in that, for a priest to go whispering at the roadside to a hooded crook, and hand him a few coins for a forgiveness unsanctioned.

My breath steamed in the cold air. Sarah would be shivering in front of a fire by now with her shawl swaddling her, or lying in bed in fear of what the dean had seen, or else in fear of death. She was dying because she was a pawn in the Lord's testing of me, dying in order to prove my faithfulness to him – in light of that, it seemed not so daring to ask him a favour, or otherwise so daring that you had to ask him, since nobody else could grant it. Would you send that western wind, to blow away the spirits and as a sign that Newman's soul has gone across and as a sign that you aren't disappointed in me, and would you send it while the dean is here? And if that's too much, Lord, or if you can do it but not in the time I ask, then will you send another sign of a more modest type?

I stood quite still, and fully frozen. The back-and-forth call of two owls sharpened the night. The dean wanted a sign – a sign must be delivered. Imagine, the sound and softness of that wind, meeting my face and neck in the same way soothing hands might, blowing high and low across Oakham's fields. It was then that I thought of the velvety blackness of the rushes rising like arms through the fog, and of how those arms signified the worshipping arms of the people, and I thought of my mother and Moses and her irrational faith in me.

If I was the bow and the arrow, that which harboured God, and that which shot towards him, couldn't I not only ask for him to come to me, but go to him myself? Be the bearer of the sign, and not only the one requesting it? I could take Thomas Newman's shirt and, *on the Lord's behalf*, hang it on those rushes in order to symbolise the deliverance of his soul, out of the river, into the arms of his people, offered up to God. A meek and peaceable deliverance, a deliverable deliverance – one, unlike the more ostentatious and unpredictable wind, I could guarantee to occur while the dean was here.

I found I was drawing circles on my palms with my thumbs; I was agitated and wishful, suddenly excited. As for the wind from the west, I'd wait for that too, and when it came, it would be proof that he still believed in me. That would not be a sign for the dean, but a sign for me; a pact, if God made such things.

And what else was possible besides? If the shirt was found, why not a sighting of the body, to banish the villagers' fear of a soul suspended? They needed to be rid of this fear of ghosts and half-deads and devil forms, for if they weren't, they'd become superstitious and hysterical and give the dean much to deride. The body couldn't be buried, but it could be seen, or purport-edly seen, a thrashed and mangled bag of river-swollen flesh no more ghostly than a hock of ham. If seen at the same time as the shirt in the rushes, it could be known that the soul had escaped and transcended its earthly torment.

It couldn't be me who claimed to find the body, though; what would make the dean believe me? It had to be someone else, who seemed to the dean with nothing to gain or lose – and that person could only be Herry Carter. So I'd go to him and explain: you need to dig up Newman's shirt, you need to go to the river and hang it on the rushes; you'll say you were down there to see about a tree that's fallen, and while there you saw Newman's body pinned up against by the thrust of the current; then you need to run to tell me. Together we'll go, I with the host and the holy oil, just in case. When we get there, the body will be gone, of course, but then you'll find the shirt, a sad and miracu-lous sign. We'll run back to the village together.

And Carter will argue – he'll say, I won't do it, it's a deceit, the body won't be gone because it was never really there, how can I lie, how can I claim to find a shirt that I myself put there, I won't do it. I'll tell him: a piece of theatre is of no harm if it's towards a holy end – think of the Miracle Plays they put on (though Oakham has never), think how they elevate our Lord and his works. This is our miracle to perform, you see? We'll act it out together, you just come to me when you've done what I ask with the shirt. Do it soon, but not tomorrow, not too soon else the dean will wonder at the coincidence of asking for a sign, and the sign being instantly given. But do it by Shrove Tuesday, before the dean leaves.

Carter would argue; he'd say, I won't do it. And I'd say, For the good of Oakham, the dean needs a sign. Carter would reply, The dean needs a sign from God, not from us, and if we've done no wrong, God will help, don't you trust him? To which there was no answer I could give with full dignity, since God, unlike Carter, knew that not only had Newman committed the sin of self-murder, but I'd refused to save him, shrive him or stop him. No, I might have answered – I cannot fully trust God.

But a priest can't answer this way to his people, so I'd have to distract from his question with a new motivation: do you want to be forgiven for your part in Newman's death and have the chance to atone? Well then, this is your atonement; do this unquestioningly for me. Carter would argue, and he'd finally concede. He'd argue with the righteousness of grief, but he'd concede with the pain of guilt.

I hurried back across the road to my croft, took his belt from behind the pail, went at a brisk walk to his house and knocked on his door with the side of my fist, a dull, low knock that might not be heard by the houses around. He answered with his wife behind him.

'I need to talk to you, Herry,' I whispered. 'Let me in.'

Carter didn't argue. He looked at his belt – which I set on the table – with a moment of horror. Then he looked at me with suspicion when I explained what I needed him to do; then, when I'd finished, he looked at me with contempt. Lastly I spoke to him about forgiveness and atonement, and his contempt turned to desperation, and he agreed. It was all the worse for this lack of argument, since without having to persuade him, I found myself momentarily less convinced. His wife said nothing, but rinsed the belt clean, hung it by the fire to dry and brought us warm milk.

He drank, slouched and listless, and was left with a milky upper lip, which his wife wordlessly wiped clean with the cuff of her sleeve. 'No one'll ever believe us,' he said, without concern. 'All we'll do is make things suspect – a shirt and body washing up all of a sudden, three days after that body's gone in, when by that time the body would've got much further than West Fields. Who'll believe us?'

That last wasn't a question but a dismissal, which I dismissed. 'A body washing downstream to West Fields would have to navigate the Odd Mill and Burn Wood oxbows,' I said, 'and would get impeded at any pass – not to mention the new impediment of that fallen tree.'

Against which a body could wash up and stay pinned with all the reasonableness of science. I told him he had to put his faith in our scheme, which, being theatre, enacted the truth – the truth being that Newman's body was somewhere mangled, and his soul was on its way to heaven. What was Carter's look? I can only say desperate, and within that, relief at being given a chance to atone, and within that relief, more desperation that a bit of make-believe wasn't enough.

'So you'll come to me, Herry Carter,' I said, 'Monday or Tuesday, you'll come and find me early, before dawn, and you'll say you've seen a man washed up against that felled tree.' I lifted his chin where it had dropped. 'You'll come and find me, Herry, and you'll say what?'

As drab and unenthusiastic as a waterless fish: 'There's a man washed up, drowned.'

'The better you act it, the less an act it becomes, the more it resembles the truth, the better a sign it'll be. The truer a sign, as if really from God.' To which I added, 'The more complete your atonement.'

'A drowned man in the river at West Fields, Father.'

'Washed up – '

'Like an old rag.'

I put my hand on his shoulder, which still felt chilled from his morning in the river. Cat Carter was at his other side, her hand at that shoulder. She didn't look at me, only at him. I saw us then, me and Carter, some days hence, caught in a moment that was more than a charade. It was a moment of manufactured hope, one in which Newman was there, available to be saved – neither alive nor dead, a forehead ready to receive the holy oil, a mouth open for the host, time arrested, or reversed. We'd take the oil, the host, our hearts expectant and legs urgent. And we two would run.

Later I sat on the step by the altar with the bell chiming nine and the village asleep. I might have expected Newman to walk in, living, or undead, defiant in any case. It felt to me that he'd been dead for ever, and not only this one day – it felt like there wasn't a time before his death.

I got up and blew out each of the wall lights, until the church was dark except for my one candle. Oliver Townshend found me thus, alone in near-darkness on the altar steps. The rain was a scit-scatter across the windows, which at first I'd mistaken for mice. He came in light-footed, that's how I knew it was him – that and the squat and solid shape that was nobody else in Oakham. Everybody but Tunley was thriftily made, only the Townshends were different. Cecily was slender but broad in the beam, and her husband was compact and as if a fillet of pure boneless meat. Yet cat-footed, his toes tending outwards when he walked. He tapped a smooth path to the altar and sat by me. He put down his lantern.

'Pews,' he said, holding his back, 'are what we need. Did you know they even have them at Bourne now?'

'Windows, pews, a bridge, a trade. What don't we need?'

'It's late, are you planning to sleep here, Reve?'

He smelt all homely of cloves and smoke and cooked pork. He asked, 'Don't tell me it was you who invited that pestilent rural dean?'

'Fine, I won't tell you.'

'What in God's name did you do it for?'

'He's a decent man.'

'As decent as a bout of the pox.'

Hours ago I'd have argued against that; now I said nothing. I didn't know if our rural dean was decent or not. His manner towards me had turned – he'd thought I was a man worth standing by, then he'd begun to wonder if I wasn't; but did that make him indecent? Or did it make me?

'He's just been up to see me,' Townshend said, 'asking about what land I own, and what land Newman owns, and when Newman bought my land, and how it was procured, and why. He drank a half-bottle of my wine. He even asked if he could see the plans and deeds.'

'Couldn't he?'

Townshend must have found the question naïve, because he blew it away, 'Ffff', and lightly slapped his own knee.

'He's trying to find out what he can so he's ready with answers, that's all. If he gets questioned by higher authorities, he needs to have something to tell them. Try to trust him.'

'I don't trust him.' Townshend turned to me. His shadow was flung monstrous behind him, his head the size of an oxen's. 'He's scuttling around with something to prove,' he said. 'Before he leaves here, one of us is going to pay for Newman's death. One of us will be up in flames, it'll probably be me.'

The enormous shadow of Townshend's hand, floating northwards in the direction of the barn, was a frivolous shadow-animal children make; a bird taking flight, a hare leaping. The hand itself was small and soft in contrast. Just then I thought I could grab that hand, hold it and confess to him my sin over Newman's death – not that he could forgive it as a holy man, but he could hear it, and I could that way get it out of my heart.

'I'm telling you, Reve, he'll stop at nothing. We even have a barn full of good dry rushes waiting for the pyre.'

'You have the dean wrong,' I said. 'Whatever he is, he's not a tyrant or one for throwing folk on a pyre for sport.'

'I have bad feelings about him.'

Don't be a fool, I thought. But he *was* a fool, with his old silk stockings snug around his thighs, a de-feathered and dusty brimmed hat, his ridiculous shoulders that he'd padded, it seemed, when he heard the dean was in town, and the tatty puffed sleeves he'd dug from some dark cupboard in the same hurry. If the abbey at Bruton decided in earnest to make Oakham into their grange, what use would Townshend be, with his puffs and pads and silken thighs?

The candle flame flickered, though, so as to give an orangey light to that round thigh, and I couldn't but think of a pyre, now he'd said it, nor ignore the idea of his thigh applied to it. I had for an alarming instant the notion of him strapped to that pyre on Ash Wednesday at the dean's will – for the dean had hardly been in Oakham half an hour before he cast a suspicious glance at Townshend. Newman dead, Townshend dead, and Oakham a doomed village in the hands of a priest with uncon-fessed sins. What then would I do, but go to a travelling friar and confess what I'd done? I'd give the account backwards in my attempt to deliver Townshend from death and leave him in some way alive. Here, in the flesh, his silk thighs still hopeful of their future.

Of course I couldn't confess to Townshend, nor could he save me. Only the reverse was ever true. If my projection, which was ridiculous and born only of fear, ever looked likely to come to pass, I could save him – that was what a priest did for the lord of his parish. I squeezed his hand briefly, though not wholeheartedly.

'Be comforted, Townshend,' I said. 'If it came to pyres or nooses, I'd sooner climb up and sacrifice myself before I saw a single of my parish die.'

Townshend turned his face to me, and while I expected a *nonsense*, or a notional word of thanks for a sacrifice we knew would never be made, his grey eyes were instead distinctly moist and grateful, and he took my hands. The candle, in its holder in one of those grasped hands, spilled a pool of wax on my thumb. I let it cool and set without a wince.

'Thank you,' he said. 'Thank you. I never doubt you. What's Oakham with no John Reve? You're every man, every woman and child, I've said it to my wife many times – we may be struggling but we have our priest, and any parish with a priest like John Reve will be looked on kindly by God. You hold the soul of every animal in Oakham, every tree and flower, every furlong of soil. You're God's word to us and his wish, you're next to Jesus.'

At this I did wince. No, not next to Jesus. Perhaps I didn't mean it about the giving of my life? (What a thin but sharp line between a gesture and an offer.) Townshend kissed my thumb where the wax had set, took his lantern and stood up to leave. The lantern's light bobbed evenly away before his thick silhouette. *I'd sooner climb up and sacrifice myself before I saw a single of my parish die.*

What a thing to say, if it was said with meaning. I didn't know if I meant it. It didn't matter; it would never come to be.

penguin.co.uk/vintage